ACCLAIM FOR ALEX RIDER:

"Explosive, thrilling, action-packed – meet Alex Rider."
Guardian

"Horowitz is pure class, stylish but action-packed ... being James Bond in miniature is way cooler than being a wizard."
Daily Mirror

"Horowitz will grip you with suspense, daring and cheek – and that's just the first page! ... Prepare for action scenes as fast as a movie."
The Times

"Anthony Horowitz is the lion of children's literature."
Michael Morpurgo

"Fast and furious."
Telegraph

"The perfect hero ... genuine 21st century stuff."
Daily Telegraph

"Brings new meaning to the phrase 'action-packed'."
Sunday Times

"Every bored schoolboy's fantasy, only a thousand times funnier, slicker and more exciting ... genius."
Independent on Sunday

"Perfect escapism for all teenage boys."
The Times

"Addictive, pacey novels."
Financial Times

"Adults as well as kids will be hooked on the adventures of Alex Rider ... Harry Potter with attitude."
Daily Express

Titles by Anthony Horowitz

The Alex Rider series:
Stormbreaker
Point Blanc
Skeleton Key
Eagle Strike
Scorpia
Ark Angel
Snakehead
Crocodile Tears
Scorpia Rising
Russian Roulette
Never Say Die

The Power of Five (Book One): *Raven's Gate*
The Power of Five (Book Two): *Evil Star*
The Power of Five (Book Three): *Nightrise*
The Power of Five (Book Four): *Necropolis*
The Power of Five (Book Five): *Oblivion*

The Devil and His Boy
Granny
Groosham Grange
Return to Groosham Grange
The Switch
More Bloody Horowitz

The Diamond Brothers books:
The Falcon's Malteser
Public Enemy Number Two
South by South East
The French Confection
The Greek Who Stole Christmas
The Blurred Man
I Know What You Did Last Wednesday

ALEX RIDER
NEVER SAY DIE

For JW – with thanks

First published 2017 by Walker Books Ltd
87 Vauxhall Walk, London SE11 5HJ

2 4 6 8 10 9 7 5 3 1

Text © 2017 Stormbreaker Productions Ltd
Cover illustration © 2017 Walker Books Ltd
Trademarks Alex Rider™; Boy with Torch Logo™
© 2017 Stormbreaker Productions Ltd

The right of Anthony Horowitz to be identified as author
of this work has been asserted by him in accordance with
the Copyright, Designs and Patents Act 1988

This book has been typeset in Officina Sans

Printed and bound in Great Britain by Clays Ltd, St Ives plc

British Library Cataloguing in Publication Data:
a catalogue record for this book is available from the British Library

ISBN 978-1-4063-7705-7
ISBN 978-1-4063-7783-5

www.walker.co.uk

ALEX RIDER

NEVER SAY DIE

ANTHONY HOROWITZ

**WALKER
BOOKS**

CONTENTS

THIN AIR

Fifty thousand people had come to the Suffolk Air Show on the east coast of England. But only one of them was there to commit murder.

It was the end of August, the last week of the summer holiday. The schools were closed and whole families had taken advantage of the fine weather to arrive at the old airbase, less than a mile from the sea. They had strolled around vintage planes from the First and Second World Wars: single-seat biplanes parked next to Spitfires and Hurricanes. That morning, the Red Arrows had put on a dazzling display, twisting and criss-crossing each other in the sky before swooping down, trailing plumes of red, white and blue. There had been fly-pasts by the Tornado GR4, the two-seat attack aircraft that had been used in Iraq and Libya and by the Lightning II Joint Strike Fighter, one of the most sophisticated and – at one hundred million pounds – one of the most expensive aircrafts in the world. The grounds were packed with simulator rides, motorbike displays, drones, face-painting and fairground stalls. Everyone was having a good time.

As with every public event in the UK, an extensive, almost invisible security net had been put in place. It was impossible to stop and search all the cars but CCTV cameras recorded every arrival and every number plate was instantly checked. People might notice police and even a few sniffer dogs moving among them. These were a common sight. But they would be unaware of the plain-clothes policemen, many of them with concealed weapons, mingling with the crowd. In fact the Joint Terrorism Analysis Centre (JTAC) had met in their offices close to the Houses of Parliament just a few days before and had agreed that the threat level at the Suffolk Air Show would remain at MODERATE. They weren't expecting any trouble.

And so nobody paid very much attention to the woman who arrived just after three o'clock. She had driven into the car park in a Ford Transit van which, according to the Automatic Number Plate Recognition system, belonged to the St John Ambulance service. This is the country's leading first-aid charity and, indeed, the woman was dressed in the green and black uniform of a local volunteer. She was carrying a nylon bag marked with a white cross which, if opened, would reveal medicine and bandages.

She was short and round-shouldered with dark red hair that had been cut so badly that it stuck out straight on one side of her head and curled in on the other. There was something quite aggressive about the way she walked, like a boxer about to enter the ring. She was overweight, breathing heavily, with beads of sweat on her upper lip. She had a lot of make-up on but it did nothing to make her more attractive, sitting uselessly on her leathery skin. As she walked, she put on a pair of cheap sunglasses. They concealed the smouldering violence in her eyes.

There was a separate entrance leading into the airbase, reserved for paramedics, technicians, organizers ... anyone working at the event. She stopped and showed a pass which identified her as Jane Smith but this was not her real name. Nor had she ever worked for the St John Ambulance service. The security man at the gate might have wondered why she had arrived so late in the day, when the Air Show was almost over. He might have asked her why she was alone. But he was tired and he was looking forward to getting home. He glanced at her pass and waved her through. He didn't even look inside the bag.

The woman's real name was Dragana Novak. She was forty-six years old and until recently she had been a lieutenant colonel in the Serbian Air Force; a high-flyer in every sense of the word. Her career had ended following a drunken fight with another pilot. He had been twice her size, but even so, she had put him in hospital. In fact he was still there.

Inevitably, there had been a court martial and she had been looking at an uncertain future – perhaps returning to the turnip farm where she had been brought up. That was when she had received the telephone call. There was a unique job opportunity. It would pay two hundred thousand pounds for two days' work. Was she interested?

Dragana didn't need to think for a minute. She had met her contact in a local tavern in Belgrade where she had tucked into her favourite dish of *sarma* – spicy beef wrapped in cabbage leaves – washed down with a large glass of *rakija*, the local plum brandy. The man, who had never given her his name, had told her what was needed. It was a tricky operation that would demand all her skills. Dragana hadn't asked any questions. All she cared about was the money. It was more than she had been paid in her life.

She was still dreaming about jewellery, fast cars and expensive chocolates as she made her way past the various exhibition stands, the bars, the fast-food outlets. People were already drifting towards the seats for the last flying display of the afternoon. For many of them it was the high point of the entire show. The aircraft was sitting out on the tarmac, patiently waiting for the pilot to walk over and take the controls. Dragana stopped at the barrier that ran the full length of the runway and took out a pair of binoculars. Without removing her dark glasses, she raised them to her eyes.

Slowly, unable to help herself, she smiled.

This was what she had come to steal.

The American-built Sikorsky CH-53E is also known as the Super Stallion and there's really no helicopter in the world that's quite like it. To look at, it's hard to believe that it can fly at all. For a start, it's huge: as tall as a three-storey building and longer than three London buses standing end to end. It's also surprisingly ugly, bolted together as if the designers had never actually had any plans.

The Super Stallion *can* fly – at two-hundred miles an hour – and what makes it special is that it can carry an enormous load. It is the workhorse for the United States military, capable of lifting sixteen tonnes of cargo. When the Americans mount an assault, it can transport a platoon with enough weapons to obliterate an entire army. How does it even get off the ground? Part of the answer is the fact that it has no fewer than three hugely powerful turboshaft engines. It also has gigantic titanium-fibreglass rotor blades, twenty-four metres in diameter. Most helicopters have just four blades. The Super Stallion has seven.

Dragana Novak examined it, running her eyes over the grey-painted fuselage, the cockpit, the tail rotor. The Serbian Air Force couldn't possibly afford a machine like this, but Dragana had briefly flown one when she was on a training exercise with the United Nations and still remembered the thrill it had given her. In less than thirty minutes' time, it would be hers. She had no children. She had never married. But right now, looking at the helicopter, she felt its power reaching out to her and knew that she was completely in love.

It was time to move. Everything had been planned down to the last second and she had been shown exactly where to go. There were several hangars on the other side of the runway but two buildings dominated the airfield closer by, both of them left over from the last war. One was the control tower. The other was a low, red-brick building with about twenty evenly-spaced windows and several doors. This had been an office complex but it was being used to house the pilots and technicians during the show, with changing rooms, rest areas and a cafeteria at the far end.

Hoisting her medicine bag over her shoulder, Dragana strolled towards the entrance where two more uniformed officials were standing behind a conveyor belt that fed into an X-ray machine – exactly the same sort of device that could be found at any airport. First, visitors would have their cases and carrier bags scanned. Then there was a metal detector which everyone had to pass through.

"Hello," she said. "I'm here to see Sergeant Perkins." She had spent five years studying in London before qualifying as a pilot and spoke good English, but with a heavy accent that made her seem as if she disliked everything she was saying.

"Why?" The officials glanced at each other, puzzled. They had been here all day and this was the first time they had seen her.

Dragana smiled, showing grey teeth, discoloured by wine and cigarettes. Her right hand slipped into the pocket of her jacket. "He has a headache. I have some aspirin for him."

Of course the story was ridiculous. The two men should have rung the control tower to get confirmation. But just like the guard at the events gate, they came to all the wrong conclusions. This was a single woman. She was wearing a St John Ambulance uniform. It was the end of the day, almost the end of the entire event. What possible harm could there be? "All right," one of them said. "Your bag has to go through the machine and remove any metal objects from your pockets."

"Of course." Dragana placed the medicine bag on the belt and watched as it was carried slowly into the machine. She knew that there was nothing inside to cause any alarm. Next, she stepped through the metal detector and smiled to herself as the light flashed green. She collected her things and continued on her way. This was going to be even easier than she had thought.

She made her way down a long corridor with a wooden floor and old-fashioned hanging lights.

A few people passed her but didn't give her a second glance. Again, the uniform saw to that. She came to a door at the end and knocked politely.

"Come in!" With just two words, she could detect the American accent.

There were two men sitting in the room, both wearing flight suits. Sergeant Brad Perkins was in his early thirties but looked much younger: clean-shaven, fair-haired, with blue eyes. He had recently graduated as a pilot from the US Army Aviation Center at Fort Rucker in Alabama and this was one of his first deployments. He was a little annoyed to find himself not just in England but in some place he'd never heard of. Suffolk? Where the hell was that? There was a co-pilot sitting with him, also American, about the same age, drinking Coke. Dragana didn't know his name. Nor did she care.

"How can we help you?" Perkins asked.

"Well, actually, you can die." Dragana had taken an unusual-looking gun out of her jacket pocket. It was white and made of ceramic, which was why it had passed unnoticed through the metal detector. She squeezed the trigger twice. The gun used a small chamber of compressed air to fire not bullets but plastic needles, each one tipped with tetrodotoxin, one of the deadliest poisons on the planet. Tetrodotoxin, or TTX as it's known, is a neurotoxin found in certain fish and octopuses and is extremely fast-acting, shutting down a person's nervous system in minutes. Perkins struggled to his feet but died before he was halfway there. His partner tried to say something, then collapsed.

Dragana put the gun away and went over to the two men. Sergeant Brad Perkins stared up at her with empty eyes. He was the smaller of the two, about her height. She reached down and unbuttoned his uniform.

Ten minutes later, she walked out of the building, now dressed in a flight suit and carrying a leather folder. Nobody stopped her as she reached the Super Stallion and climbed inside. The ground staff had been expecting two men, not a lone woman. And she was a few minutes early. But still nobody challenged her. After all, she looked as if she knew what she was doing. She was dressed for the part. And the very idea that somebody might be about to steal a gigantic helicopter in broad daylight was so bizarre, so outrageous that nobody even considered it.

And so Dragana was completely relaxed as she slipped on a set of headphones and strapped herself in. Quickly, she ran her eye over the various gauges, checking the fuel levels. She flicked on the master battery, the avionics and the fuel valve master, then watched as the seven huge blades began to turn, picking up speed until they were no more than a blur. Even with the headphones, she was deafened by the engines. She rested her left hand on the collective control, then leaned over and adjusted the throttle. She could feel the downdraught underneath her, beating down onto the tarmac at ninety miles an hour.

"Stallion One. You are clear for take-off..."

The voice came from the control tower; a young man, very English, stupidly cheerful.

A final check. She had reached proper operating rpm (revs per minute). Using the throttle and the foot pedals, she steered the Super Stallion along the runway, gently guiding it. This was the moment she loved, when this huge machine belonged only to her. She found herself whispering to it in her own language, urging it to obey her command.

As they left the ground she thought briefly of the two men she had killed. She had no pity for them. After all, she was a military officer who had been trained to kill people although she had never had the opportunity until today. Ten minutes in the air and two hundred thousand dollars in the bank. She would have killed fifty more people for that. She reached out and pressed on the cyclic lever, bringing the nose of the helicopter down and urging it on. The Super Stallion shot out beyond the coastline and over the sea.

"Stallion One. Turn left heading zero five zero and ascend flight level one hundred, over."

The man in the control tower was still jabbering in her ear. Of course she wasn't going to do what he said. In fact, he was beginning to annoy her. She reached down and switched the volume off. Then she turned right.

It would be obvious almost at once that something was wrong. The path of the helicopter would be traced by primary and secondary radar systems. Very soon, there would be a red alert at the Air Traffic Control centre at Swanwick. It might have happened already. They would know that she had strayed from the agreed flight path and was not responding to their commands. They would already be tracking her. There were dozens of satellites in outer space and they would be directed to watch her every move. And of course, the Super Stallion was filled with communications equipment, which she had been unable to neutralize and would be transmitting even now. She loved the helicopter. It belonged to her. But she couldn't stop it giving the two of them away.

Timing was everything. She had memorized the exact route she had to take and made the necessary adjustments. The grey surface of the North Sea was beneath her but now she brought the helicopter round, travelling south. Looking out of the window, she saw the port of Felixstowe, the cranes and gantries lined up along the docks, the two rivers – the Stour and the Orwell – stretching inland. She checked her course and accelerated, sweeping low over the pier and the seafront. She knew she would be seen but that didn't matter. In a way, it would help.

The field she was looking for was just east of the A12, the road that led from Suffolk to London. There was a scattering of buildings, an abandoned farm. She had already been shown the maps and photographs and had studied them so many times that she recognized the location instantly. She noticed a few cars parked around the edge. She knew that there would be half a dozen men waiting for her to complete her short journey.

And there was her target. She saw it from two thousand feet and immediately began her descent. It was a rectangular block of steel lying flat in the grass, a landing pad, just big enough for the helicopter to fit onto. Three thick metal hoops had been welded into the steel, one at the top and two below, forming the shape of a triangle. This was the difficult part. The Super Stallion had three huge wheels. Each one had to be positioned right next to the hoops. Otherwise, the plan wouldn't work.

There was no way that Dragana was going to fail. She was in command of the helicopter and it would do everything she asked. It weighed fifteen thousand kilograms but she brought it down as gently as a falling leaf. For a few seconds she hovered over the metal plate, then dropped. She felt the hydraulics take the great weight and immediately flicked the engines off. The rotors began to slow down. Already, the men who had been waiting for her were running forward, carrying with them fixing devices that looked remarkably like wheel clamps, the sort of thing the police used to immobilize cars.

Nobody hesitated. Dragana got out of the cockpit and walked over to one of the cars. At the same time, the men were kneeling underneath the helicopter, locking the wheels to the three hoops. The clamps they were using were made of magnesium alloy, the lightest and the strongest metal in the world.

It took them two minutes. Before they had even finished, Dragana Novak had already left the field, sitting in the back of a fast car, on her way to London. The Super Stallion was securely locked in place. It was only thirty miles from the airfield where it had been stolen.

One of the men had a remote control device with two buttons. He waited for a signal, then pressed down. At once, hydraulics hidden beneath the metal slab sprang to life and slowly, inch by inch, the slab began to rise. It was like the lid of a trapdoor opening in the ground, even though there was nothing underneath it. The Super Stallion tilted backwards, the cockpit pointing up.

Finally, it was vertical. The next part of the operation could begin.

"And then?"

Sitting in her office on the sixteenth floor of the building in Liverpool Street, London, the Chief Executive of the Special Operations division of MI6 examined the report that had just been pressed into her hands.

It was only three weeks since Mrs Jones had been appointed head of Special Operations, moving into the office that had once been occupied by her boss, Alan Blunt. Slim and dark-haired, she was wearing a black suit with only one piece of jewellery: a silver brooch shaped like a dagger. She looked exhausted. From the moment Blunt had resigned, she had felt the weight on her shoulders, understanding what it was like to be responsible for the security of the entire country. And now this! There had been problems, fears, dangers. But this was the first real crisis she had encountered since she had taken charge.

There were four men facing her across the desk: two from Special Operations and two others in uniform, from the regular armed forces. She had addressed her question to her Chief of Staff. John Crawley had been with the service for as long as anyone could remember. He had once been an extremely effective field agent. In fact it was said that in just one year, three rival organizations had tried to recruit him while three more had tried to assassinate him. Now, with his thinning hair, his tired eyes and his very ordinary appearance, it was all too easy to underestimate him. That would be a serious mistake.

"The helicopter went out to sea, heading towards the Continent," he explained. "Our first thought was that it was being taken to Russia. But then, after travelling four and a half miles, it turned south and headed back towards the coast. It was tracked by the Air Traffic Control centre primary and secondary radar systems from Swanwick.

It was last seen flying over Felixstowe. And then it vanished into thin air."

"What do you mean?"

"Exactly what I say, Mrs Jones. It was tracked by our satellite systems. We have the signal from its own transponder. And then nothing."

"So where did it go?"

Crawley shook his head. "We have absolutely no idea. It may have crashed into the River Orwell. That seems most likely. But we've already got people on the scene and there's no sign of anything whatsoever."

Mrs Jones turned to the man sitting next to Crawley. "Do we have anything from the site?"

The second agent was the youngest person in the room, in his late twenties, black, with very intelligent eyes and hair cut close to the scalp. He was smartly dressed with a crisp, white shirt and bright tie. He moved slowly as the result of a gunshot wound which he had suffered recently, on duty in the Timor Sea. He had recovered with amazing speed and had insisted on returning to work. Mrs Jones liked him. It was she who had recruited him from the SAS and brought him under her wing. His name was Ben Daniels.

He opened a laptop and tapped a button. At once, an image appeared on a seventy-two-inch screen, mounted on the wall. "All the data shows that the helicopter came down in one of these fields," he said. "We tracked it right up to the last minute but then, as Mr Crawley says, it just disappeared." He pointed. "As you can see, there are some farm buildings, a barn, a windmill and some houses. There's a church nearby. The trouble is, none of them are big enough to conceal a helicopter the size of the Super Stallion ... even if you somehow took off the roof and landed inside."

Mrs Jones examined the photographs. There was indeed a barn – but it was half-collapsed. Could the helicopter have been buried in the straw? Surely someone would have checked. She had seen plenty of windmills in Suffolk and this one was typical: wooden-fronted with white blades, used for corn grinding long ago but now abandoned. What about the church? No. Just as Crawley had said, it was too small. She looked through the other photographs. A hill, a haystack, two electricity pylons, the river. If it wasn't here, where was it?

"It could have landed on a truck," Ben Daniels continued. "That way, it could have been driven off and we'd have no way of knowing where. You'd need a very big truck, though."

"This really isn't good enough, Mrs Jones." It was one of the military men who had spoken. His name was Air Chief Marshal Sir Norman Clarke and he was the Vice Chief of the Defence Staff, the second most powerful man in the British Armed Forces. He was small, bald and angry-looking with a ginger moustache. He tended to bark every word.

"The Americans aren't too pleased. They lost two of their men. Murdered!"

"I can understand that, Sir Norman. But we're doing everything we can."

"We're clearly not doing enough. We need to search the area again. And if the Super Stallion was transported by truck, surely to goodness we should be able to get some sort of CCTV picture?"

"There's a rather more serious question we should be asking ourselves." It was the other military man who had spoken. His name was Chichester and he worked in naval intelligence. He was a very gaunt, serious man. He spoke slowly, as if he was testing his every word. "What exactly are they going to do with the helicopter?" he went on. "Could this be the prelude to some sort of terrorist attack?"

"It seems unlikely." Mrs Jones had already considered the possibility. It had been her first thought when she heard the helicopter had been taken. "The Super Stallion only has a range of a thousand kilometres and although it can carry machine guns, this one wasn't armed. It's a transport vehicle."

"Yes, of course. But who is transporting what?" Sir Norman snapped. From the way he was talking, the whole thing could have been Mrs Jones's fault. "The prime minister is extremely concerned," he went on. "We're talking about a massive piece of equipment here. We can't just have lost it."

"We haven't stopped looking," Crawley said. "We

have the police out in full force. Our agents are all over Suffolk. We've managed to keep this out of the newspapers and we're on full alert."

Mrs Jones sighed. Her instinct was telling her that this had all the hallmarks of a Scorpia operation. Firstly, the theft had been completely ruthless. Why had it been necessary to kill the two American pilots? They could just as easily have been knocked out. It had also been extremely efficient. And finally, it was completely unfathomable, a bit like a magic trick.

But that was impossible. The criminal organization known as Scorpia was finished. Its members were either dead, under arrest or on the run.

"We need to go back to the immediate area around Felixstowe," she said. "Let's get divers into the river and into the sea." She gestured at the photographs. And we need to search here ... the farm, the hills, everything!"

"We've already searched it," Crawley said.

Mrs Jones looked straight into the eyes of her Chief of Staff. "Then search it again."

Even as she spoke, MI6 agents were sweeping the area. It was already getting dark but they had powerful torches. The beams swept across the grass, picking out the trees, the electricity pylons, the empty and derelict barns. They didn't go into the windmill. It was too small. There was no point.

Nobody saw that the outer shell was actually

very flimsy, made out of plywood that had been bolted together very recently.

Nor did they notice that, unusually, the windmill had seven blades.

ONE OF THE FAMILY

Five thousand miles away, in San Francisco, Alex Rider woke up and took in his surroundings.

He had been living here for a while now, but still it seemed new to him – a bright, colourful house at the top of Lyon Street in the area known as Presidio Heights. He had his own room on the fourth floor, tucked into the rafters. It was reached by a single, narrow staircase that went nowhere else. Every morning, the sunlight streamed in through a window that slanted over his bed and as he got dressed he had a view all the way down to the ocean with Alcatraz – the famous prison – and Angel Island in the distance. The house was old, built in the Victorian style, with extra rooms bolted on almost haphazardly. Inside, it was a jumble of corridors, archways and stripped wooden stairs. There was a garden at the back – a "backyard", he had to call it – and it was a lovely place to sit in the evenings, overgrown with ivy trailing everywhere, orange and lemon trees and wild flowers tumbling out of terracotta pots.

Sometimes he would remember how far he was from home. Then he would correct himself. That wasn't true any more. This *was* his home.

It was the house that Edward Pleasure had bought when he had moved to America to continue his career as a writer and journalist. In a strange way, Alex had helped to pay for it. Edward Pleasure was the author of *The Devil You Know*, the true story of international pop singer, anti-drugs campaigner and multi-billionaire businessman Damian Cray. The book had become a huge bestseller, turning its author into a celebrity. But it was Alex who had unmasked Damian Cray, almost getting himself killed in the process. The book was full of information that only he could have supplied.

Edward Pleasure had more or less adopted Alex after his last mission in Egypt had gone terribly wrong. To the journalist, it seemed that Alex had been completely broken by what had happened. He had barely spoken as the two of them had passed through Heathrow Airport and had simply stared out of the window as they sat together on the plane.

Alex, I want you to think of yourself as one of our family. Edward had spoken the words as the plane dipped down over the American coast. *It's going to be a new beginning for you and we're going to do everything we can to make it work.*

And maybe it had worked. After weeks in

California, Alex seemed a little more like his old self. He'd managed to put on some weight, even if he was still a little lean for a boy who had recently turned fifteen. But he went to the gym and seemed to enjoy hiking or hanging out at the beach at weekends. He had cut his fair hair short and occasionally Edward noticed a haunted quality in his eyes. It was also true that his grades at school were giving some cause for concern – but it was early days. Of course it would take him time to settle in. All in all, though, Edward was optimistic. He knew what Alex had been through but believed that, slowly, he was putting it behind him.

The start of another day.

Alex went into the bathroom, showered and cleaned his teeth. Then he got dressed. He had started school at the beginning of the fall semester – the autumn term, he would have called it back in London. There was no uniform at the Elmer E. Robinson High School. Today, Alex threw on sweats, a T-shirt and a hoodie – all of them bought from the same branch of Hollister on Market Street. Glancing at himself in the full-length mirror next to the bed, he decided that he looked American and anonymous. It was only when he spoke that he stood out. Of course, everyone said how much they loved his British accent.

There was a homework assignment on his desk. "Do animals have a conscious life?" It was an essay he'd been given for his Human Geography class but Alex wasn't even sure that he understood the question. He'd managed to scrawl out the five hundred words demanded but he was fairly certain that he'd get a bad grade ... a C or even a fail. When Alex was at Brookland – the school he had gone to in south London – he'd always done well, even when he was missing classes, dragged out of school by MI6. But there was a part of him now that just didn't care. He picked up the pages and stuffed them into his backpack. Then he went downstairs.

Sabina was already in the kitchen with her mother, sitting down to breakfast. Liz Pleasure had set out pancakes and fresh fruit, cereal and coffee. Alex remembered the first time he had met the family – when they had invited him on a surfing holiday in Cornwall. He had thought then how close they were and had secretly envied them. His own parents had died soon after he was born and he had never had a proper family of his own. Well, now he was one of them. He had become a son to Edward and Liz, a younger brother to Sabina (she was three months older than him). So why didn't he feel that he belonged? Why did he still walk into the room like an invited guest?

"Good morning, Alex!" Liz beamed at him and poured him a glass of freshly-squeezed orange juice. She was a large, round-faced woman who was always cheerful. If she worried about Alex, she was careful never to show it. "Did you get your homework done?"

"Yes. I finished it last night." Alex sat down next to Sabina. In the corner, Rocky, the family Labrador, thumped his tail lazily against the floor as if he was glad to see Alex too.

"I had two pages of Math," Sabina complained. "It took me ages!"

"Well, you should have started it when you got in," her mother scolded her. "Instead of watching all that TV."

"Math" not "Maths". Alex noticed what Sabina had said. She had been in America for less than a year but it seemed to him that she had quickly folded herself into her new life.

Edward Pleasure was away. He was working on a news story in Los Angeles and wouldn't be back for a couple of weeks. Liz was also a writer, finishing a book about fashion. She had a study at the back of the house, overlooking the garden and worked from there. "Did you sleep OK?" she asked.

Alex looked up. He hesitated for just a moment, then answered automatically. "Yes. I slept fine."

He hadn't. The nightmare had woken him again. He was back in the chapel at the eighteenth-century fort in the desert outside Cairo. Razim was there – the madman and agent of Scorpia who hoped to make a name for himself by finding an exact measurement for pain. And Julius Grief was standing in front of him, bobbing up and down in excitement. The boy was also mad in his own way. He had been surgically altered to turn him into an exact replica of Alex and it was as if Alex was looking into a fairground mirror, seeing a distorted version of himself.

Alex was tied to a chair, unable to take his eyes off the television screen in front of him. Wires had been attached to different parts of his body: his neck, his fingers, his forehead, his naked chest. He could feel the chill of the air conditioning against his skin. But there was something even colder in the room. It was his own terror. Razim and Julius Grief were about to murder the person he most loved and they were forcing him to watch.

Once again he saw Jack Starbright on the screen. She was his closest friend. She had looked after him for most of his life. But there was nothing he could do for her now. She had managed to escape from her cell by prising out one of the bars in the window. She had found a car, parked in the courtyard outside. The keys had been left in the ignition. She climbed in, unaware that this was what they wanted her to do – that her every move was being monitored. In his dream Alex screamed at her to stop. He was twisting in the chair, straining against the ropes that held him. Julius Grief was laughing.

The car drove out of the fort and into the desert. And then, as it had done the night before and every night after Alex had finally managed to fall asleep, it blew up. There had been a bomb concealed inside. Razim had stage-managed the entire escape simply to torture him. Alex saw the flames as he had seen them fifty times before and woke up in his room on the fourth floor, his pillow damp with sweat and tears.

Sabina's mother had served him a pancake but he pushed the plate away, unable to eat. She noticed this and eyed him warily. "Aren't you hungry, Alex?"

"No, thanks." Alex tried to smile. "I'm fine with orange juice."

"Well, make sure you eat at midday. Sabina – keep an eye on him!"

"Yes, Mum," Sabina said. She couldn't keep the worry out of her voice. She knew there was something wrong.

A few minutes later, Alex and Sabina left. They were both at the same high school, just a few blocks north, close to the huge park – the Presidio – that gave the area its name. To Alex, the Elmer E. Robinson High School looked more like a university, with half a dozen low-rise buildings spread across beautifully kept lawns and an oversized Stars & Stripes fluttering at the entrance. There was a theatre, a brand-new library, a thousand-seat auditorium, tennis courts, basketball courts and, of course, an American football field. It was home to over two thousand students and made Brookland seem small and old-fashioned.

"Are you sure you're OK?" Sabina asked as they approached the fountain that stood outside the main entrance. "I know how hard this must be for you."

"I'm fine, Sab. Really."

"Maybe you should change your mind about Los Angeles. We can have lots of fun down there and Dad really wants to see you."

Normally, Edward Pleasure came home at weekends but he had a Saturday meeting and the family had decided to take advantage of the warm weather and spend some time together on the coast at Santa Monica.

"No. I'll be fine and it's good that the three of you have a bit of time on your own." They'd reached the steps leading up to the main door. "I'll see you later. Have a good day."

"You too."

The two of them went their separate ways. Sabina had deliberately stayed close to Alex in his first week as he tried to settle in, but they'd agreed that it would probably be easier for both of them if they moved apart, allowing Alex to make his own friends. Anyway, Alex had noticed that Sabina had met someone else. Blake was seventeen, broad-shouldered, blond-haired with an easy smile. He was the senior basketball captain and one of the most popular boys in the school. Alex had taken an immediate dislike to him and then felt annoyed with himself for doing so. What was wrong with him?

He'd never been like this when he was in the UK.

It wasn't working out. He had to admit it. Most of the students at EERHS had been welcoming but somehow he was still on his own ... and he understood why. You can't make friends unless you're completely honest and there was simply too much mystery about Alex, too much that he couldn't explain. He couldn't tell anyone why he had no parents, why he was living with Sabina and her family, what he had been doing for the past year, why he had come to the United States or even how he had managed to get a visa. He just hoped things would get better in time. After a year, or maybe two years, people would begin to accept him.

The bell was about to go for the first class of the day. Alex strolled over to his locker to take out some books but as he opened the metal door, a hand came out of nowhere and slammed it shut again. Alex felt a tightness in his stomach as he turned round. Yes. It was just as he had thought. Clayton Miller and Colin Maguire. CM and CM. The two of them had decided to give him another dose of their daily medicine.

Alex knew that there were boys like them in every school in the world and no matter how hard teachers tried or how many parents complained, nothing would make them go away. They were bullies. Nobody knew quite why they did what they did. Perhaps they were victims themselves, damaged in some way by their own families. Perhaps they were unwell. But they were always together. They were always picking on someone. EERHS had a Student Code of Conduct that forbade any sort of abuse ... physical, mental or cyber. Unfortunately, it seemed they hadn't read it.

Colin was the younger of the two, sixteen with curly black hair, bad skin and freckles. He wasn't exactly fat but he had the sort of flabbiness that comes with bad diet, no exercise and smoking. Clayton was a year older, with blond hair slicked back and a lazy eye. He worked out obsessively – in his bedroom and at the gym where his brother worked – and it showed. If Colin was the brains, Clayton was the muscle. Colin made the decisions. Clayton made sure they were carried out.

"How are you doing, England?" Colin asked. That was what he had called Alex ever since he had learned he was from the UK.

"I'm OK," Alex said, quietly.

"I gotta question for you," Colin continued and Clayton sniggered, waiting for what was to come. "How come you got no mommy? What happened to your mommy, England? I heard she dropped you because she didn't like you. Is that true?"

"My mother's dead," Alex said.

"Oooh! I'm so sorry!" Colin was jeering at him, screwing up his face in mock sympathy. "But now you got Sabina to look after you. Is she your mommy now?"

Alex felt a wave of cold fury shudder through him. It would be so easy to take out these two creeps. He was a first-grade *Dan*, a black belt in karate. He imagined an elbow strike to the side of Colin's head, followed by a jab punch – using the index and middle fingers – straight into Clayton's throat. In less than three seconds, they would be writhing on the floor. He could actually feel the muscles in his arms tensing up as they prepared for action and he had to force himself to remain calm. Hitting back wasn't the answer. If he did that, he would be as bad as them. And anyway, he was the stranger here, the freshman. It would only cause him trouble if he attacked these two kids.

Fortunately the bell rang. Clayton flicked a hand against the side of Alex's face and Colin sniggered. The two of them lumbered away. Alex took his things out of the locker and headed off for the first class.

The rest of the school day was much like any other. In the morning, there were two classes of ninety minutes each, then lunch, then two more classes. In the afternoon, he had a session with his counsellor, a pleasant African-American woman called Mrs Masterson who had been assigned to him the day he had arrived. This was their third meeting and Alex had quickly learned how to lie to her, how to make her believe that everything was going well. It was only when the final bell went and he drifted back outside that he realized that he had barely spoken to anyone his own age. Once again, he was annoyed with himself. He had to make more of an effort. Surely he could do better than this?

He had brought his laptop with him and, sitting in the sun waiting for Sabina, he opened it and connected to the school's high-speed wireless network. It was something he'd been doing more and more recently. He liked to see how Chelsea FC were doing, picking up the scores of games he hadn't actually seen. He glanced at a few news stories – what was on TV, stuff on social media – and even checked out the weather in London. He knew it was stupid, but it somehow made him feel less far away. He still got emails from Tom Harris, his best friend at Brookland, and Jane Bedfordshire, the school secretary, had contacted him too. He knew they were both worried about him and he always tried to answer as cheerfully as he could. There had never been anything from Smithers, from Mrs Jones or anyone else at MI6 – but nor did he expect it. They had probably forgotten about him and if they did want to reach him, they wouldn't send anything as insecure as an email.

It was four o'clock in San Francisco, which meant it was nearly midnight in London: too late for any new emails. However, there was one message in Alex's inbox. It was from a company called HERMOSA. Alex had never heard of it. The message had no subject. It was probably spam and he was about to delete it when, at the last moment, something guided his hand and he double-clicked and opened it instead.

Three words appeared on the screen.

ALEXX
I'M AL

That was it. No sign-off. No image. No link. No explanation. But Alex stared at the screen as if he had been electrocuted. He sat there, utterly unaware of the other students walking past, climbing into the yellow buses that would take them home. He didn't see or hear anything. He didn't feel the sunshine on his neck and arms. At that moment, Alex even forgot that he was in America. Everything that had happened in the past month was wiped away.

He slammed the laptop shut and went to find Sabina.

FROM LIMA WITH LOVE?

"It's from Jack," Alex said.

"Alex..." Sabina looked at him darkly. She didn't know what to say.

"I know it is." Alex's voice was low. He was speaking slowly. But there was a fire in his eyes that Sabina hadn't seen for a long time and he was leaning forward with his whole body tensed, as if he was about to break into a run.

She shook her head. "It's just three words, Alex. And the last word doesn't even make sense. 'I'm Al.' What does that mean?"

"'I'm alive'. That's what she was trying to tell me. She managed to get her hands on a computer – but only for a few moments. Someone came in before she finished typing the word."

"You can't know that." Alex had opened his laptop a second time and she gazed at the screen, trying to make sense of it. "It could be from someone called Al. It could be Alexander or Alistair or Alice. Or it could be the start of something else.

'I'm alone.' Or 'I'm always thinking of you.'"

"But it isn't," Alex insisted. "It's from Jack."

He had found Sabina as she came out of the Art Studio. She had been talking to two other girls and without a word of explanation he had pounced on her and dragged her away. Now the two of them were sitting at one of the picnic tables near the fountain, opposite the main entrance. The campus was almost empty. The field hockey team was training on the pitch behind them and they could hear drum rolls and the wail of trumpets coming from the school jazz band, who were practising in the theatre. But the buses had left, the teachers had gone and only a few last students were still trickling out of the doors.

Sabina didn't know what to think. She had heard her parents talking and knew that both of them were desperately worried about Alex and had even been thinking of sending him back to get proper help, closer to home. For her part, she had been really excited when she heard that he was going to live with them in San Francisco, but from the moment he got off the plane, she had known it wasn't going to work, that this wasn't the same Alex she had met at Wimbledon Tennis Club one year before. Of course she understood what he had been through but at the same time there was something else. The two of them had grown apart. It wasn't anyone's fault. Maybe it was simply the fact that they hadn't seen each other for so long.

Now she wasn't sure how to respond.

"It doesn't even say it's from Jack," she said.

"It doesn't need to." Alex tapped the screen. "Look what she calls me. Alexx with an extra X."

"Isn't that a typing error?"

"No! It was a sort of joke between us. She always did it. It's my name followed by a kiss. It was her way of saying 'with love'."

Sabina still looked doubtful. "What about HERMOSA? What's that?"

Alex shook his head. "I don't know. I've googled it. *Hermosa* is the Spanish word for beautiful. It's the name of a beach here in California and an old subway station in Chicago. There's a place called Hermosa in Mexico City. It could mean anything – it's just the name of the account."

"Do you think Jack is in Mexico City?"

"I don't know, Sabina." Alex sighed. "I suppose she could be anywhere."

"But she's dead, Alex." Sabina hadn't meant to be so cruel but the words had simply slipped out and now it was too late. "You saw what happened. You were there!"

Alex fell silent. He didn't want to think back but he had no choice. Jack had been driving a car that had blown up in front of his eyes. He pictured it now as he had seen it then ... tied up, the television screen in front of him, the car exploding in a ball of flame. Could it have been somehow faked? Of course it was possible. Alex had seen New York and San Francisco utterly destroyed any number of times in big Hollywood films. These days, with special effects, it was possible to do anything.

But he had to ask himself – what would have been the point? Razim had no reason to spare Jack's life. She was no use to him. And if she wasn't dead, where was she? It had been six weeks since Alex had left Egypt. Why wouldn't she have got in touch with him before now? And where was Hermosa? Mexico City, Chicago, California ... none of those destinations made any sense at all.

"I don't know what happened any more, Sabina," he said – and his voice was husky. "I just opened my laptop after the last lesson and I saw this message and somehow I know it's from Jack."

The two of them sat in silence. Just then, a boy came out of the main door and began to walk down to the street. Alex recognized him. All sorts of different groups hung out together at EERHS. There were the artsy kids, the athletic kids, the drama kids, the nerds and the geeks. The boy was called Johnny Feldman and he definitely belonged to the last category. He was small and reedy with long, fair hair and glasses. He was wearing a zip-up sweater and skinny jeans. He and Alex had only one thing in common: Johnny had also been picked on by Colin and Clayton. Alex had once seen him come out of the toilet with his glasses crooked and blood dripping from his nose, although, following the unwritten school code, Johnny had insisted that he had "slipped".

Sabina called out to him and he strolled over, a surprised look on his face. "What do you want, Sabina?" he asked.

"Can you help us, Johnny?" Before Alex could stop her, she gestured at the screen. "We just got this message. We want to know where it came from. Can you do that?"

The boy shrugged. "That's easy. Just look at the IP address."

"I don't even know what that is," Sabina said.

Johnny sat down at the computer. Alex saw that he was pleased to have been invited over – and for once he was in command. "Do you mind?" he asked. He swung Alex's laptop round and pressed a few keys. At once a string of computer code appeared on the screen. Alex tried to read it. "Return-Path ... Thread-Topic ... Message-ID..." It was all gobbledegook as far as he was concerned.

"This is the email header section," Johnny explained. "The message has been bounced around a bit. From what I can see, it was sent to somewhere in London and then redirected via SBC Global over here." He pointed at a series of numbers. "That's the originating IP address and it's pretty simple to find out where it is." Without asking, Johnny began to type, his fingers moving incredibly quickly over the keyboard. "I'm using a trace email analyser," he said. He copied and pasted the email header into the analyser and stabbed ENTER. A map came up on the screen. "There you are!" He sat back triumphantly.

Alex and Sabina leaned forward. It took them a moment to realize that they were looking at the centre of Lima, in Peru. The map covered an area from the National Stadium to the sea and must have been at least five miles square.

"It won't go any closer than that," Johnny said. "If you want to know exactly where the email came from, you have to look for something you recognize."

"How about Hermosa?" Sabina asked.

"We can try." Johnny called up a search engine and tapped in the seven-letter word, this time adding the name of the city. The extra information helped. He was directed to a specific street. "Hermosa is the name of a shop in the middle of Lima," he said. "It sells products made out of alpaca wool."

Alex was disappointed. For a moment he had thought that this was leading somewhere. But even if he was ready to believe that Jack Starbright was still alive, he couldn't see her in a shop in Lima, selling luxury jerseys and scarves.

"Is there anything else you need?" Johnny asked hopefully.

"No, Johnny," Sabina said. "Thanks for your help."

"That's cool, Sabina." Johnny got to his feet. "I'll see you around, you guys!"

Sabina waited until he had gone. Then she turned to Alex. "Well?"

The three words were back on the screen. ALEXX. I'M AL. When he had first seen them, he had felt a great rush of hope. But now they had become a lifeline that was rapidly falling to pieces in his hands. "I don't know," he said, simply.

"Alpaca wool," Sabina said. "Maybe that's what the 'al' means."

"I suppose so." He reached out and closed the laptop. "I'm sorry, Sabina," he said. "I didn't mean to come running up to you like that. But when I saw it..."

"That's all right, Alex." She laid her hand on his and just for a moment they were together again, the way they had been in England. "I know how tough this has been for you. I just want you to be happy again."

"I am happy," Alex said. He wondered if he had convinced Sabina. He certainly hadn't convinced himself.

They walked home together, then went to their separate rooms to do their homework assignments. Neither of them mentioned the email again.

The week passed, one day slipping into the next with the same warm sunshine and cloudless skies so that there was almost nothing to tell them apart. At last the weekend arrived and Liz Pleasure brought down the cases and began to pack the car for the trip to Los Angeles. Rocky, the Labrador was going too and didn't seem too happy about it, whining and making a fuss of Alex as if he knew that something was wrong.

Liz Pleasure felt it too. She hadn't wanted to leave Alex "home alone" in the first place and had only agreed because it was going to be such a short trip. Even so, she had talked to their neighbour, a retired teacher, who had promised to look in on him twice a day and she had cooked enough food to keep him going for a week. She had also made Alex promise to call her if anything went wrong. Despite her misgivings, she had to admit that Alex had quite suddenly become more relaxed and cheerful. The difference was quite remarkable. Perhaps a little time by himself was what he needed after all.

Alex was at the door when they left in the family's Ford Mustang. Liz had taken the roof down and Rocky was curled up on the back seat. Sabina was sitting in the front, already plugged into her iPhone.

"Alex, remember, if you need anything..." Liz began.

"I'll call you," Alex said.

"And if you change your mind, you can jump on a plane and come down any time. We're staying at Shutters. I've left the name and the address on the table."

"Have a great weekend," Alex said.

The car drove off. Alex stood in the doorway for a minute. The house seemed very strange and empty. It felt as if he had only just arrived, as if he had never actually lived here. He crossed the hallway and went up the main stairs, then took the little staircase that led to his room, the wooden boards creaking under his feet.

He had already written the letter. He read it one more time.

Dear Liz and Edward (and Sab),

You've all been incredibly kind to me since I came to America. I don't know how to thank you for all you've done for me. You picked me up after everything that happened and took me into your family, and I don't know how I would have been able to go on if it hadn't been for you.

I know it hasn't been easy for you. I know I haven't managed to fit in the way I would have liked ... at home and at school. I really have tried. But I can't forget Egypt. I can't get it out of my head. Sometimes it's like I'm going mad. I'm sorry about that. And I'm also sorry about what I'm doing now.

Something has happened. Sabina will explain. I got an email and it's made me think that perhaps Razim managed to lie to me and that Jack may be alive after all. Maybe I'm wasting my time and causing you all this worry for nothing but I know I won't be able to sleep until I've found the truth. So by the time you read

49

this I will have gone. Please, please don't send the police after me and whatever you do, don't tell Mrs Jones or anyone at MI6. Please don't try to follow me. I know what I'm doing. I'm fifteen now, and anyway, if you think about all the things that happened to me last year, I hope you'll agree that I can look after myself.

I don't think I'll be more than a couple of weeks. Can you tell them at school that I'm sick? And apologize to Mrs Stevens that my essay on conscious life was so rubbish? I promise you that I will text and email to let you know I'm OK.

Thank you again. I'm sorry.
With love,
Alex

He propped the letter up on the kitchen table. He had already packed his backpack, taking just a few clothes and his laptop, before Sabina and her mother had left. He had his passport and he had five hundred dollars which he'd taken from his savings, money that had come to him when his uncle, Ian Rider, had died. Alex also had a debit card that was tied to an account controlled by Edward Pleasure. It was his own money that he would be using and unless Edward blocked the account, he would be able to support himself while he was away. He had already used the card to buy a ticket online.

The taxi arrived ten minutes later. Alex left the house, locking the front door behind him and posting through the keys. He threw his backpack into the back seat and was about to get in when he noticed something on the other side of the street. Three boys. One of them dark and thickset. The other taller and more muscular. Colin Maguire and Clayton Miller. The third boy was very small, about ten years old. He was holding an ice cream. He looked scared.

Alex went round to the driver. "Do you mind waiting a moment?" he asked.

"Sure." The driver was young, Chinese American. "Take as long as you like. The meter's running!"

Alex straightened up, then crossed the road. It wasn't so surprising that Colin and Clayton should be here. They lived quite close by and Alex had often seen them in the neighbourhood. He had always taken care to avoid them.

But not today.

The two of them were towering over the young boy and as Alex approached, he saw Clayton flick his fingers almost lazily. He hit the side of the ice cream cone and knocked it out of the boy's hand, falling to the ground. "Oh, I'm sorry!" Clayton squealed in a falsetto voice. "Did I knock your ice cream over? Are you going to buy another one?"

"Why don't you buy us one too?" Colin crooned.

Alex reached them before they saw him. "Why don't you leave him alone?" he said.

51

Colin looked up, hesitated, then smiled. Clayton wanted to be sure there was no danger, but now he did the same, his own smile tugging at his lazy eye. This was exactly what they both wanted. Alex was on his own and outside the protection of the school. Apart from a taxi parked opposite, there was nobody in the street: no witnesses.

"Well, well," Colin sneered. "What are you doing here, England? You got a problem?"

"Yes, I have," Alex said. "The two of you make me sick." He glanced at the smaller boy who was staring, wide-eyed. "Go!" he said.

The boy didn't need telling twice. He turned and ran. His ice cream lay in the gutter, melting in the sun.

"I want the two of you to turn round and get lost," Alex said. "And I want you to know that if I ever hear you've hurt anyone else at the school, I swear I'll come back and deal with you."

"Oh yeah?" Even before he started speaking, Alex knew that Colin wouldn't listen to him. He still wanted to give him one last chance. But Colin had calculated the odds. There were two of them and only one of Alex. Clayton alone must weigh at least four and a half kilograms more than Alex. And there was something else Alex didn't know. Clayton gestured and Colin reached into his back pocket and took out the flick knife that he always carried when he was out of school. He pressed a button with his thumb. A short silver blade sprang out, slanting up towards Alex's face. Both of the bullies giggled.

Even as he had crossed the road, Alex had promised himself he wasn't going to physically harm the two of them. He would defend himself if he had to, but he wasn't like them. He wasn't going to start a fight on purpose. Seeing the knife made no difference. Colin had raised the stakes but Alex was still going to play the game according to his own rules.

"You're making a mistake," he said.

"And you're a loser!" Colin replied. "Why don't you run away while you can?"

"I'm not going anywhere," Alex said.

For just one moment, Colin hesitated. Clayton was also looking worried. Like most bullies, they weren't used to people standing up to them. But they still couldn't see that there was any problem. Alex was unarmed. He was a lightweight. Anyway, it was too late to back out now. They made their decision.

It was the wrong decision.

Everything happened very quickly. Colin swung the knife, aiming for Alex's chest. It seemed to the two boys that Alex did very little, but then they didn't know that he was using basic moves from *aikido*, a Japanese martial art that he had learned when his uncle was still alive. Aikido is an unusual form of self-defence in that it is entirely non-aggressive. Its aim is to bring any attacker under control "without the necessity of inflicting injury" and, more than strength, it demands total relaxation in both body and mind.

The first move was called *gokyo*. It was designed purposely to ward off a knife attack. As Colin swung forward, Alex lightly took hold of his wrist with one hand and his elbow with the other. At the same time, he seemed to shimmer sideways as he twisted round to get out of the way. Colin's hand with the knife rushed past him. Unfortunately, Alex wasn't to know that Clayton had chosen that precise moment to creep up on him from behind, hoping to use his size and strength to pinion him. The knife sliced across Clayton's arm. Clayton screamed. His hand flailed out, knocking the knife out of Colin's hand. He grabbed hold of the wound and stood there, stunned.

Colin stared, his mouth falling open in shock. Alex waited for him to make his move. It came a second later. He had lost the knife so now he lashed out with his fist, which was exactly what Alex was expecting. His second move – *tai sabaki* – was also evasive. Stepping forward, he swivelled round on his hips so that the fist swept past him, inches away from his face. Alex was standing next to a lamp post. Colin's fist slammed into the metal. Alex actually heard his fingers break. Colin fell to his knees, cradling his injured hand and howling. Behind him, Clayton was still clutching his wound. Blood was trickling between his fingers

There was only one more thing to do. Alex took

out his mobile and dialled 911. "There's been an accident in Lyon Street," he said. "Two young guys seem to have damaged each other. Can you send an ambulance?" He hung up.

He didn't think Clayton was too badly injured and he was quietly pleased with the way it had all gone. He hadn't actually hurt either of the boys. Their injuries were entirely self-inflicted ... and when word got out about what had happened, they would become a laughing stock and at that moment they would lose whatever power they'd ever had.

He went back to the taxi.

"What was all that about?" the driver asked.

"Just saying goodbye to a couple of friends," Alex replied.

The taxi drove Alex straight to San Francisco International Airport. Two hours after that, he was settling into his economy-class seat on Flight UAL 8900. He wasn't heading for Lima, even if that was where Jack's email had come from. Johnny Feldman had said it had been bounced all over the world and Alex knew he had to go back to the last place he had seen her. That was Egypt. In eighteen hours he would be landing in Cairo.

And what would he do when he got there? Alex didn't think of that. He sat back and closed his eyes as the engines roared and the plane jolted forward. Jack was alive. He was sure of it. He was going to find her.

BACK TO SIWA

Cairo Airport was worse than Alex remembered.

The last time he had arrived here – less than two months ago – he had been with Jack and the two of them had been met by a pleasant, smartly-dressed man from the British embassy who had whisked them through passport control and into an air-conditioned car. This time it was a completely different experience as he stood on his own at the back of the long line that stretched towards the booths where every tourist had to buy their entry visa. Half an hour later and twenty-five dollars poorer, Alex finally presented himself at passport control.

This was the moment he had been dreading. He wondered if he would even be allowed into the country. It wasn't just that he was a fifteen-year-old boy, travelling on his own – although that was unusual in itself. He was also well known to the Egyptian authorities. As he handed over his passport to the young, scowling official behind his

glass window, Alex imagined the word SPY pop-
ping up on his computer screen. And then what?
The political situation in Egypt was fragile, to say
the least. The authorities were constantly on the
lookout for trouble. There was every chance that
he would be dragged off to jail.

The passport officer tapped a few buttons on his
keypad. Alex watched. He was aware of the sweat
trickling down his face and hoped he didn't look
as nervous as he felt. But everyone was sweating.
The air-conditioning system inside the airport had
broken down. Or perhaps it simply wasn't up to the
job of cooling so many people.

"What is the purpose of your visit?" The passport officer spoke good English. He held Alex with
his eyes.

"I'm on holiday," Alex said.

"You have come here alone?"

"My aunt is waiting for me outside. She lives in
Shobra Street." It was a name that Alex had picked
at random from the Internet.

"What is her name?"

"Susan."

Alex hadn't been expecting the question and
it was the first name that came into his head.
Fortunately, the officer wasn't interested. His fist
came punching down, stamping the passport. Alex
was through.

Next came the shock of the city itself. Emerging
from the airport, Alex was hit by the full heat

of the sun, the stale gusts of air and the stink of petrol fumes. He climbed into the first taxi he saw, and it was only after he had closed the door and given the driver the name of his hotel that he realized it had no meter and he would end up paying two or three times the correct price for the journey. That didn't matter. He was just glad to be away. He leaned back, the springs creaking underneath him as he was carried once again into the noise and the confusion of Cairo; the traffic at permanent standstill, the crumbling offices and apartment blocks with their washed-out advertising hoardings, the rubble and the dust. There were thousands of people crowding the pavements, some of them carrying huge bundles, some of them arguing at market stalls, many of them simply standing motionless as if pinned down by the sun.

After the calm of San Francisco, he felt utterly lost and it was only now that he began to think about what he had done. He had run away, leaving his home and crossing the entire world – and all because of an email that might have originated in Peru! Did he really think Jack had sent it? Yes. He had to believe that. It was much too late to go back.

The taxi took him to a hotel which he had also chosen online. He wanted somewhere not too expensive, close to the centre of town. Somewhere that wouldn't ask too many questions. The Hotel Neheb was recommended on TripAdvisor as a secure base for student travellers. That sounded about right. It only cost four hundred Egyptian pounds – about thirty British pounds – a night. It turned out to be a small, whitewashed building, half covered in scaffolding, close to Tahrir Square. Alex had booked for just one day and one night. He hoped he wouldn't have to stay even as long as that.

The reception area was small and shabby with a fridge selling drinks and a slowly turning fan. A couple of backpackers were sitting on a low sofa, smoking cigarettes and drinking Coke. There was a wooden counter and, behind it, a receptionist – young and unshaven – sitting with a number of old-fashioned keys hanging on hooks behind him. He checked Alex's passport and then photocopied it, using a machine that wheezed as it scanned the page with a blinding green light. He took an imprint from Alex's bank card, then directed him towards a narrow staircase. There was no lift.

Alex's room was at the far end of a gloomy corridor on the third floor. All the light bulbs were broken and someone had left a basket of dirty laundry right outside the door. The room itself was square and basic and about as comfortable as a prison cell. It had a single bed with a dark, patterned bedspread, an outdated TV and a locked window with a view of a concrete flyover. An ancient air-conditioning unit clung to the wall. There were no curtains. As Alex went in, a large cockroach scuttled across the floorboards and disappeared under the bed but Alex was too hot and tired to care. He stripped off and went into the bathroom, which contained a sink, a toilet and shower, the three of them so close that it would have been possible to use all of them at the same time. The shower spat out a dribble of lukewarm water but Alex made the best of it, drying himself on the thinnest and roughest of towels.

Finally, he turned on the air conditioner – which whined and rattled but made no immediate difference to the temperature of the room – and threw himself onto the bed. He fell asleep almost at once to the sound of car horns blaring, police whistles blasting, people shouting and above it all, the serene call to prayer.

Meanwhile, only one mile away, a man was sitting behind a desk in an oversized room, examining the file that had just been placed in front of him. The man was short but he had a powerful presence with thickset shoulders and intense, dark eyes. His neck seemed to be melting into his collar and his black hair shone with the grease that he had used to keep it in place. He was wearing a suit that had been tailor-made for him in Paris, along with a white shirt and no tie. The man liked gold. There was a chunky gold chain around his neck and three huge gold rings, weighing down his fingers.

There was a long silence. The man was angry. He looked as if he was about to explode.

"Alex Rider," he muttered at length.

"Yes, sir. He arrived two hours ago."

"Why was I not informed immediately?"

The conversation was in Arabic. The man standing opposite him was younger, also dressed in a suit. But his was cheaper and fitted him badly. It clearly showed the outline of the handgun that he was carrying in a holster beside his left arm. "It wasn't our fault, sir," he explained. "There was a computer malfunction at the airport. The passport officer did not receive the correct information until it was too late to take action."

The man with the gold rings swore, using a particularly filthy collection of words. "Does nothing work in this city any more?" he demanded. "This whole country is going to the dogs!" He took a deep breath. "So where is he now?"

"We don't know, sir." The younger man blinked and continued quickly. "But we will find him very soon. The hotels have to hand in the names of their guests."

"I know that!"

"Some of the lists arrive later than others but we are scanning them now and as soon as we've found him—"

"You will collect him personally, Ibrahim. And take someone with you. Alex Rider is a very tricky, very dangerous customer. I want you to find him. Rough him up if he causes you any trouble. Don't break anything." The man slammed his fist down on the desk. "Just make sure you bring him to me!"

*   *   *

It was half past six when Alex woke up, once again covered in sweat. He had another shower and put on a fresh T-shirt. He had decided to leave the hotel. According to the Internet, a bus left for Siwa every night at eleven o'clock and that suited him well. It was better to keep on the move. He could grab another few hours' sleep on the way.

Siwa.

The location of Razim's desert fort. The place where Jack had died. Even thinking about it made him feel sick.

It was only a short distance to the Cairo Gateway bus station and Alex decided to walk. The city was quieter and cooler now that the evening had come, and he could grab some street food on the way. He glanced out of the window and was about to leave when the screech of tyres on the road told him that a car had just pulled in and that it was in a hurry. He looked down and saw a black SUV outside the hotel. Even as he watched, two men climbed out and disappeared through the front door. He knew at once that they had come for him. It wasn't just the fact that they were wearing suits in a hotel where the dress code was most definitely torn jeans and T-shirts. There was something too definite, too serious about the way they moved. Police? Military intelligence? Or something worse? It didn't matter. He had less than a minute to work something out.

The receptionist would have already told them he was here. In another few seconds they would be on their way upstairs.

There was no lift. There was only one staircase. Alex could go up or he could go down. He could try to find somewhere to hide in the hotel – but where? All the doors along the corridor were closed. There was nowhere to hide inside the room. He had tested the window. It didn't open. He couldn't climb out and he could already hear footsteps at the end of the corridor, coming up the stairs. Somehow, he had to disappear immediately.

Thirty seconds later, the two men reached the third floor and began to move down the corridor. They pushed past an old Arab woman wrapped in a traditional cloak – an abaya – with a huge basket of laundry on her head, and continued down to the door. It was locked. Ibrahim pounded his fist on the door and waited for it to open.

Meanwhile, Alex Rider turned the corner and hurried down the stairs. The disguise would only have worked in the darkness of the corridor. The cloak was his bedspread, the basket taken from outside the room. In the shadows, his face had been invisible to the two men. Now he ran down the three floors and out through the reception area, still carrying the basket. Outside, the sun was setting but it was still light and he knew that the trick would no longer work. Sure enough, he saw the black car parked in front of the hotel.

Inside there was a third man, a driver, rising out of his seat, reaching inside his jacket for a gun. Alex didn't hesitate. The man was half out of the car when Alex hurled the bedspread and laundry basket at him, dirty clothes spilling over his face. Alex kicked out, slamming the door. The man shouted and fell back, and at the same time Alex slid over the bonnet and ran across the road, dodging between the traffic.

He didn't stop when he reached the other side. There were three men after him and he had only held them up briefly. He ducked down an alleyway between a café and a stall selling pancakes. Breathless and already sweating – the shower had been a waste of time – he emerged into another main road and flagged down the first taxi he saw. Once again, the car had no meter. The driver was a smiling, bearded man, missing one of his front teeth. Wooden beads and several air fresheners hung from the mirror beside his head.

"Yes, sir. Yes, sir. You want to see Pyramids? You want felucca ride on the Nile?"

Alex twisted round and looked out of the window. He hadn't been followed. "Take me to the Gateway bus station," he commanded.

"The bus station?" The driver's face fell. It was only a few streets away and he'd been hoping for a better fare.

"Just go!" Alex took out his wallet. "I'll pay you ten dollars."

It was a lot of money. The driver grinned and rammed the cab into gear, steering it into the traffic.

The Cairo Gateway bus station was huge and surprisingly modern. It also contained shops, offices and restaurants. Alex hadn't eaten for eight hours and he was hungry. He paid the driver and went inside, passing through a security checkpoint where his bag was searched. He had noticed a lot of soldiers and policemen out on the street and guessed that people must have grown used to living their entire lives in a state of alert. There was a row of offices – they were actually little more than booths – on either side of the entrance and he quickly found the one for Siwa. The name was advertised in English as well as Arabic. It was closed. He glanced at his watch. It was seven o'clock. The bus was due to leave in four hours. Perhaps the office would open later.

"No bus!" The man in the next booth had been watching him. He signalled Alex over. "No bus today. No bus tomorrow. Maybe day after."

"Why?" Alex felt exhausted. He didn't know what else to say.

The man shrugged. "You come back another time."

But Alex realized he might not have another time. He couldn't go back to the Hotel Neheb. That much was certain. Somebody was looking for him and although there were seven million people in

Cairo, he knew that a solitary English teenager would stand out like a sore thumb. He had to be on his way. Could he perhaps take a bus or a train to Alexandria and work his way down from there? Or what about a taxi...?

The man who had brought him here was still waiting outside, hoping for a new passenger. Alex examined the dusty black and white cab with its crumpled side panels and cracked wing mirror. It must be at least thirty years old. Would it even be able to manage a journey of four hundred and fifty miles? He went over to the driver.

"I want to go to Siwa."

"Siwa far, far away!" The driver rolled his eyes and grinned, showing his missing tooth. "I take you but you pay five hundred dollar."

"Forget it." Alex knew that the man was being ridiculous. The bus would have cost less than ten dollars.

"All right, English. How much you pay?"

"Fifty dollars." Alex had the beginnings of a headache. He just wanted to be on the road.

"Two hundred and fifty."

"A hundred. If you don't like it, I'll find someone else."

"A hundred dollar is good! I like it!"

"Great."

Alex got into the car. The driver rubbed his hands gleefully and started the engine. A few seconds later, they were away.

*   *   *

They drove through the night, taking the Alexandria Desert Road west from the city. It took them an hour and a half to leave the street lights and the buildings behind them, and suddenly they were cutting through the desert with nothing except darkness on either side of them. There was very little traffic. Occasionally, a car or a lorry would come shooting past. It seemed every vehicle on the road was going faster than they were. Slumped on the back seat, his arms and legs sticking to the plastic, Alex wished that he'd found time to grab some dinner before they'd gone. They'd stopped once at a garage on the outskirts of Cairo and he'd been able to buy a sandwich and two bottles of water but his stomach still felt empty. He gazed out of the window, pressing his face against the glass. There was no view whatsoever.

Another hour passed. The driver had introduced himself as Yusuf and they had talked a little as they fought their way out of Cairo. But any conversation had dried up like the land that surrounded them and Alex had surrendered himself to the monotony of the journey, the wooden beads and air fresheners swaying hypnotically and the entire car rattling every time they came to a pothole or a bump in the road.

Somehow Alex managed to fall asleep because the next thing he knew, the sun had risen and there were other vehicles on the road. He looked out of the window at the blue sky and the end-lessly stretching sand. He saw a cluster of buildings ahead of them.

Yusuf noticed him moving. "Siwa!" he exclaimed.

Alex blinked. Siwa was a small, dusty town in the middle of nowhere, surrounded by palm trees with the mountains stretching out behind. Everything was built of sand-coloured bricks, beaten into different shades of grey and yellow by the desert sun. Yusuf pulled in and parked at a junction with cafés and shops spilling out onto the pavement, oil drums, crates and boxes, great sacks filled with spices and overhead, a tangle of telephone wires that seemed to be holding every-thing together. Alex noticed that there was a second, more ancient town looming over Siwa on a hillside. It was deserted and, bizarrely, looked as if it had somehow melted. He had read about it on his laptop and knew that it had done just that. The town was called Shali Ghadi and it had been built out of salt and mud bricks. Three days of heavy rain – back in 1926 – had nearly destroyed it.

Yusuf turned off the engine. "Finish!" he said.

Alex shook his head. This wasn't where he wanted to be. "There's a place in the desert," he explained. "A fort. It's ten miles from here."

"I don't drive fort. I drive Cairo to Siwa. This Siwa!"

Alex took out another twenty-dollar bill and handed it to him. "We can ask," he said.

"Someone must know how to get there."

Yusuf took the money reluctantly, stuffing it in his shirt pocket, then went across the road to a coffee bar where a group of men were sitting, smoking cigarettes and talking. Alex went into a shop and bought himself a can of Coke. The shop-keeper had taken it out of a fridge but it was cool rather than cold and tasted well past its sell-by date. He noticed that Yusuf was busily talking to two of the men outside the coffee bar, but some-thing was wrong. The men weren't looking at Yusuf. They were looking past him, their eyes fixed on Alex. And they didn't look pleased.

Both the men were Berbers, North Africans rather than Arabs, clean-cut, slightly European-looking. Most of the people in Siwa were wearing traditional Arab clothes but these men were dressed in a modern style – jeans and loose-fitting shirts – although one of them had a skullcap and the other an ornate silver cross around his neck. As Alex watched, a third man got to his feet and stepped forward. He was bearded, scowling, with thick arms and a paunch. He had recently been injured. There were grimy bandages wrapped around his neck. He muttered something and Yusuf nodded slowly.

Alex finished his Coke. Yusuf came back over. "What was all that about?" Alex asked.

"I ask the way," Yusuf explained but there was something in his eyes that made Alex wonder if he was telling the whole truth. "They say fort bad place," he added.

"It is a bad place," Alex agreed. "Do you know how to get there?"

"Yes."

"Then let's go."

They got back into the cab and with one last glance in the direction of the coffee bar, Yusuf started the engine. A road that was little more than a dirt track led out of the town and into the great emptiness of the surrounding desert. Alex had never driven on it before. On both occasions when he had been taken to the fort, he had flown in by helicopter. They left the palm trees and the mountains behind them and, for a while, there was only sand stretching out in every direction. Heat haze shimmered ahead of them, obscuring the view.

And then, quite suddenly, Alex saw the outer walls of the fort rising up in the distance. He had known that the first sighting would be difficult but it was worse than that. It was like being punched in the head. His heart felt as if it was beating at twice the right speed.

Perhaps Yusuf understood something of what Alex was going through. He was muttering what might have been a prayer in Arabic as he steered the cab round to the great arched gateway that was the main entrance. The wooden gates were hanging open but he didn't drive in. He pulled up outside and waited for Alex to get out.

70

"I'll be about an hour," Alex said. In fact, he thought he might be longer but he had given Yusuf twenty dollars ... more than enough for his time. It also occurred to him that the taxi driver might be hoping to take him back to Cairo, earning a second fare.

Yusuf said nothing. Alex began to walk towards the gateway.

His legs felt heavy. It was as if the sand was dragging him down. He saw the sun-bleached walls looming up in front of him, still pock-marked with machine-gun bullets from the night when Unit 777, the Egyptian counter-terrorism squad, had launched its attack. Not wanting to, but knowing that he had to, Alex turned his head and looked for the burnt-out Land Rover that Jack had been driving moments before her death. It wasn't there. Someone had cleared it away.

He reached the gates and was trying to find the strength to walk through when he heard the sound of a car engine starting up. He turned again, just in time to see Yusuf reversing away from the fort, the wheels of his taxi spinning in the sand. The car twisted round, then shot off. Alex opened his mouth to call out, then realized there was no point. The taxi disappeared very quickly, swallowed up by the desert.

What was that all about? It didn't matter. Alex had all his things in his backpack. He knew the way back to Siwa. He would make the return journey later that evening, as soon as the sun began to set.

He took a breath, steeling himself for what lay ahead. Then he went in.

NIGHTMARE LAND

It was the worst place in the world.

Alex could never have imagined coming here again. He had done everything he could to keep the fort out of his mind. He had dreaded going to sleep in case he saw it in his dreams and even during the day he had felt its shadow stretching out towards him. His counsellor had told him that it would be better to confront what had happened at Siwa – but what could she possibly know, sitting in her comfortable office in a modern San Francisco school?

Well, he was confronting it now. Here it was, right in front of him – and suddenly he was seeing everything again. The wires attached to his chest. Razim's mad eyes and the glowing tip of his cigarette. The knives and the scalpels in the brightly-lit room and the television screen that was going to make everything so much worse.

Are you ready, Alex? There's something I want you to see...

They had killed Jack Starbright and they had forced him to watch. Standing here, with his heart thundering in his chest and his head pounding, Alex knew how much they had hurt him. He would never fully recover.

Unless Jack was alive.

It was hope that had brought him here and now it spurred him on. He had to do this – for her. Clenching his fists, he forced himself to continue forward, leaving the ruined gate behind him. His feet made no sound as they brushed against the sand. He felt the sun beating down on his neck.

He was surrounded once again by the four walls of the fortress and even though the gate was open and there was nobody in sight, he still felt trapped. Guard towers rose up at each corner and he could imagine Razim's men with their machine guns watching his every step. A movement caught his eye and he froze. But it was only a scrap of paper floating in the breeze.

He glanced towards the chapel that stood at the far end of the compound: circular, with a white dome. It looked small, even picturesque. But he knew that this was the one building he wouldn't be able to enter, no matter what happened.

The screen.

The car exploding.

Julius Grief laughing. Wasn't that great! Wasn't that cool!

Swallowing hard, Alex turned his head away.

Where to start? The entire fortress was unnaturally still and silent. It hadn't just been abandoned. It had been completely forgotten and stood here now, a fading memory of itself. Alex needed to get out of the sun and he walked purposefully towards the nearest open door. It led into the old bakery, which had been the control centre for all the sophisticated machinery that Razim used to protect himself. The chimney, which had once risen from the oven, was now broken in half, the brickwork smashed. Alex had thrown the grenade that had done the damage, knocking out the lights and the power supply and making it possible for the Egyptian special forces to invade. Once again he heard the machine-gun fire and the explosions all around him as he padded into the gloomy interior. There was nothing here but it was cooler in the shade. Alex stood still for a moment. His pulse was still in overdrive. He took several breaths, forcing himself to calm down.

It was obvious that the entire fortress had been stripped bare. Alex guessed that the Egyptian authorities had been in. They would have taken away the TV cameras, the computers, the security lights, the huge arsenal of weapons, which included machine guns, rocket launchers and flame-throwers. What about the rest of it? The local people wouldn't have been very far behind. Alex could imagine the free-for-all after the last government vehicle had left.

Televisions, furniture, fridges, coffee machines, even the stone table that had once stood outside Razim's home ... everything would have gone, probably ending up in the many street bazaars in Alexandria or Cairo.

He went out into the sunlight. His backpack was weighing down on his shoulders but he was glad that he hadn't left it in the cab. He turned up his collar to protect his neck. It was even hotter than he remembered. What now? He looked around him. The building where Razim had lived was over to the right but the fountain which had once given the illusion of cool was broken and still. The dwarf palms in front of the house were dead but there was a cactus garden that had survived. A clothes line hung between two trees. There was no sign of any clothes.

Why had he actually come here? What was he expecting to find? Alex had convinced himself that Jack was alive but he knew that he would need proof if he was going to persuade anyone else – and this was the only place he was going to find it. If the car explosion had been faked in some way, surely he would stumble across a clue or something that would tell him how it had been done. Even now he could see the route that the Land Rover had taken, across the courtyard and out the gate. Jack was smart. If she had somehow survived, she would have wanted him to know and he was certain that she would have left some sort of message behind.

That was what he had thought. But now that he was here, standing alone in the empty fort, he wasn't so sure. A single bird, some sort of vulture, swooped overhead, silhouetted against the sun. It seemed to mock him. There was nothing here. He didn't even have a lift back to Siwa.

Alex crossed the courtyard, past a well, making for the entrance to a long, narrow building with barred windows and a slanting roof made out of sheets of grey plastic. This was the prison block. It was where he and Jack had been held and it was an obvious place to start. It was also where he had seen her for the last time. *I'll come for you. I promise.* He remembered the last words she had spoken to him and at the same time it struck him that it was actually the other way round. He had come for her. He quickened his pace, shaking off the sense of helplessness that he had been feeling only moments before. He had to make this journey. He owed it to her.

The prison block door was open, hanging off its hinges, and he walked into a corridor, following it past the empty cells. Ahead of him, a scorpion froze for a moment, then scurried into the shadows. There were eight cells, all of them identical, but he recognized his own from its position, two down on the right. He didn't go in. The room with its four blank walls, barred window and wooden bunk held only bad memories. Jack had been kept a little further down, on the opposite side. Her cell was easy enough to find. It was the one with a bar missing from its window. Jack had prised it free, thinking she was escaping when all she was doing was walking into Razim's trap. Fighting his emotions, doing his best to stay calm, Alex stepped inside. His eyes swept over ... nothing. Apart from the window, the cell was no different to his own, an empty box. Even the mattress on the bunk had been taken away.

Still, he went in. He pulled himself up to the window and looked out. There was a drop of four or five metres to the ground and suddenly – a jolting flash of memory – he saw Jack falling after she had made her way out. He closed his eyes, then set about searching the room. Briefly, he examined the walls. He found nothing. The bunk was a bare slab of wood. He knelt down and looked underneath it.

And that was when he saw it. There were scratch marks on the wall, right in the corner, close to the ground. He tried to move the bunk but it was screwed into place. He could make out letters. There was a G followed by an R and maybe an N. He reached into his backpack and took out a bottle of water, splashed some on his hands and crawled under the bunk. When he was close enough, he wiped his hand across the wall, removing the surface dust. Now he could read what had been written. It wasn't an N. It was an M. Part of a name.

GRIMALDI

The letters were about one centimetre high and might have been carved with a loose nail. Still on his knees, Alex considered what it might mean. First – the most obvious question – was this the message from Jack that he had hoped for or was it simply the name of someone who had been held in the cell before her? After all, it was something that prisoners often did. They would carve their name in the wall to show that they had once been there.

On the other hand, why would they have chosen the wall under the bunk, where it wouldn't be seen? That suggested someone trying to pass on a secret. It was impossible to tell if this was Jack's handwriting and even if she was responsible, what was she trying to tell him? Grimaldi could be a person or a place. It sounded Italian. What exactly would that signify ... in the middle of Egypt? Alex had his laptop with him but he would need to get back to the town to get a signal – then, maybe, the Internet might provide an answer.

He heard something outside. The slightest sound carried across the desert and this was very distinct. It was a car approaching. Well, that was something anyway. It seemed that Yusuf had changed his mind and had come back to pick him up. Alex used his mobile phone to take a picture of the name, then got to his feet, dusting himself down. Before he left, he took one last, quick look around the cell. There was nothing else. He put the phone away, lifted the backpack over his shoulders and followed the corridor back to the main door.

As he emerged, blinking, into the sunlight, he saw that he was wrong. It wasn't Yusuf. An old dumper truck with flat tyres and rusting bodywork had driven right into the fort and even as Alex watched, it pulled up beside the well. There were four men squatting in the back and two more in the front. The driver got out and Alex recognized him. It was the man he had seen in the town, the Berber with the dirty bandages around his neck.

He was carrying a rifle.

In fact, all six men were armed. Two of them had knives. The others were carrying different sorts of clubs including, bizarrely, a brightly-coloured American baseball bat. The man with the silver cross and the man with the skullcap were part of the group. Alex knew instantly that he had been set up, that they had come for him. Yusuf had agreed to bring him here and then to abandon him; he was probably well on his way back down the road to Cairo. The men he had spoken to had collected a few friends and together, they had driven out to the fort. Why? Had they once worked for Razim? If so, it was possible that they had recognized him when he returned to Siwa – but even so, he couldn't see what they hoped to gain. Beating him up or killing him wouldn't change anything. Razim was dead. Game over.

There was no point discussing it with them. The odds were six against one and the men clearly hadn't come here for a quiet chat. Somehow Alex had to get back to the relative safety of the town. Whatever they were planning, they wouldn't be able to go through with it if there were witnesses. He took one look at them as they spread out and began their search, giving each one of them a name.

BANDAGE. He was carrying the rifle and seemed to be in charge.

SKULLCAP. Carrying a knife.

SILVER CROSS. Another knife.

BASEBALL BAT. Named after his weapon.

ANT.

DEC.

Alex didn't know why he had named the last two after popular television presenters, except that they were both short and dark-haired and looked a bit like each other. They were carrying what looked like axe handles – fortunately, without the metal blades.

So that was the enemy. At least he had them pinned down in his mind. Alex backed into the doorway, allowing the prison block to conceal him. Already he was considering his options. He was alone and unarmed. Apart from Yusuf, nobody knew he was here. He could try to hide but the men would find him eventually. It would be better to run. What then? Even if he made it out of the fort, he'd find himself in the desert, surrounded by flat sand with nowhere to hide, ten miles from the town. The men would spot him instantly and then they would jump in the truck and run him down.

Without making a sound, he doubled back along the corridor and into Jack's cell. He glanced one last time at the bunk, thinking of the name he had found underneath it. He was glad he had captured it on his phone ... the one fragment of proof that he actually had. But there was no time to think about that now. He needed to get out of the building, fast, and thanks to Jack he knew how to do it.

Once again, he pulled himself up to the window that was missing its bar and, pushing his backpack ahead of him, squeezed through the gap. The ground was a long way down and he fell with a soft thump. He snatched up the backpack, wishing that he had brought along a weapon. Where was Smithers when he needed him? A couple of exploding coins, a miniature smoke bomb, a mobile phone with an anaesthetic dart ... he would have been grateful for anything. He heard a voice coming from the other side of the building, someone giving orders in Arabic. He guessed it was Bandage. He was the most dangerous of them. He was the one with the gun.

Alex knew that, whatever happened, he had to stay out of sight. It was his only advantage. This was going to be a cat-and-mouse game and fortunately there were plenty of holes for the mouse to hide. Even so, he couldn't just let them hunt him down. Time was on their side. They could stay here all night if they wanted, while he had no food and little water. Somehow he had to reduce the odds. They had split up and that was their first mistake. It gave him the chance to sneak up on them one at a time. And what then...? He arrived at one of the salt piles – Razim's men had once collected salt from the desert – and scooped up a handful of the white crystals. Briefly, he considered hiding himself in the pile but he knew it was out of the question. The chemicals in the salt were too toxic. He remembered what they had done to Razim.

He reached the corner and peered round just as Skullcap appeared. He looked enormous, walking with the sunlight behind him, a dark shadow looming over Alex as he headed towards him.

Skullcap was even more surprised to see Alex than Alex was to see him. Both of them reacted at once but Alex was faster. Skullcap lifted his knife, the seven-inch blade glinting in the sun. But before he could use it, Alex threw his hand forward, his fingers splayed, as if he was casting a spell. Skullcap gasped and fell back. It wasn't magic. Alex had been holding the salt that he had taken from the pile and had thrown it into the man's eyes, blinding him. He quickly followed through, twisting round and bringing his right knee to his chest, then striking out with his heel, putting all his body weight behind it.

Skullcap crumpled without making another sound.

Five against one. And Alex now had a knife. He grabbed it.

Alex didn't waste a second. There was always a chance that one of the others might have heard the brief confrontation and he needed to move away fast. A flight of stone steps led up to the parapet, a wide ledge which ran high up along the inner wall, all the way round the courtyard. Alex took the steps three at a time, then threw himself flat when he reached the top, lying on his stomach with the battlements rising up behind him. Nobody had seen him. Catching his breath, he looked around. An ancient cannon stood a short distance away, facing out into the desert. The fort had been built during the French invasion of Egypt and the weapon must have been left behind by the armies of Napoleon. It was useless now, cracked and rusting and too heavy to move. Even a museum would probably have said it was without value. He also noticed a couple of old cannonballs, black and mottled, about the size of coconuts. Tentatively, he reached out with his foot and tested the nearest one. It was heavy but it moved.

Alex twisted onto his side and examined the courtyard. Lying on the parapet, he knew that he would be hidden from the men who were searching for him ... even if they happened to look up. He saw one of them come out of the chapel about fifteen metres away. It was Baseball Bat. He seemed to be taking a more relaxed attitude to the search.

As Alex watched, the man fumbled in his pockets, took out a cigarette and lit it. Alex measured the distance between them. He'd had an idea. As quickly as he could, he took off his wristwatch and threw it down into the sand. It was an Omega, given to him by Ian Rider, and he didn't want to lose it, but if things went well, he would get it back later. If things went badly, he wouldn't need it anyway. Baseball Bat didn't see the watch fall but he heard something hit the ground and that caught his attention. He lowered the cigarette and almost at once he saw the shine of the metal band reflecting the sun. He smiled to himself and began to move forward.

Alex curled himself behind the cannonball with his back against the wall. It was more dangerous sitting up. The top half of his body was exposed and if anyone looked up, he would be seen. But this was only going to take a moment. Alex watched as Baseball Bat drew nearer, walking towards the wall. He stopped directly beneath him and reached down for the watch. Alex lashed out with both feet, propelling the solid iron ball towards the edge. At the same time, he jerked forward so that he could see what happened.

The man was leaning down, his hand stretched out to pick up the watch, when the cannonball hit him on the side of his head. In a way, he was lucky. An inch to the right and it might have broken his neck. Instead, he received a glancing blow – but it was still enough to knock him out instantly. He fell and lay still, a pool of blood seeping into the sand.

Four against one.

Once again, Alex was on the move. Crouching down and keeping as close as he could to the battlements, he scurried like a crab ... all the way round the parapet, past the chapel and over to the house where Razim had lived. Then, he heard a shout from the other side. Skullcap had just been discovered, lying unconscious outside the prison. That changed things. They knew he was dangerous now. They would be more careful. And Bandage still had his gun.

Alex found a flight of steps leading behind the house and threw himself down them, glad to be dipping out of sight. Was it too much to hope that with two of their colleagues injured – one of them badly – the others might give up? Unfortunately, they seemed to be doing the exact opposite. Alex saw Bandage checking his gun. It was an old Lee–Enfield self-loading battle rifle, the sort used by the British Army in the Second World War. Alex guessed there would be twenty bullets in the box magazine – if it was fully loaded. It was clearly the game-changer here. Whoever had the gun had control of the entire courtyard and the gate. At the moment that wasn't him. Was there anything he could do?

The four survivors had gathered on the other side of the well. Squatting behind Razim's cactus garden, Alex could see them clearly. Bandage was rasping out orders in Arabic. Clearly, he had decided that some sort of plan was required before there were any more casualties. Sure enough, one of the men – Dec – climbed up to the parapet, taking the same steps that Alex had used. From there, he would have a view across the entire courtyard and could warn the rest if Alex made a move. The two others set off towards the bakery. They obviously thought they would be safer as a pair. Bandage positioned himself at the very centre, next to the well. He had a good view of the main gate and most of the buildings. Wherever Alex appeared, he would be in the line of fire.

Alex had to do something – and soon. Dec was moving slowly round the parapet and it was only a matter of seconds before he reached the corner from where he would have no trouble spotting him. Bandage had his back to him. Alex thought about running across the courtyard, trying to surprise him. But it wouldn't work. He was too far away. Could he throw the knife? He examined the weapon in his hand. It was sharp but it was also heavy and might not fly straight. Anyway, there was something in him that recoiled at the idea of stabbing a man in the back.

Was there another way?

Yes. Alex took one quick look around him and set to work.

Bandage had also lit a cigarette. It was about the most stupid thing he could have done – and not just because smoking would kill him. Taking the packet out of his pocket, sliding the cigarette, finding a match ... all this had demanded his attention and when the man on the parapet cried out a warning, it was already too late. He turned slowly and saw that the boy had appeared, running towards him swinging something above his head. The two men had come out of the bakery and they saw it too. At first they thought it was some kind of spiked ball on a chain, the sort of thing used by a medieval knight and they were puzzled. Where could he have found a weapon like that?

Alex had used the knife to cut a length off the washing line he had seen. Then he had looped it around a barrel cactus growing in Razim's garden, pulling it tight. The cactus was about the same shape and size as the cannonball. It was covered in vicious, yellow spines – dozens of them – and Alex had been careful not to touch it. He knew how much it would hurt. Now Alex swung it round his head once, twice, while Bandage dropped his cigarette and fumbled with his gun. He was too late. Alex released the rope. The cactus flew free.

The green ball soared across the courtyard and found its target perfectly, hitting Bandage full in the face. It didn't bounce off or fall to the ground. Instead it hung there, with at least a dozen spikes piercing his lips, his cheeks, the side of his nose and one of his eyes, each one of them injecting its poison into his nervous system. Bandage shouted something. Panicking and momentarily blinded, he fired the rifle but it had been pointing in the air and the bullets went nowhere near Alex. There was a scream from the parapet and the man who had been sent up there fell to his knees, clutching his stomach with blood seeping through his hands. He had taken the full force of the blast. Alex couldn't believe his luck – but he didn't stop to congratulate himself. He was already sprinting across the courtyard. He had just a few seconds to reach Bandage before he recovered enough to fire again. Out of the corner of his eye, he saw the other two men running towards him.

Bandage was sobbing. He looked as if he had an alien growth on his face and he was puncturing his fingers, inflicting more pain on himself as he tried to rip it off. In truth, he had forgotten about Alex. He had dropped the gun. Alex reached him and, leaning backwards so that he didn't have to come too close, put him out of his misery with a single roundhouse kick. The man and the cactus went down. Alex swept the rifle off the ground and swung round just in time to bring it to aim at the two men who were only a few metres away.

They stumbled to a halt. Silver Cross and Ant. They looked at each other uncertainly. Alex gripped the gun tighter. He wanted them to believe that he was prepared to use it.

"Who are you?" Alex demanded. "Why did you come here?"

There was no answer. Alex pointed the gun at Silver Cross and took aim. "I work for Razim," the man said, simply.

"Razim's dead."

"Yes. Because of you. Now we have no jobs. We lose all our money. You take everything from us."

So Alex had been right. They had come out here – to hurt him or even kill him – purely out of revenge. He could hardly believe it. Didn't these people ever give up? At the same time, he wasn't sure what to do. He had no real interest in them. He certainly wasn't going to shoot them. Perhaps he could use the gun to persuade them to give him a lift back to Siwa.

It was the younger of the two who alerted him. Silver Cross hadn't reacted but Ant suddenly smiled. Why? Alex realized that both of them were looking past him and turned just in time to see that Bandage had recovered and was rushing towards him with a hideous look on his face, a knife in his hand. He had managed to get rid of the barrel cactus, although his flesh was horribly swollen. There was a huge bulge between his nose and his eye and his lips were twice the size they should be, with a few needles still sticking out like tribal ornaments. Alex hadn't kicked him quite hard enough.

Alex brought the gun round, pointing it at the

ground just in front of him, and squeezed the trigger. He intended to fire a warning shot, to stop him in his tracks. But nothing happened. Either there was some sort of safety catch or the old Lee–Enfield had jammed. He could only watch as Bandage took three more steps and then slashed down with the knife, aiming at his throat.

There was a single shot. Bandage screamed as his hand became a splash of red and the knife spun away. A second shot and he was thrown onto his back. Alex knew at once that he wouldn't be getting up again. He turned to see Silver Cross and his friend dropping to their knees, their hands behind their heads, surrendering.

Four more men had come bursting through the main gate. They looked like soldiers, dressed in desert khaki and carrying automatic pistols and sub-machine guns. For a horrible moment, Alex thought that new trouble had arrived, that they had come for him too. But that couldn't be the case. They had killed Bandage. They had actually saved him.

And then a fifth man appeared. He was short and dark, his black hair slicked back with too much oil. He was also dressed in desert khaki, although it somehow didn't quite suit him and, Alex noticed, he wasn't carrying any weapons. Rather oddly, there were several gold signet rings on his fingers. They certainly didn't go with the military uniform. He stomped into the courtyard with a scowl on his face, glanced at the two kneeling men, then went over to Bandage, prodded him with his foot and sniffed. Finally, he seemed to notice Alex, who was still holding the Lee-Enfield. He held out a hand. Alex handed him the gun.

The man took it. He nodded slowly, then waved one of his fingers, close to Alex's face.

"Alex Rider," he said, in an almost exaggerated Arabic accent. "You are a very naughty boy."

FREEZE-FRAME

Alex knew exactly who the man was. The two of them had met following the attempted assassination of the American Secretary of State just two months before. The man was Colonel Ali Manzour and he was the head of Jihaz Amn al Daoula, the Egyptian State Security Service. He had taken charge of the situation then and presumably had come here to do the same now. Alex wondered how Manzour had found out he was here. Could it be that Edward Pleasure had contacted MI6 after all and that they had in turn informed the Egyptians?

Alex had barely spoken to Manzour when the two of them were in Cairo. He had been so shocked by what had happened – by the death of Jack – that he'd been in a sort of daze. But now, on this second occasion, he found himself taking a liking to the intelligence chief who was already drawing a cigar out of his top pocket, biting the end off and lighting it. Despite the battledress and gold jewellery, he looked like an overworked teacher and was actually telling Alex off as if he was one.

"If you were going to come to Egypt, you should have told me first," he was saying. "We cannot have English schoolboys running around the place killing people, even scum like these. It is against the law and it is very annoying."

"I didn't kill anyone," Alex said. Even as he spoke, one of the men who had attacked him was carried past on a stretcher. It was the one he had hit with the cannonball.

"You may not have killed this one," Manzour agreed. "But I suspect that it will be a long time before he can tie up his shoelaces or even remember his own name."

"How did you find me?" Alex asked.

Manzour blew out smoke and gestured angrily with the cigar. "Do you think I am so stupid that I do not know who is coming in and out of my country? I was alerted by the officer who made the very grave mistake of stamping your passport in the first place." So that was interesting. MI6 hadn't been involved after all. "For this act of folly, he shall be sent for six months' retraining!" Manzour went on. "I hope you were comfortable at the Hotel Neheb. Yes! That is the flea pit in Cairo where you stayed. We looked for you there and when we did not find you I guessed that you must have returned here. I followed you by helicopter ... at great expense, I might add. And lucky for you! If I had arrived one minute later you would have been shish kebab!"

That wasn't quite true. Even if the Lee–Enfield had jammed, he could still have used it as a club to defend himself. But Alex didn't argue. "Thank you," he said.

"You're welcome." Manzour didn't smile.

"The people who attacked me ... they worked for Razim." Alex watched as Bandage was dragged out feet first, his head and shoulders trailing across the sand.

"They were nothing but dogs of the gutter," Manzour snapped. "It was stupid of them to come after you. Now one of them is dead and several of the others are seriously maimed. But forget about them! I hope you are satisfied with yourself, Alex. You have, I am sure, caused great upset to the people who were looking after you in America and you have achieved nothing. What exactly were you hoping to find?"

"I don't know, really," Alex said. "But I did find something. I'll show you."

Alex walked back through the fortress, snatching up his watch as he went. The strange thing was that he felt a lot better than he had in a long time. It was as if the brief burst of action had jolted something inside him and woken him up after a long sleep. He was back in control. Manzour followed him into the prison block and into Jack's cell. Alex crouched down and pointed to the word he had found, scratched into the wall beneath the bunk.

"Grimaldi." Manzour was squatting beside him. From the way he spoke the name, Alex was certain that it meant something to him. "You think your friend wrote this?"

"She may have."

"Many poor, wretched souls will have been in this prison cell. Any one of them could have been responsible."

"It looks recent."

"In the desert, everything looks old and everything looks new. It's hard to tell which is which." Manzour straightened up. "At any event, this proves nothing at all. I'm sorry. You should go back to America."

"I'm not going anywhere until I've found Jack," Alex said.

Manzour was still holding his cigar. He sucked at it, the tip glowing red. "Are you arguing with me, Alex? People do not argue with me. It is not good for my health and it is very bad for theirs." He paused and suddenly he was less threatening. "Miss Starbright is dead. You are deluding yourself if you think otherwise and it will do you no good. However, this is not the right time to discuss this. I take it you do not wish to remain in Siwa? No. I do not think you would find the town very welcoming after you have taken out half a dozen of its finest citizens. You can return with us to Cairo and we will discuss this tomorrow, after I have made further enquiries. You can travel with us by helicopter and I will arrange for you to stay in a hotel."

"That's very kind of you," Alex said.

"It is remarkably stupid of me. Really, I should have you arrested and deported." Manzour still wasn't smiling but there was a certain twinkle in his eye. "I am glad to see you again, Alex Rider. The last time that we met, it was not in pleasant circumstances but now it seems to me that you are different. That is a good thing, I would say. Come along. It's a long journey, even by air, and there is nothing more to be done here."

The two of them left the prison block and stood together in the sunshine. Manzour rapped out an order and a few moments later, a jeep came tearing through the main gate and pulled up next to them. A soldier leapt out and held the door open for them. Alex climbed into the back.

"Grimaldi," Alex said. "You know that name. Don't you!"

Manzour said nothing. He climbed into the front seat and tapped the dashboard impatiently. The driver understood. The three of them sped away.

The following morning, Alex woke up in a king-sized bed on the top floor of the luxurious Four Seasons Hotel in Cairo. It was a far cry from the Hotel Neheb where he had begun. Although Colonel Manzour had grumbled about the price, he had booked Alex into a penthouse suite. A whole wall was taken up by a huge picture window with a private balcony on the other side. Even the sheets felt expensive. Sitting in bed, Alex could see the Nile with a line of skyscrapers on the other side and, behind them, the Great Pyramids rising up in the desert, somehow mysterious and magical even at this distance. For a long time, he lay where he was, watching the river with its feluccas – traditional wooden sailing boats – and tour boats darting past. Then he got up, showered – this time in a proper jet of hot water – dressed and went downstairs for breakfast.

The Colonel had reserved a table next to the swimming pool, surrounded by white umbrellas and palm trees. He was wearing a pale suit and a light blue shirt, which was open at the collar to reveal a gold chain around his neck. He looked like a successful businessman and the outfit certainly suited him better than combat dress. As Alex sat down, a waiter brought croissants and bread rolls, fruit and tea.

"Do you want bacon and eggs?" Manzour asked.

"No. I'm fine with this," Alex said.

"I thought all English boys ate bacon and eggs and sausage and chips," Manzour said, adding unnecessarily, "it is beef bacon, of course. The tea is peppermint. Is that all right?"

"Thank you."

The two of them began to eat. Alex hadn't realized how hungry he was. He'd collapsed into bed the night before and it only occurred to him now that he'd had nothing since the sandwich on the way to Siwa.

"So we need to talk," Manzour said, suddenly serious. He had deliberately chosen a table in the corner, away from everyone else. He leaned forward, speaking softly. "I am afraid that what I told you yesterday was correct. You have wasted your time, Alex. I have gone over the evidence again and there is simply no chance that your friend is alive. I wish I could say otherwise because I can see that she meant a great deal to you. But I have seen what I have seen..." He stopped and picked up a croissant, which he tore in half as if it was to blame for the bad news. "However," he went on, "I will admit that there is one thing of great interest that you have brought to my attention. I am not sure that it is relevant but I will admit, at least, that you were right. The name in the prison cell ... it is known to me."

"Grimaldi."

"It is an Italian name and it is not that uncommon. In any other place, I might have been inclined to ignore it. But this was the fort at Siwa." He paused, glanced at the two pieces of croissant then took a bite. "You are of course aware that Abdul-Aziz al-Razim was working for the filthy criminal organization known as Scorpia. Following their last, failed operation, Scorpia have disbanded. They are finished. I have to say that this is largely thanks to you. It would seem that most of its members killed each other at one time or another and the rest of them have been arrested – but unfortunately there are two of them who are still at large. They are twin brothers. Their father was a major criminal working with the Mafia but they took over his operation after – it is said – they murdered him. Their names are Giovanni and Eduardo Grimaldi."

"They were there ... at the fort!"

"You do not know that. You do not know who wrote the name on the wall and when. You do not even know if it is the same Grimaldi. It could just be a coincidence."

"But if it was Jack who wrote it—"

"Wait!" Manzour finished eating his croissant, sipped some tea, then took out a handkerchief and wiped his lips. "Alex, you are a remarkable boy," he said. "Joe Byrne of the CIA told me a great deal about you when you were here in Cairo, but of course I had already heard much of it myself. You are not often wrong – but this time you must listen to what I say. I have looked at the evidence ... not once but several times. We have the TV images that were shown to you when you were Razim's prisoner. I examined them only last night. Do you need to be persuaded? Do you really have to see them again?"

Alex thought for a moment. He was sitting in the shade and it was almost as if a cold breeze touched the back of his neck. Could he really bring himself to watch the last moments of Jack's life? He still remembered the pain that had ripped through him. Even if Jack did somehow turn out to be alive, even if she walked up to him right now, he would never forget it. The film had almost destroyed him. But he had to see it for himself. Colonel Manzour hadn't been there. He had no real interest in finding Jack. There was still a chance that there might be something he had missed.

"All right," Alex said. "Show me."

There was a black Jaguar XJ40 waiting for them outside the hotel. It was an Eighties model made in Britain, and as Alex opened the back door to let himself in, he was surprised how heavy it was. He guessed the whole thing must be armour-plated. The driver was a huge man, bald with dark glasses. Alex suspected he was armed.

Colonel Manzour got in the front and a moment later they set off, following the river south to the Kasr Al Nile Bridge. Alex settled into the plush leather seat. The interior of the car was soft and comfortable and the air conditioning filtered out most of the noise, but even so, it looked as if the journey was going to be painfully slow. They had joined a long line of traffic that, as usual, seemed to be going nowhere but then they crossed the Nile and turned off at a roundabout, and almost at once they found themselves in an area that was quite different to the rest of Cairo. The horns, the exhaust fumes, the glare of the sun, even the heat of the city disappeared behind them as they cruised through a maze of narrow, twisting streets lined by trees that turned the light into a soft green. There were no modern offices here, no ugly, neon-lit shops. Instead, they drove past handsome villas and immaculate lawns, tucked away behind ornamental metal fences. With their grey brick walls and classical pillars, they looked more European than Arabic. Alex had seen similar architecture in the smarter streets of Paris and Rome.

Manzour twisted round in his seat. "This is called the Garden City," he explained. "It is the most expensive area of Cairo. The British and the American embassies are here. Also, some of our wealthiest citizens. My organization was fortunate to get a house in this neighbourhood. We didn't even have to threaten the owner. Well, not that much."

Alex didn't know if he was joking or not. He knew that the Egyptian intelligence service was ruthless. He had seen them at work. He didn't like to think how far they would go to get what they wanted.

The car drew in outside what looked like an abandoned building. It was four storeys high and almost invisible behind a screen of trees and shrubs that had been carefully planted to keep it private. With its balconies, arched windows and balustrades, it reminded Alex of a museum or even a church. Manzour got out and Alex followed. The driver stayed where he was. Alex was surprised to see that the front door was hanging open and nobody seemed to notice the two of them as they walked up through a garden that had been left to grow wild. A statue of a man wearing a fez stood on a plinth, a hand raised as if in welcome. Alex glanced at it, then looked a second time. There had been no sound but he was certain that the head had turned slightly, swivelling to allow the eyes to watch them as they continued forward. That was ridiculous. He had to be imagining it.

They entered a dark, wood-panelled hallway with three doors leading further into the house, all of them closed. The hall was almost empty. It had been stripped bare apart from a broken table and chair and, on the far wall, a mirror so old and dusty that it showed no reflection at all. It was only the tiny blink of a red light behind the glass that warned Alex, once again, that things might not be quite as they seemed. There was some sort of equipment, a scanner or a surveillance camera, concealed there. He remembered the house that Smithers had once occupied in Cairo. That too had looked ordinary ... until the moment when it had come under attack.

Manzour marched across the hallway and slid part of the wood panelling back to reveal a sophisticated entry system: a touchpad and a glass fingerprint reader. He entered a code, then placed his hand against the glass and a moment later there was a soft hiss and a whole section of the wall rose silently into the ceiling. Looking through, Alex saw bright lights, an open-plan area with men and women – most of them young – sitting at desks, dozens of computers, printers, monitors and other machines that he couldn't recognize. Nobody looked up as they walked through. The wall slid down behind them.

"Welcome to Jihaz Amn al Daoula," Manzour said. "I designed the entrance myself and persuaded the Americans to pay for it. They will do anything to show that we are all on the same side. Please come this way."

Alex followed him through the first room and up a modern metal staircase to the next floor. He had already noticed that although the building had plenty of windows when he had seen it from the outside, there were actually none at all now that he was inside. It was as if they had built a house within a house – with air conditioning and artificial light. They passed a series of glass-panelled offices and arrived at a desk with an attractive, serious-looking woman wearing a suit and a headscarf. She spoke a few words to Manzour in Arabic and he replied. There was a door behind the desk. They went through.

This was Manzour's office. It somehow suited him with its oversized, antique furniture, comfortable chairs, fireplace and Persian rug. There were portraits on the wall: different presidents of Egypt, including Anwar Sadat. A table had been set up to one side with a computer and two chairs. He gestured and, with a heavy feeling in his stomach, Alex sat down in front of the screen.

He stared at the grey glass, knowing what was coming. He wasn't ready for it. Suddenly he was back in Siwa with another screen in front of him. He could feel the cords attached to his wrists, the wires running down from his chest.

Are you afraid, Alex? It was Razim talking – Razim's ghost.

Alex jerked round as a hand rested briefly on his shoulder. But it wasn't Razim. It was Manzour. "Are you sure about this?" he asked. "I do not want to hurt you any more than you have been hurt already and I very much fear that it will all be for nothing."

Alex nodded. He didn't trust himself to speak.

Manzour leaned forward and clicked the mouse. The computer screen lit up and Alex saw Jack Starbright as she made her escape. Manzour was not showing him the entire sequence. These were the last minutes of what had happened. The camera and the desert light had sucked most of the colour of the image but it was still as if she was there with him in the room and he almost had an urge to call out to her, to warn her not to do what she was about to do. Alex's heart was pounding. He could feel the blood pulsing through his veins. He didn't want to watch this but he had to. This time *he* was torturing *himself*.

Once again, Jack knocked out the guard, using the iron bar that she had taken from her own cell. Once again, she hurried across the courtyard of the Siwa fort and climbed into the waiting Land Rover. He watched her start the car and drive out through the gates. Now the scene was being filmed by a second camera outside the fort, following her as she drove through the desert. Alex knew what was about to come and braced himself. The car had made it about thirty metres from the gate. It was picking up speed.

It blew up.

Manzour left the film running. The Land Rover had been completely destroyed. There was absolutely no way that anyone could have survived the explosion. Bright orange flames filled the screen. At last, he leaned forward and closed the file.

"I'm sorry," he said. "Really, I am."

"I want to see it again."

"Alex..."

"Please, Colonel!"

Manzour didn't move so Alex reached out and used the mouse himself. He dragged the film back to the same point and pressed the arrow to replay. But this time he watched it more clinically. Somehow, he managed to push his emotions to one side. Jack had sent him an email. She had left a message for him, scratched onto the wall of her cell. Alex had flown all the way to Egypt in the belief that she was alive and he wasn't going to give up now. What was it that Razim had said to him when they were together at the fort? *Have you not yet learned? I am a master of manipulation.* He remembered the words now. Somehow he had been tricked. He was going to find out how.

The guard falling.

Jack running.

The car starting.

It had driven through the gate. It was in the desert.

The explosion.

Manzour was no longer looking at the computer. He was looking at Alex and his face was full of concern. Alex was ignoring him, hardly aware that he was still in the room. He was hunched forward, one hand gripping the mouse – his whole body tense as if he was about to project himself through the screen and into the actual film itself.

And he had seen something!

It was so tiny, so insignificant that of course it had been easy to miss. Alex dragged the bar back and pressed PLAY. Had he imagined it? Was he trying to convince himself about something that wasn't there? He let the film run a third time, then stabbed down with his finger, freezing the image half a second before the car blew up.

"There!" he said.

"I don't see..." Manzour began.

Alex reached out and touched the screen. Manzour saw what looked like a scrap of paper floating in the air. Then he looked more closely and saw that it was a bird, flying high above the car. Alex used the mouse to move forward two more seconds. This was the actual moment of the explosion. The Land Rover was out of focus as it burst apart. The smoke and the flames had been captured in a strange orange and grey bubble. Alex sat back triumphantly. Despite the cool of the room, he was soaked in sweat.

The bird was no longer there.

"I know what you are thinking," Manzour said. "But you are wrong. All that has happened is that the bird was frightened by the explosion and flew away."

"No." Alex was utterly certain. "The whole thing was faked. Jack knocked out the guard. She stole the car – and she was being watched all the time. But they've cut a whole section out. Part of the sequence is missing! They stopped the car and dragged her out. Then they blew it up ... when it was empty. Razim and Julius Grief just pretended to press the button to make me think that every-thing was happening in real time when actually the film they were showing me was recorded. The bird gives it away. It was there when they started filming but it wasn't there at the end – and that's why it disappears."

"But why, Alex? What would be the point?"

Alex sighed. "I don't know, Colonel. Razim was interested in measuring pain. He wanted to hurt me the worst way he could. And he succeeded. To be honest, what he did that day almost killed me. But it didn't matter to him whether Jack lived or died. He didn't care about her either way."

"Easier to kill her, then."

"Maybe he had another use for her."

"How could she possibly be useful to him?"

"I don't know."

"Where is she now?"

"I don't know that either. But wherever she is, she managed to contact me. She sent me an email. She tried to tell me she was alive."

Colonel Manzour thought for a minute. Then he strode over to the desk, picked up the phone and barked a few orders in Arabic. He put it down again and turned to Alex. "All right," he said. "Then let's try and find her."

THE ONION ROUTE

They took a lift down to the basement. This was where the technical section of Jihaz Amn al Daoula operated. As the doors slid open, Alex found himself in a corridor that stretched into the distance, with doorways and plate-glass windows looking onto a series of laboratories and work-shops. The area extended well beyond the house. As Alex followed Colonel Manzour, he guessed they must be walking underneath the garden. He glimpsed scientists and technicians in white coats, bent over computer screens, talking in low voices. An armed soldier passed them, going the other way, followed by two men he recognized. They were the agents who had been sent to the Hotel Neheb and who had missed Alex as he walked past them, disguised, in the corridor. Now they briefly made eye contact but said nothing.

The Colonel arrived at an office and went in without knocking. A young woman was sitting at a desk talking on the telephone, but she hung up as soon as she saw him. She was in her twenties, slim and dark-haired, wearing a blue silk suit and a headscarf. She had very soft, gentle features and it immediately struck Alex that she was a little out of place, working here. She alone in the compound actually looked friendly.

"This is Shadia," Manzour said – and the strange thing was that he had suddenly become a little uncomfortable. "She is the head of our technical section. Give her your computer."

Alex was reluctant to hand over his laptop but he did as he was told. As she took it from him, she met his eyes and smiled. "So you're the famous Alex Rider. I watched you arrive on the garden cameras." Alex remembered the statue with the swivelling head. "How are you enjoying Cairo?"

"It's been interesting so far," Alex said.

"And the sooner he's out of Cairo, the happier I'll be," Manzour cut in. "He has received an email which seems to have come from Peru. I suspect it has been rerouted..." He added a few words in Arabic and Shadia opened the laptop.

"Do you want my password?" Alex asked.

Manzour let out a bark of laughter. "Shadia has hacked into the computers of almost every world leader," he said. "The White House, the Kremlin, Downing Street, the Elysée Palace... If she asked for your password, I would fire her on the spot!"

Alex watched as Shadia's fingers swept lightly over his keyboard. He had a screen saver – a view of the River Thames – but it disappeared almost at once to be replaced by a mass of text. She worked for about fifteen seconds then looked up with mischief in her eyes. Alex saw that she had opened his email page. "You should change your password," she said. "It's far too easy."

She pulled up the email that he had received from Lima and went through the same procedure as Sabina's friend in San Francisco. That had been just days ago but to Alex it felt much longer. He wondered what time it was in California. He hadn't spoken to Sabina or her parents since he had left and suddenly he felt bad about it. He would contact them as soon as he had the opportunity. "Whoever sent this used Guerrilla Mail," Shadia said. "And you're right, Colonel. The message was routed through TOR network."

TOR stands for The Onion Router. Alex vaguely understood how it worked. Johnny Feldman had already told him that the message had been bounced around the world. In fact, it would have been sent through a network of proxy servers – computers that might not even know they were being used. The alpaca business in Lima would have been one of them. To make things more complicated, the message would have been encrypted every step of the way. It was the worst news he could have heard. As far as he could see, it would be impossible to find out where the email had begun.

Shadia must have seen the look on his face.

"Don't worry," she said. "TOR network is very hard to crack. It's like a huge maze with the messenger changing his identity at every turning. It's almost completely secure but it has two weak spots: the point you go in and the point you come out. In order to send the message in the first place, they'll have had to access a wireless network. I can run a special program – it's called a correlation program – and it'll look at all the Internet traffic being sent at exactly that time. That way, I should be able to find out where this thing started."

Alex understood what she was saying. There was a wireless network at the Elmer E. Robinson High School. Every time he logged on, it was as if he was using his own private key to open a public door and he couldn't go in without leaving certain clues behind. This is where I work. This is where I can be found. Of course, there were some networks – schools, libraries – that only a small number of people could use. There were others that were open to everyone. "What if it's somewhere public?" Alex asked. "A Starbucks or a McDonald's or something like that?"

"That will make it a bit more difficult," Shadia admitted. "But fast-food restaurants and coffee shops with free Wi-Fi nearly always have CCTV. If someone sent this from a Starbucks, we can look at the film and get the time code and we might be able to identify them."

"How long will it take?" Manzour demanded.

"As long as it has to!" Shadia snapped back, and Alex was surprised that she didn't care how she spoke to her boss. "A few hours," she added.

"Then there's no point waiting here." Manzour turned to Alex. "We'll leave Shadia to get on with it. I'll get my driver to take you back to the hotel. I have other things to do apart from child-minding an English schoolboy. Do you want to do some tourism? The Great Pyramid perhaps? I can arrange to have them closed for you, if you like."

Alex was tempted but he shook his head. "No thanks, Colonel."

"Very well. Wait for us at the hotel. We will come to you as soon as we have any news."

Alex spent the rest of the day beside the pool. He'd found an old Stephen King novel in the hotel library and he read about fifty pages. He swam twenty lengths. At one o'clock, a waiter brought him lunch. He assumed that Manzour had arranged it. Hopefully, he'd paid for it too. As the day wore on and there was no sign of Shadia or her boss, he became restless. He thought about the Grimaldi brothers and their link to Scorpia. Could it be that they had been in Siwa and that for some reason they had taken Jack with them? Would the email lead him to them? Alex felt guilty just sitting there in the sunshine. At the very least he should be at school. In America, in England ... somewhere!

That reminded him of the promise he had made
to himself. The day was drawing to a close and,
with the nine-hour time difference, he knew that
it would be early morning in San Francisco. He put
his shirt on and went into the hotel's business
centre. It was ice-cold inside with the air conditioning turned on full and he was grateful for the
long sleeves. There were half a dozen computers
to choose from and, once again, nothing to pay.
Alex sat down and put in a video messaging call
to Edward Pleasure. The call tone sounded twice
before it was answered and the journalist appeared
on the screen. Looking at the background on the
screen, Alex saw that Edward was back home.

"Alex! Where are you? Are you in Lima?"

"No. I'm in Cairo."

"Egypt!"

"Yes. I'm at the Four Seasons."

"Are you all right?"

"I'm fine."

The journalist looked relieved and Alex could
see the strain in his eyes and knew that he was
responsible. "You shouldn't have taken off like
that. You should have talked to us first."

"I know. I'm sorry. But I'm certain that Jack is
alive. I went back to Siwa. And I found something."

Quickly, Alex told Edward Pleasure about the
name scratched onto the cell wall, the arrival of
Colonel Manzour, the fake film. He didn't say anything about the fight. He didn't want to cause any

more worry. "They're trying to find out where she is," he concluded. "They think they can trace the email back to where it was sent."

"I'm just glad someone's looking after you." Edward paused. "I guess we let you down."

"You didn't. You were always there for me. You were great. And you're right. I should have talked to you before I left."

Just then, Sabina came into the room. She saw Alex on the screen and her face lit up. She leaned over her father and waved at the screen. "Hi, Alex!"

"Hi, Sabina!"

"Are you OK?" She didn't wait for an answer. "Everyone's talking about you at school. Clayton Miller is in hospital and Colin Maguire has been arrested. There was a witness – some taxi driver – who saw what happened. And then you disappeared. Everyone's been asking me about you, but of course I haven't said anything."

They talked for about ten minutes and right then Alex felt that things were the way they had been, when they first met. No matter what happened, she would always be his friend.

"When do you think you'll come back to San Francisco?" Sabina asked.

"I don't know," Alex answered truthfully. "I've got to go where this takes me."

"The door's always open for you, Alex," Edward Pleasure said. "Let us know if there's anything you need or anything we can do."

"I miss you, Alex." Sabina smiled at him from the other side of the world. "Come back soon!"

The screen went blank.

Shadia arrived half an hour later, carrying a motorbike helmet, with Alex's laptop in her backpack. The sun had just set and the sky was an intense red as the heat of the day finally began to lift. Alex was in the lounge. "Did you have a good day?" she asked.

"Yes, thanks. I got some rest."

"The Colonel will be here in a few minutes," she said. "We left at the same time but I got ahead of him. A motorbike's the only way to get around Cairo." She sat down opposite him. "He really likes you."

"Does he?" Alex was surprised. "How do you know?"

"Didn't he tell you?" She paused. "He's my dad."

Alex looked at her a second time, seeing her in a completely new light. So that explained the slightly odd relationship between them! There was no family resemblance at all.

Shadia knew what he was thinking. "He never tells anyone if he can help it. I think it embarrasses him, having his daughter working for him. I have three sisters and no brothers and he complains about it all the time. If you want the truth, I think he looks on you a bit like the son he never had. Don't tell him I said that though. He'd kill me."

A few minutes later, Manzour came stamping over. He had ordered fruit juices for all three of them and a waiter brought them on a tray. "Have you told him?" he asked Shadia.

She shook her head. "I was waiting for you." She turned to Alex. "It's good news and bad news," she said. "I managed to find the starting point of the message that you received – that's the good news. It was a public network, just like I thought. But it was a very odd one..."

"It was sent from the South of France," Manzour said.

"That's right. They used the Wi-Fi service at the tourist office in Saint-Tropez."

"Saint-Tropez? Are you sure?" It was the last thing that Alex had expected to hear. Saint-Tropez was a very smart, fashionable town on the Côte d'Azur. He had passed through it once with his uncle. Ian Rider hadn't been impressed. "Overcrowded and overpriced." That was how he had summed it up. What could Jack possibly be doing there? To Alex, the location was almost as strange as the alpaca wool shop in Lima.

"There's no doubt about it," Shadia said. "I've checked, by the way. It was sent early in the morning last Monday. And that's the bad news. Anyone could have gone in the tourist office. There are no security cameras on the Quai Jean Jaurès – which is where it's situated. It's going to be very difficult to prove that it was your friend,

Jack Starbright. It could have been anyone."

"And why there of all places?" Manzour added. "Did she go on holiday without telling you?" At least he had accepted that she might still be alive. Alex made a note of it but didn't say anything.

"I wish I could be more helpful, Alex," Shadia said. She took out his laptop and gave it back to him. "But that's the best I can do."

Alex thought for a moment. "I'm going to Saint-Tropez," he said.

"Oh, really!" Manzour exclaimed. He picked up his juice, drank it in one go, then put down the glass. "Is that what you think? You can just go chasing off to the South of France and sort this out on your own?" He shook his head. "We can look into this for you. I can contact the DGSE – the French intelligence service. I can speak to Mrs Jones in London. This is a job for professionals." He jabbed a finger in Alex's direction. "You should be at school."

"No, Colonel." Alex had already made up his mind. "Jack wrote to me. She wanted me to find her. I'm not going back to San Francisco. Not until I've found out what happened."

"You are a very difficult boy!" Manzour looked at his empty glass regretfully, then leaned forward. "All right! All right! As it happens, I have a friend in the Egyptian Air Force. In fact, he's the commander if you really want to know. He's in charge of the whole thing. He mentioned to me that he's got a training exercise – a couple of Alpha Jets heading up to France. I'll see if he can get you a seat on one of them. They can drop you off at Nice Airport. If you behave yourself, they might even land first. Is that acceptable to you?"

"Thank you, Colonel." Alex couldn't help smiling.

"I have spoken to nobody about this. Even your own people do not know where you are going. I take it you prefer it that way."

"Yes. I'll contact them if I need to."

"Very well." Suddenly Manzour was serious again. He was a man who could switch moods in a moment. "But there is something else I must tell you. You remember the name, Grimaldi, that you found in the cell?"

"Giovanni and Eduardo Grimaldi. Yes. You told me..."

"They worked for Scorpia. Scorpia are finished now – but that does not make them any less dangerous. I have made enquiries and although nobody is certain, there are strong rumours that they are themselves in the South of France, possibly even in Saint-Tropez."

"Maybe they took Jack with them!"

"Why would they do that? What possible reason could they have?" Manzour stopped himself. "You may not want to know the answer to that particular question. Never mind! I have arranged things for you, Alex, but what I am saying to you is that you should be careful ... think about what you are walking into." He stood up. "My driver will come for you at six o'clock tomorrow morning. I hope I will see you again in Cairo."

"I'll let you know," Alex said.

"I will know anyway."

Shadia had also got to her feet. "I've added a couple of things to your computer," she said. "I hope you don't mind but I thought they might come in useful. They're standard equipment for our own agents. Press CONTROL three times followed by S and I'll be able to see you through the camera. I'll hear everything you say. That way you can get in touch with me if you need any help. Press CONTROL – again, three times – and M and you'll send out a Mayday signal which will be picked up by the nearest intelligence service. And if you're in real trouble, press CONTROL three times, then X."

"What does that do?"

"It gives you fifteen seconds to get under the table or out of the room. After that, your computer will explode."

"Just don't do it by accident." Manzour turned to his daughter. "Do you remember Khaled in communications? He sent an email to his mother and signed it with a kiss. He blew off three of his fingers!"

Manzour roared with laughter, then grabbed Alex in a powerful bear hug. "Take care of yourself!" he exclaimed.

The two of them left.

PEPPERMINT TEA

Eighteen hours later, Alex was sitting in a café on the seafront at Saint-Tropez. It was the first week in September but this was the sort of town where the summer never seemed to end and the streets and cafés were still crowded. He had chosen a table at the corner, giving him an unobstructed view of the area around him. This was the old harbour. The quayside swept around a great expanse of water with about a hundred boats bobbing up and down in their moorings: everything from little dinghies, yachts and fishing boats to the single multimillion-pound cruiser that towered over everything else. A long sea wall stretched out like a protective arm. The Mediterranean was on the other side, with Alexandria and the north coast of Egypt more than two thousand miles away.

The café was one of several. There was a long line of restaurants packed together with their different-coloured canopies stretching out over the pavement. From where he was sitting, Alex could

see waiters moving like circus performers, balancing
great piles of plates and glasses as they curved and
twisted expertly between the tables. Behind them,
pink and white apartment blocks rose up with balconies providing front-row seats over the seafront.
It was one o'clock and everyone had chosen to have
lunch at the same time. The street was full of cars
and motorbikes, ice cream sellers, postcard stands,
street performers, tourists and travellers.

Had Jack been here?

It was impossible to say.

Alex sat quietly. He still hadn't fully recovered
from the flight that had brought him here.
Strapped into the rear cockpit of the Alpha Jet
MSI, he had felt every bone in his body contract
with the G-force as it blasted down the runway
and into the air, rising at eleven-thousand feet
a minute. The Alpha wasn't the most modern jet
in operation but it was still incredibly powerful,
cruising comfortably at six-hundred miles an hour.
Alex had been given a jumpsuit and headphones to
protect him from the deafening howl of the turbo-
fans and he had sat in a sort of cocoon throughout
the flight. The Egyptian pilot hadn't spoken to
him. He clearly wasn't too pleased to find himself
carrying a civilian passenger and one who was only
fifteen years old at that. But he was too nervous
to argue with the head of Jihaz Amn al Daoula and
even managed a brief smile and a nod once they
touched down at Nice Airport.

Alex had been taken to a side room, where he changed. Then, carrying his backpack with the rest of his clothes and his laptop, he had been escorted through passport control by a puzzled French official. Nobody asked any questions. A second official took a quick glance at his passport, nodded, and Alex suddenly found himself back in Europe and once again on his own. He had always liked the South of France with its palm trees, long beaches and unbroken sunshine. He took a local bus down to Saint-Tropez, arriving shortly before eleven o'clock. First, there was the boring business of checking into a hotel, this one an attractive, dusty pink building behind the main square. It was market day and Alex strolled between the various stalls, picking out fresh croissants, fruit and cheese ... some of the best food he had ever eaten. He wolfed it down as he walked. He didn't want to waste any time.

After that he'd gone directly to the tourist office in the Quai Jean Jaurès. He still had his eye on it now. It was on a corner, set back slightly from the harbour; a large, simple room with two arched windows and a tired-looking agent sitting at a computer. There were posters on the walls, various stands with brochures advertising local attractions – beaches, boat trips, the Butterfly Museum – but no other furniture; no obvious place to sit. Alex spent just five minutes there before coming out and finding a café where he had ordered a glass of grenadine, the bright red drink made from pomegranates that was his favourite drink when he was in France. He needed time to think.

Had Jack really been in Saint-Tropez? Could she have walked into the tourist office, carrying a laptop? Why hadn't she used her phone? The more Alex thought about it, the more improbable it seemed. Alex had already checked that a signal could be picked up anywhere in the harbour. She could have been anywhere near by. She had started sending a message – and what then? Someone had seen her and stopped her before she could write more than a few words?

And where was she now? The trouble was – Alex had to admit it – Shadia was right. There were no CCTV cameras anywhere near. Jack could have come from any one of a number of directions and nobody would have had any reason to notice her. He considered going to the local police – but what could he ask them? "Have you seen a cheerful, red-haired English woman, aged twenty-nine, carrying a laptop? She was here about a week ago and may have been kidnapped..." They would laugh at him.

He was aware of a rustle of clothing, a light coat, as a woman sat down next to him. She hadn't asked to share his table and he looked up, annoyed. Then he recognized who it was and he shook his head, accepting the inevitable. He should have expected it.

"How did you find me?" He sighed.

"Please, Alex! Do you really need to ask?"

It had been a long time since he had seen Mrs Jones. When they had last met, it had been at his home in Chelsea. She had come to visit him following the sniper attack at his school and she – along with Alan Blunt – had persuaded him to leave for Cairo. It struck him at once that she had changed. She had always been a darkly serious woman, so wrapped up in her secret world that she seemed out-of-reach, unknowable. But right now, sitting in the sunshine, she looked strangely relaxed. He could tell that she was pleased to see him.

"You can't fly into a country without being seen," she said. "Not these days. And certainly not in an Egyptian military jet. I'm actually quite annoyed with Colonel Manzour for not contacting me the moment you turned up in Cairo. You don't mind if I join you, do you?" She had ordered a cup of mint tea. She paused as the waiter brought a teabag and a cup of boiling water to the table, then went on. "As it happens, I was just down the coast in Marseille. A rather dull conference on international border controls. As soon as I heard you'd landed, I called Manzour and he told me where I might find you." She tore open the wrapper and dipped the bag into the water. Alex remembered that she'd always had a fondness for peppermint. "How are you?" she asked.

"Jack Starbright is alive," Alex said.

"That's not what I asked."

"I'm fine." Alex looked her in the eye. "Jack's alive."

"That's highly unlikely. But if so, you should let us find her."

"No. She's my friend. I'm responsible for her."

"Is that why you left America? I was very sorry to hear it, Alex. You were safe there. Why would you want to put yourself in harm's way?"

"That never bothered you in the past," Alex said.

Mrs Jones raised an eyebrow. "Actually, that's not true. For what it's worth, I was against the idea of using you from the very start. Oh yes – I could see at once that you were special. Your uncle, Ian Rider, used to talk about you and about all the things he was teaching you. He turned you into a spy without you even knowing it! And then, that first day when you came to Liverpool Street, I saw it for myself. I actually watched you climb out of a window on the fifteenth floor just to get what you wanted. That was Alan's idea, by the way, that little test. You passed with flying colours.

"Alan knew he'd found the perfect weapon when he sent you after Herod Sayle and, of course, you proved him right, not just on that occasion but time and time again. But I was always concerned. You were a child! Quite apart from anything else, there were the security implications to consider. It would have been quite difficult for us if any-one had noticed that we were employing a minor!"

She paused and Alex wondered if she had said more than she intended. "Of course, it was much more than that," she went on hastily. "I worried about what we were doing to you. You were missing school. You were lying to your friends. You saw things that no young person should ever see. And you were badly hurt. You were almost killed when you were shot outside our office! Maybe it was the mother in me, Alex. I once had children myself. But I knew that what we were doing was wrong and that's the reason why I've tracked you down today. I'm not going to allow it to go on."

Alex's ears pricked up when Mrs Jones mentioned her children. He had seen a photograph of them in her flat and had often wondered what had happened to them. But he wasn't going to ask her about that now. Instead, he said, "I don't see how you can stop me."

"I can stop you very easily," Mrs Jones replied. "I could snap my fingers and in five seconds you'd be bundled into a car and on your way to San Francisco. I hope it won't come to that." She sighed. "Things have changed at Special Operations, Alex. Alan Blunt has resigned. I'm in charge now and we're doing things my way. Smithers has also left, by the way. I thought you might like to know, as I'm aware that he was your friend."

"What do you want me to do?" Alex asked.

"I want you to go back to America." She reached into her handbag and took out an envelope, which she laid on the table. "Here's a single ticket. Nice to San Francisco with Air France. The flight leaves tomorrow morning at seven o'clock."

"What about Jack?" Alex's voice was heavy.

"I've asked my Chief of Staff, John Crawley, to look into it and he's putting a team together even now. I'll be honest with you, Alex. I don't think you should raise your hopes too high. Even if Razim didn't kill her, it's unlikely she's still alive. You have to ask yourself – where is she? Why hasn't she tried to contact you a second time?" She glanced at her tea as if she had forgotten it was there. "Do you have your mobile phone with you?"

"Yes." The question took Alex by surprise.

"Make sure it's on and keep it with you the whole time. If we have any news, we'll let you know at once."

Mrs Jones stood up. She hadn't drunk anything, not so much as a sip. "I always enjoyed knowing you – and don't think I'm not grateful for everything you've done. Although you may not see it this way, I'm doing you a favour. The trouble with danger is that it's a drug. You get addicted and you keep wanting more, until finally, it kills you, like your uncle. I always thought America was a good idea for you. A fresh start. Stay there. Stay away from us."

She turned round and walked back down the quay.

Alex opened the envelope. Sure enough, there

was a ticket inside, Air France direct to San Francisco. He noticed that he had been booked in as an unaccompanied minor. After everything he had been through, after missions that had put him in danger all over the world, someone at MI6 had arranged for a member of the cabin crew to meet him at the airport and guide him to his seat! Slowly, deliberately, Alex tore the ticket into about fifty pieces and scattered them in an ashtray. He felt better after that.

There was something that Mrs Jones had said, something that unlocked the puzzle he had been considering when she had sat down next to him. Alex glanced at the teacup with the bag still floating in the water. What was it? He had to think. There was something he was missing and he was sure that she had provided him with the answer.

He retraced his thoughts. Suppose Jack had been here. She would have to be a prisoner – otherwise she would simply have gone to a phone and called him. He imagined her, locked in a room. Somehow, just for a few seconds, she had got her hands on a computer and she had logged in using the nearest signal, the Office of Tourism. Of course she didn't need to go into the building. She could have simply been somewhere near by. But where? Alex ran his eye over the apartment buildings with their tall windows and balconies. It could have been any one of them. But that didn't make any sense. Why would they have wanted to lock her up here?

And then, suddenly, he had it. That was what Mrs Jones had said! *You can't fly into a country without being seen*. Alex had been smuggled in by the Egyptian Air Force but even so, he had been noticed. With so much fear of terrorism, every airfield was closely monitored, every flight and every passenger checked. But suppose she had come in by boat! It was the obvious answer! From Egypt, it would have been a journey of about seven days, first across the Mediterranean to Malta, then up past Sardinia and finally along the French coast from Monaco to Nice and round to Saint-Tropez. The answer was staring him in the face. Jack had been locked in a cabin, not a room. She had never actually stepped onto the quay.

Alex called for the waiter and took out a twenty-euro note. *"Madame a réglé,"* the waiter told him. Well, that was something anyway. Mrs Jones had paid for the drinks.

He knew what he had to do. Hoisting his backpack onto his shoulder, he hurried over to the harbour office, which he had already noticed when he had scouted the area. It was housed in an attractive, circular tower on the nearby Quai de l'Epi. Alex was lucky that he spoke excellent French – it was just one of the things that Ian Rider had taught him when he was growing up. He was able to persuade the elderly woman behind the desk that he was working on a school project and needed to know the names of all the large yachts that had been moored in the harbour of Saint-Tropez on a certain Monday.

"What size yachts?" the woman asked. She peered at him through glasses attached to a cord looped behind her neck.

Obviously, it would narrow the search. Alex thought about the long journey from Egypt, perhaps Jack had slipped unnoticed from one cabin to another. "At least sixty metres," he said. "Maybe bigger."

The woman tapped a few keys and gazed at her computer screen. "There was only one boat of that size on the day you are asking about," she said. "It's September and generally we are less busy here at this time of the year." She pressed a button, then went over to a printer which spat out a sheet of paper. "Here you are." She handed it to Alex.

The boat was called *Quicksilver*. It was huge – around eighty metres long, with four decks, saloons, staterooms, gym, Jacuzzi and swimming pool. Alex looked at the image for a few seconds, then went outside. He found a bench, sat down and took out his laptop. Resting it on his knees, he booted it up, then pressed CONTROL three times and pressed S. Nothing happened. "Shadia?" he said. "Can you hear me?"

The screen flickered and a moment later Shadia appeared. She was sitting in her office. "Hello, Alex. How's Saint-Tropez?"

"It's hot."

"It might be getting hotter. I was going to warn you. MI6 called us. I think they're looking for you."

"It's OK, Shadia. They found me." Alex got straight to the point. "What can you tell me about a boat called *Quicksilver*?"

Shadia leaned forward and Alex could imagine her inputting the information into her computer. He could have googled it himself but she was bound to have more on her system. A moment later, she looked up. "Manufactured by Benetti in Livorno, Italy. Seventy-nine metres. Maximum speed – sixteen knots. Range – four thousand nautical miles. It was sold five years ago to an olive oil company called Draco d'Olivo, based in Naples. They paid one hundred and ninety million euros." She frowned. "That's interesting. Wait a minute..." There was another pause as she searched her database. Then she looked up again. "Yes. I thought I knew the name. You remember my father told you about the Grimaldi brothers?"

"Yes."

"They own a great many companies. They use them as a front, hiding behind them. We're not certain, but there are suspicions that Draco d'Olivo is one of theirs." She paused. "Why are you asking, Alex? Do you need help?"

"No. I'm fine. Thanks, Shadia." Alex signed off and closed his laptop.

He sat where he was, still holding the piece of paper that the woman in the harbour office had given him. He looked at it one last time, then crumpled it in his hand. He didn't need the photograph. He had recognized the boat the moment he had seen it. He could see it now. The actual superyacht was right in front of him, moored beside the Quai Jean Jaurès where he had been sitting just a few minutes ago.

He had found it. He might even have found Jack.

Now all he had to do was get on board.

QUICKSILVER

It was a beautiful boat, massive in size and yet somehow sleek and delicate, perching on the water as if it weighed nothing at all. Apart from the tinted windows, the whole thing was a dazzling white with silver railings polished until they gleamed. There was a main deck with outdoor seating, sunloungers and a shaded area with doors opening into the main saloon. An upper deck contained the bridge and the captain's quarters and a range of aerials and satellite dishes mounted on the roof. There were at least two lower decks with the smallest portholes – crew quarters – closest to the sea.

The wind had dropped and an Italian flag – green, white and red – hung limply at the back. A gangplank sloped down to the side of the harbour. It was the only way in and out. Two guards, both dressed in jeans and T-shirts with sunglasses, stood on the aft deck, guarding it. One was completely bald, with a head that reminded Alex of a punctured football. He was in his late forties. The other was younger – around twenty-five or six, skinny and endlessly fidgeting. They had been standing there for hours.

Alex had positioned himself in another café, a little further down from the one where he had met Mrs Jones, directly opposite the quay where *Quicksilver* was moored. After he had left the harbour office, he had gone back to the hotel and changed into darker clothes, which would help him with what lay ahead. It might be cold later in the evening, so he put on a crumpled jacket and a long-sleeved shirt. There was no safe in the room so he had brought his passport and wallet with him. They were in his inside pocket. He also had his phone and his laptop in his backpack. He had a nasty feeling he was going to need them.

The sky had changed from red to mauve to the deepest blue. Suddenly it was night. Alex had been sitting where he was for a long time, watching the boat, trying to see who was on board. Apart from the guards, there was nothing; no movement at all. But watching the two of them, he knew that they weren't ordinary security men. They weren't there simply to nod politely at the public and keep them moving along. Alex knew it at once from the way they stood, their blank expressions, their empty eyes. The younger man was pale with the sort of vacant, hungry look that reminded him of Colin Maguire, the bully he had taken out in

San Francisco. Some sort of skin rash had eaten away at the corner of his mouth and his eyes and if he lay still, it would be quite easy to mistake him for someone who had recently died. The other man was in charge. He looked ferocious. As well as being completely bald, he had very dark, angry eyes and a nose that seemed to have been pushed back into his face. His T-shirt was stretched out over a bodybuilder's chest and there was a tattoo – a bright red flame – on the back of his right hand.

These gangsters were all the same. Alex had met them at Herod Sayle's computer manufacturing plant in Port Tallon, then again at Sarov's hideaway in Skeleton Key, and on Flamingo Bay, the Caribbean island where Nikolei Drevin had planned to launch his rocket into outer space. Some things never changed. Rich, powerful men surrounded themselves with people who would protect them at any cost. Pay the guards enough money and point them in the right direction and they would kill anyone without a second thought.

This yacht belonged to the Grimaldi brothers – Giovanni and Eduardo. Alex remembered what Colonel Manzour had told him about them. They were ex-Mafia and ex-Scorpia. It was possible that they had killed their own father. Alex smiled grimly: two more charmers to add to the long line of people he had come up against. Well, if they had taken Jack, they had made a big mistake. He wasn't going to let them stand in his way.

The two guards still hadn't left, not even to
go to the toilet. Alex knew that he was going
to have to make his move soon. Apart from
anything else, the waiters were getting a little irri-
tated. He had managed to sip his way through two
glasses of grenadine and had ordered a cheese-
burger and chips, which he had eaten as slowly as
he could, but even so, they were wondering how
much longer he was going to occupy the table.
The trouble was, there was no obvious way he was
going to get on board *Quicksilver*. It wasn't as if
the Grimaldi brothers were throwing a party so he
could slip in with the crowd. There had been no
deliveries, no chance to pretend he was carrying in
supplies. It might be possible to swim round to the
bow but he wasn't sure he would be able to climb
up. The main deck was too high and anyway, he
would almost certainly be heard.

The yacht looked empty. No lights had come
on behind the tinted windows, at least not as
far as he could see. Nobody had come onto the
deck. But Alex was certain there must be someone there. Otherwise, why would there be any
need for the guards? It had to be Jack Starbright.
This was where she was being kept. If he stood up
and shouted her name, she might even hear him.
Unfortunately, so would the guards.

As he sat there with his empty glass in front of
him, all sorts of memories came tumbling through
his mind. Jack dragging him out of bed, getting

him ready for school. Jack making him breakfast, cutting his toast into soldiers, even though
she knew he was far too old for it. Jack sticking
an Elastoplast on his knee after that first fight in
Stryker's car demolition yard. Jack always worrying
about him, waiting for him when he came home
from every mission. Alex had no parents and MI6
had more or less torn his life apart. In the end,
she had been the only constant, the one person he
could rely on. He had thought she was dead. Now it
was possible that she was just a few metres away.
She had managed to send him a message, perhaps
risking her life. He was going to get her out.

Alex didn't much like it but he had worked out
a plan and knew what he had to do. He paid his
bill, then got up and walked along the harbour
to the far end where steps led down to a strip of
shingle with shallow water and small waves breaking against the shore. He had thought he might
need a torch but the moon was out and there was
enough light to see around him. He was looking
for something and soon found it: part of an old
wooden crate, thrown out by a fisherman perhaps
and washed up here. He dragged it towards him
and examined it. It was exactly the right size. It
would do perfectly.

He waited another hour, hoping that the moon
would disappear behind a cloud and give him the
cover of darkness, but it was a clear, still night and
eventually he realized it wasn't going to happen.

Alex was getting tired. He was still jet-lagged after flying from San Francisco to Cairo and knew he needed to make his move. He took the laptop out of his backpack and laid it flat on the wooden lid of the crate. He would be sorry to lose it. It wasn't just a question of the cost. It wasn't even the data that it held. He'd already uploaded everything that was important and emailed it back to himself. It was the machine itself. He remembered saving up for it. He'd had it for two years and it had become a part of him. Well, there was no other way. It simply had to go.

He waded out into the water, shivering as it rose up to his thighs. The temperature had already begun to drop as autumn drew near. Three more steps and he was swimming, kicking quietly with his legs and at the same time pushing the little raft with his computer ahead of him. *Quicksilver* was over to his left, towering above him.

He wasn't too worried about being seen by the two men. They were high up and their eyes were fixed on the quayside. Once he got closer, he would be well concealed by the bulk of the yacht itself. Alex was more afraid of being spotted by someone in one of the restaurants or perhaps on one of the other, smaller boats moored further out. If they saw a lunatic kid going for a midnight swim and decided to raise the alarm, the police would arrive and then it would definitely be game over.

Six ... seven ... eight ... he tried to keep his

movements as rhythmic as possible, counting the strokes. His hands were still stretched out, guiding the raft. He felt his clothes tugging at him as he swam. Perhaps it would have been more sensible to strip off before he went in – but it was too late to think about that now.

He swam until he reached the slanting white wall of *Quicksilver*, then made his way back towards the quay until he was underneath the gangplank. This was the crucial moment. Treading water and being careful not to make any sound, he drew the laptop towards him, then partly opened it, keeping the glow of the screen concealed. It occurred to him that he had never asked Shadia to turn the computer into a weapon and although he was grateful to her, there was a part of him that resented it too. What was it she had said? Pressing CONTROL three times and X would turn the laptop into a bomb with a fifteen-second fuse. With difficulty, kicking out to keep himself afloat, Alex did exactly that, then gently pushed the raft so that it floated towards the front of the ship, taking the computer with it. Then, he swam under the gangplank and out the other side, putting as much distance as he could between himself and what was about to happen. He could imagine the two men standing directly above him, unaware that anything was wrong. That was about to change.

Alex counted to fifteen. Nothing. Had Shadia got it wrong? Could she have been joking? Alex swore quietly. Then, a second later, the computer exploded, an orange fireball blossoming out of the surface of the sea. It looked more like a giant firework than an actual bomb. It had made little noise but the flames were reflected in the water and seemed to spread across the entire harbour. The computer didn't sink immediately. It was almost as if it had decided to help Alex one last time. What was left of it stayed where it was, floating on the piece of crate, cheerfully burning.

Alex had started moving the moment it had detonated. He lunged upwards and grabbed hold of the gangplank with both hands, then drew himself out of the water. The two men had vanished. Everything was happening exactly as he had hoped. They had run down to the front of the boat to see what was going on. Of course! They needed to see what was burning on the surface of the water. They might be under attack. His greatest fear had been that one of them would stay behind, but in the heat of the moment, they hadn't taken that elementary precaution. The entrance was clear. Alex hoisted himself onto the gangplank and ran on board. He was dripping water and he was afraid that the puddles would give him away but finally the moon had done him a favour and found a cloud to hide behind. There were lights in all the restaurants and the fire was illuminating the sea, but the yacht itself was dark.

He slipped through a set of double doors and

paused for a moment to allow his eyes to get used to the gloom. He was in a saloon, surrounded by expensive white sofas and chairs. Even in a house, the room would have felt huge. On a boat, it was almost beyond belief. A white grand piano stood in one corner. A whole wall was given over to a cinema screen with a sophisticated projector bolted into the ceiling. Alex noticed four shelves of DVDs, a drinks cabinet, a coffee table with a few magazines. Everything was brand new, cleaned and polished until it looked like something out of an advertisement.

He was still soaked, dripping water onto the highly polished wooden floor, and he quickly stepped onto a thick rug, then rolled on it to dry himself off. It wasn't ideal but at least when he stood up he was damp rather than drenched. He glanced out of the windows. The two guards were still out at the bow but already the fire was going out. Alex could see the flickering flames on the other side of the glass. It was time to move on. With his clothes sticking to him and his trousers already chafing between his legs, he crept over to a second door and went into a dining room with an oval table, a great expanse of shining mahogany surrounded by fourteen chairs – more white leather. There were no plates, no glasses. Alex got the sense that nobody had eaten here for some time. The ceiling was low with recessed lights, all of them turned off. But for the glow coming from the restaurants on the harbour front, he would have been unable to see. He almost sneezed, holding it back at the last moment. He was cold. He remembered the pool of water he had left in the first room. If the guards saw it, it would lead them straight to him.

He wanted to hurry on but at the same time he knew he had to take care. It was something he had learned when he had been training with the SAS in the Brecon Beacons. Two simple rules. Never enter enemy territory unless you've established your way out and never leave your path of retreat unprotected. If the guards came after him, everything would be on their side. Alex didn't know where he was going. He was unarmed. He was walking into a self-made trap and before he went any further he had to adjust the odds, to move them in his favour.

But how? He looked around him. There was nothing in the dining-room, no knives or forks or anything he could use as a weapon. A second door led into a high-tech kitchen: stainless-steel surfaces, an American fridge-freezer, an industrial-sized oven. Quickly, Alex searched through some of the drawers. There were plenty of knives to choose from but, thinking about it, he didn't fancy the idea of a knife fight, not when the guards would almost certainly have guns. He found a utility drawer with candles, matches, Sellotape, string. Everything every household ever needs. An idea came to mind. It would take him a few minutes to set it up. Was it worth the time? Alex remembered the SAS training sergeant, screaming into his face. Yes. It definitely was.

Three minutes later, Alex was on his way again, climbing down a staircase which he had found on the other side of the dining room. The steps were covered with thick-pile carpet and he was grateful for it dampening any sound. A gleaming silver handrail swept round, inviting him further into the belly of the beast. He listened for any sound of movement but there was nothing, a silence that seemed to intensify as he went down. He came to a corridor, stretching into darkness. Down below, with no windows on either side, he couldn't see anything. Alex reached into his backpack. He had managed to keep most of it out of the water while he swam. He took out his mobile phone, turning on the torch function. The sharp white beam picked out a series of doors. Bedrooms – or staterooms, he supposed he should call them. Boats had their own language, their own way of life. What did it matter? Jack might be in one of them. He was sure he was getting close.

He tried the nearest door. It opened into another oversized room with a king-sized bed, a dressing table, wardrobes, floor-to-ceiling windows. Once again, everything looked untouched, as if the entire boat was there to be shown off rather than used. Could he be wrong? Could anyone actually be living here? Perhaps the two guards had been paid simply to protect the property, the fixtures and fittings.

The next stateroom was the same. Alex padded down the corridor, the phone spilling light out of his hand. It was only when he opened the third door that he knew something was different. For a start, the air conditioning was on. He felt it stroking his face and his neck even as he tiptoed in. And this room was occupied. He saw a suitcase resting against a wall. The curtains were drawn. There were some paperback books thrown onto a table.

There was someone in the bed. Alex could tell from the shape beneath the covers. He saw red hair, spilling onto the pillow. He closed the door behind him. His heart was racing.

"Jack?" he whispered.

Nothing.

"Jack!" He tried again. He wanted to go over to her and shake her.

He didn't need to. She had become aware of his presence and he saw her body shift. She turned over. A hand reached out to turn on a lamp on a bedside table and yellow light flooded the room. She twisted round and sat up.

It wasn't Jack.

Alex found himself staring at an unattractive woman with a slightly masculine face and grey, lifeless eyes. She was much older than Jack, wearing a pink, semi-transparent nightie that hung awkwardly off her shoulders. She had gone to bed wearing lipstick. It had smeared across her mouth.

"Who are you?" Dragana Novak demanded.

"I ... I'm sorry!" Alex didn't know what to say.

"What are you doing here?" She spoke with a foreign accent that chewed the words. She was Eastern European. She looked furious to have been woken up.

"I was looking for someone," Alex said. "I came into the wrong room. I'm very sorry to have disturbed you."

He turned his back on her, reaching out for the door handle, but the woman called out to him. "Shtopp!"

There was something in her voice that made Alex hesitate. He turned around and saw that the woman had snatched up an odd-looking gun that had been resting on the table, right next to the bed in case she needed it. It was lightweight and seemed to be made out of some sort of white plastic. She brought it round to aim at Alex. At the same time, she swung herself out of the bed. Her legs, poking out beneath the pink nightie, were thick and blotchy, with a fine covering of hair.

"I was looking for a friend of mine." Alex was already thinking ahead, trying to find a way out of this situation. He was annoyed with himself. The thought of seeing Jack had made him careless. He shouldn't have just gone blundering into this room. "She told me she was staying on a boat called *Silver Streak*. I must have got the wrong one! Go back to sleep! I'll show myself out..."

"No!" The woman was still aiming the gun at him. There was a dull excitement in her eyes. She licked her lips. Alex knew at once that she wanted to fire the weapon at him. Not because he was a danger to her – but because she would enjoy it. "You are not allowed on this boat. You sneaked in. You are a spy!" She spat out this last word with a sense of triumph.

"No," Alex said. "I'm just a schoolboy. I'm just on holiday."

"You are lying."

"Please. Have a heart!"

Her eyes narrowed. "What do you mean?"

"I came here by mistake. Cross my heart!" Alex tapped his chest. "I'm fifteen. I'm nobody..."

Everything depended on the next few seconds. Either she was going to shoot him or she was going to call the guards. Alex made his move. Ignoring the woman, he half twisted round and grabbed the door handle. Dragana Novak fired. A tiny needle, two centimetres long and tipped with the deadly poison tetrodotoxin, shot silently across the room and penetrated his jacket. Alex jerked backwards, his shoulders slamming into the door, his phone dropping to the floor.

His eyes widened. He tried to speak. Slowly, he slid down to the floor and lay still.

FIRE AND WATER

Dragana Novak gazed curiously at the boy lying on the floor, in the corner. She wished now that he had told her his name before she killed him. Not that it mattered, really, but she was curious. Certainly, he had deserved to die. It wasn't just that he was an intruder, creeping into her cabin in the middle of the night. He had woken her up! It was particularly annoying, as she had gone to bed with a headache and didn't want to be disturbed.

She had spent the day shopping in Saint-Tropez. After the drabness of her life in Serbia, she felt she had come alive in the South of France: the sunshine, the bright colours, the shops so full of beautiful things. The pink nightie she was wearing had cost two hundred euros, an incredible sum of money – more than a month's salary back home. After that, she'd had lunch in a busy restaurant near the seafront. Unfortunately, she had drunk too much wine. The third bottle was definitely a mistake and she had felt quite giddy as she had climbed into the taxi which had taken her back to *Quicksilver*. She had eaten some chocolates and then collapsed gratefully into bed, falling asleep almost at once.

Who was the boy? And how had the guards let him get past them? Dragana decided that he must be carrying some sort of ID and she would check it before she called them down.

Alex heard the bedsprings creak as the woman stood up. He was lying exactly how he had fallen, his arms and legs splayed, his head to one side. His eyes were closed but he took the risk and opened them just enough so that he could see her coming towards him. He had to know exactly where she was.

She had the most hideous feet. Her toes were stumpy with the sort of nails – thick and yellow – he would expect to see on an elderly man. He could just make out the hem of her nightie. Her lower legs reminded him of joints in a butcher's shop. Her heel was a lump of dead skin.

Alex was alive because of a combination of luck and trickery. The luck was his wallet and passport in the inside pocket of his jacket. They might just have been thick enough to provide a shield for a bullet. Certainly they had protected him from the dart which, he guessed, must be tipped with some sort of poison. But he'd had to trick the woman too – and he'd done it using something else that he'd once learned from his uncle, Ian Rider. *The power of suggestion, Alex. It's what stage magicians use. They make you think you've got a free choice but actually they're secretly influencing you.* That's what Alex had remembered in the moments before the woman had fired. He had told her to have a heart. A moment later, he had repeated it, "Cross my heart." When he was pleading with her, he had deliberately tapped his chest. In reality, he was telling her where to aim and, just to be sure, he had turned his body so that the target was obvious. And she had obliged. The tip of the dart hadn't come anywhere near his flesh. After that, it was simply a case of pretending, providing her with what she expected to see.

The woman was standing over him. Alex didn't move. He tried not to breathe. She was still holding the gun and it might hold a second needle. He could actually feel the weight of her, pressing down on the floor as she caught her breath. Now he could smell her. She had soaked herself in expensive perfume, presumably bought in Saint-Tropez, and smelled like a flower shop on a hot day. There was a rustle of material as she bent down towards him and that was when Alex knew he had to act. In an instant, his entire body sprang to life. His shoulders crashed into the side of her leg and at the same time, he whipped a hand round her ankle and pulled with all his strength. The woman cried out, losing her balance. Alex rose up, still holding her ankle. The woman struggled, her arms flailing.

For a moment her eyes blazed into him. Her mouth was a snarl of rage. Then she toppled backwards.

He had hoped she would hit the floor but for once things didn't go his way. Her head and shoulders slammed into the bed – and the mattress had the effect of a trampoline, bouncing her up again, back onto him. It was the last thing Alex had been expecting. With a cry of triumph, she launched herself at him, her hands reaching for his throat, and now the two of them fell together. Alex felt the breath being driven out of his lungs as she landed on top of him. He had twisted to one side to stop the needle being pushed through the wallet and the passport but he knew at once that it was the least of his problems.

She was strangling him. The pupils were dancing in her eyes and her lips were stretched in a smile as she used her weight to press him down, her hands gripping tighter and tighter. Alex could see the chocolate smeared on her teeth. Desperately, he reached up, grabbed the needle and pulled it out. He could use it against her. But Dragana had been waiting for the move. She released his throat with one hand and lashed out. The needle was sent spinning away. Dragana giggled and began to strangle him again.

Alex couldn't breathe. The edges of the room were going dark. He stretched out his hands, searching across the carpet for anything he could use as a weapon. There was nothing. He could no longer see her face. She was going in and out of focus. He had perhaps seconds left. And then his fingers caught hold of something. A wire. His brain was shutting down and it took him a moment to work out what it was. The wire was connected to the bedside light. He pulled and it came crashing down. Somehow his fingers closed around the metal base. With the very last of his strength, he swung it into the side of the woman's head. He felt metal connect with bone. There was a satisfying clunk and a flash as the bulb shattered. Dragana keeled over and lay still.

It had been very close. Alex tore the woman's hands from him and backed away, gasping for breath. His throat felt as if it had been through a mangle. He found a plastic bottle of water on a table, tore off the top and forced himself to drink. Gradually, some of the pain subsided. He waited until he could breathe properly again. Finally, he snatched his mobile off the floor, checked it was still working and slid it into his pocket. Only then did he set to work.

Alex was desperate to search the boat. There was every chance that Jack was in the other cabin or in the crew's quarters below. But first he had to deal with the woman who had just tried to kill him. He examined her briefly. She was lying in a heap, glass fragments in her hair, breathing heavily. Alex went over to the bed, pulled off the top sheet and, using his teeth, tore it into strips. He was worried that the guards would come. Surely they must have heard the struggle, the moment when the lamp fell to the floor. They might discover the pool of water and come down anyway. He would just have to risk it. Using the strips, he tied the woman's hands and feet. She didn't seem to be in any hurry to wake up. Good. That gave him a bit of time

He found the poison dart and laid it gently on the bedside table. Then he searched the room. The woman had been shopping. There were new clothes and expensive-looking shopping bags everywhere. A half-eaten box of chocolates lay on a table on the other side of the bed and there were choco-late marks on the pillow. She had been reading a fashion magazine. It was resting on top of the bed next to a map of the UK. It showed the towns of Oxford, Cheltenham and Stratford-upon-Avon.

Alex heard a low groan. The woman had woken up. He snatched the dart and went over to her just as her eyes flickered open, staring at him with anger and disbelief.

"*Malo kopile! Ubit ću te!*" She realized that she couldn't move her arms or her legs and swore at him in a language that he didn't recognize. Her face was ashen grey and there was a nasty bruise forming where she had been hit with the lamp. The nightie had bunched up around her. All in all, she reminded Alex of a potato wrapped in a pink handkerchief.

He showed her the dart. Squatting, he brought it

close to her neck. "What is your name?" he asked.

She didn't answer. She tried to spit at him. Alex pressed the tip of the dart against her throat so that it almost pricked her skin. "Tell me your name," he said, quietly.

She could feel the tip of the needle and her eyes widened. "Dragana Novak!" She hissed the words at him.

"Where is Jack Starbright?" Alex demanded. She didn't seem to understand, so he repeated the question. "Where?"

Dragana was close to fainting. There was a terrible throbbing in her head. She felt the needle against her skin and shuddered with fear. Could this really have happened to her? This was just a child but there was a sort of ferocity about him that she had never seen before. "I don't know this person," she rasped.

"You're lying." Alex pushed the dart a little harder. "You've got a map of England on the bed. Is that where Jack is? In one of these towns?"

"No! No! I don't know who you're talking about. I haven't seen him."

I haven't seen *him*. Alex knew she was telling the truth because of that last word. She didn't know that Jack was actually a woman, so the two of them couldn't have met. Conscious that the seconds were ticking away, that the guards might still arrive, Alex tried another approach. "Who owns this boat?" he demanded. "Is it the Grimaldi brothers? Where can I find them?"

"I'm not telling you. I tell you nothing!" She glared at him defiantly.

Alex examined the tip of the dart. "What is this dipped in?" he asked. "Is it cyanide or something? Why don't we find out?"

"They will kill you!" Dragana grinned. "You will never get off this boat. They will find you and they will make you pay, I promise you. They are coming now!"

It was true. Alex heard someone shouting from above. Either the guards had discovered his footprints or they had heard the brief fight. One of them called out her name.

Dragana opened her mouth to reply but Alex was ready for her. He had another piece of the sheet and before she could say anything he shoved it between her lips and behind her neck, tying the ends to gag her. The grey eyes stared at him with all the hatred in the world. Alex stood up, taking one last look around the cabin. There was nothing else here, nothing to help him. He wanted the gun but he couldn't see it. She had been carrying it when she left the bed. It must have flown out of her hand as she fell. Never mind. It might not have been loaded and he wouldn't have been sure how to use it anyway. He heard another shout from above. There was no time left. He had to go.

He slipped out of the cabin and back down the corridor, heading the way he had come. The

staircase was ahead of him. As he moved forward, lamps came on all around him throwing a
soft light that reflected off the polished walls. Did
the guards know he was here? Were they already
looking for him?

The questions were answered almost at once.
Alex reached the top of the stairs just as the two
men entered the dining-room. They had taken off
their sunglasses to reveal the hard, narrow eyes
of trained killers. The bald man was screwing a
silencer onto an automatic pistol. Alex noticed
the red flame tattoo on the back of his hand. The
other one took out his gun and did the same.
The two of them saw Alex at the same moment as
he saw them. As one, in a single movement, they
raised their weapons. Alex turned and plunged
back down the stairs as a fan of bullets flashed
soundlessly over his shoulders, spitting and snap-
ping into the walls.

They came after him at once, chasing round the
table, but the great wooden surface provided Alex
with cover. Earlier, when he was in the dining-
room, he had pulled out some of the white leather
chairs and now they formed a barrier, forcing the
two men to continue round the other side, closer
to the kitchen. It was exactly what Alex wanted. It
was what he had planned.

Neither of the two men saw the length of string
about six inches above the floor, stretching out
from the dining-room table and disappearing

through the open door and into the galley. Neither of them could have known that the end of the string was tied round a large kitchen match, which in turn was tied to a matchbox, the whole thing taped to one leg of the kitchen table. It was the simplest, the clumsiest of booby traps but it was all Alex had been able to rig together in the time he had been given. Pulling the string dragged the match across the striking surface of the matchbox, causing it to spark.

There was more. Before he had left the kitchen, Alex had turned on all the switches on the oven. It was powered by highly flammable butane gas and the rings had been hissing away as he had continued downstairs for his encounter with Dragana. That was at least ten minutes ago. By now, the kitchen was full of gas.

The single spark ignited it. The second explosion of the evening was very different from the one that the two men had seen outside. It was as if the very air had caught fire. There was no loud bang, just the sound that an enormous paper bag might make when it was crumpled. At the same time, a strange, blue fireball came rushing out of the kitchen, utterly devouring them. They both screamed and reeled backwards, crashing into each other. The whole of the bald man's head seemed to have caught fire. Dropping his gun, he slapped himself again and again, the red flame tattoo on his hand now battling against the real thing. The other man had thrown himself down. He was rolling over and over on the carpet, his clothes blazing. The bald man didn't try to help him. For a moment he stood where he was. There were tears streaming from his eyes and red scorch marks over the bridge of his nose. With something between a snarl and a sob, he snatched up his gun and launched himself after Alex.

The automatic sprinkler system had been activated, putting out the fire, and as Alex hurtled down the stairs and along the corridor, he found himself fighting his way through a haze of falling water. He glanced back over his shoulder. It was difficult to see. The water was like a screen. Even now he wondered if he might have time to search the last cabin. No. It was out of the question. If either of the two men caught up with him, they would kill him. He had to get out of here.

He knew what he was looking for. He had glimpsed it on the way down and there it was straight ahead of him: a glass door with a staircase on the other side, leading back up onto the main deck. Alex reached for the handle and pressed. That was when he discovered that it was locked. It was the last thing he had been expecting. Because the door was glass, because it only led to a flight of steps, he had assumed it would be open. What now? He saw a fire extinguisher on one of the walls. He could use it to smash the glass. He reached out, water from the sprinklers splattering onto his head and running down his neck and shoulders.

"*Arrête!*"

The single word came from the end of the corridor. Alex twisted round and saw the bald man who had reached the bottom of the stairs at the other end. His face was streaked with red. Both his eyebrows seemed to be missing and his eyes were angrier than ever. Water was dripping off his chin. He had his gun and he was taking careful aim. In the distance, Alex heard police sirens. That was hardly surprising. There had been two explosions. The local police must have thought that war was breaking out.

There was no way they were going to get here in time. The bald man was going to shoot him. Alex saw that. Furious, in pain, he was going to pay him back for what he had done and then get rid of the body before the police arrived. Alex had nowhere to hide. He was trapped in a narrow corridor with the locked, glass door behind him, the other cabins on his left and right, and the bald man no more than ten paces away. At this range, even with the clouds of water still cascading down, it would be impossible to miss.

Three things happened at once.

Alex lunged for the fire extinguisher. He wasn't just going to stand there, an easy target. He would go out fighting.

The bald man fired.

And one of the cabin doors burst open. Dragana

Novak had managed to free herself. She had picked up her poison gun. She had come searching for Alex.

Screaming, her eyes bulging, she ran into the corridor just as the bullet spat its short distance towards him. She was blocking the way. Alex saw it hit her in the shoulder. She span round, the gun flying out of her hand. Outside, the first police car drew up. Alex actually heard the screech of tyres on the quayside. He had his hands round the fire extinguisher. He wrenched it off the wall and smashed it into the door, which shattered completely, the pieces falling like a curtain that has been cut in half. Dragana was still on her feet, between him and the bald man – who couldn't risk a second shot in case he hit her again.

Alex was already on his way, bounding up the staircase three steps at a time. Two more bullets ricocheted close to his head and he knew that it wasn't over yet. He burst out onto the deck, which was now flashing blue-white in the reflected light of a police car. He saw it, parked on the quay. Two uniformed officers were making their way up the ramp. A second police car was tearing through the darkness towards the boat.

He didn't wait to be seen. If he fell into the hands of the French police, it would all be over for him. Mrs Jones would find out that he hadn't left and he would be on the next flight out … probably in handcuffs. Without breaking pace, he dived over the edge, his arms outstretched, breaking cleanly through the surface of the water and disappearing into the night-black depths below. He had taken a deep breath as he went and he swam as far as he could – at least ten strokes – before he came up for air. Fortunately, his dive had been almost silent. Nobody had heard or seen him. Looking back, treading water, he saw at least a dozen policemen swarming onto the deck of the superyacht. There were people shouting. Crowds were pouring out of the restaurants to see what was going on.

There was no point staying here. The water was cold and covered with a thin sheen of oil. Alex realized that he would have to buy fresh clothes as soon as the shops opened in the morning. He turned round and began to swim away. As he went, he summed up the evening. On the face of it, he couldn't say it had been a great success.

He had lost his computer and he hadn't found Jack. He had also left a calling card, which would warn the enemy that he was close to them. From now on, they would take extra precautions. Nor did he know where the Grimaldis were hiding. He couldn't even be sure they were in Saint-Tropez.

But in a way, none of that mattered.

He knew what he was going to do next.

TWO RED ROSES

The Villa Siciliana was in the hills above Saint-Tropez, about five miles from the sea. It was a very private place, surrounded by pine trees and cedars and enclosed by a high stone wall. An electronic gate opened onto a drive that swept past a guardhouse with CCTV cameras mounted on either side so that nobody could enter or leave without being seen. During the day, armed guards patrolled the grounds. At night, infrared beams swept through the undergrowth searching for intruders. It was a lot of security for what was, after all, nothing more than a second home – but then the South of France is full of people who demand privacy at any cost.

The house itself was very beautiful; pink and white with old wooden shutters and ivy growing up the walls. A living room ran the entire length of the ground floor but all the windows folded back so that the interior could actually spill out into the garden. A dining-room table with seating for at least twenty people had been placed outside beneath a stone balcony that provided shade from the sun. A series of lawns rolled gently down the hillside with several terraces, an outdoor bar, a tennis court, a helicopter pad and, of course, a king-sized swimming pool surrounded by sunloungers. There were flowers everywhere – lavender, sunflowers and late-summer roses – filling the air with their scent.

The owners of the house were sitting at a table by the pool, eating the breakfast that had been brought to them by a servant, formally dressed in black trousers and a white shirt. Both of them had exactly the same: a soft-boiled egg, a croissant, a plate of melon and yoghurt, a cup of strong black coffee. They were identically dressed in white linen trousers and polo shirts. They were facing each other and, at a glance, it would have been easy enough to imagine that there was only one man there; that the other was his reflection. One was left-handed and the other right-handed and they often moved at the same time, which only added to the illusion.

Giovanni and Eduardo Grimaldi were twin brothers. They were exactly fifty years old. They had been born five seconds apart and often said that they had never been separated for any longer. Even as babies, they had been incredibly close. They had shared a pram. Otherwise they screamed. They'd eaten at the same time or not at all. They'd slept in the same cot and always fallen asleep and woken up at the same moment. Only once – when they were six years old – had a nanny tried to separate them as a punishment for making too much noise. Nobody was quite sure what happened, but that same day the nanny fell out of a third-floor window. The two little boys were seen walking past her body, hand in hand. Both of them were smiling.

It was no surprise that violent death was part of their childhood. Their father was Carlo Grimaldi, one of the most notorious Mafia bosses in North America and the founder of a family that briefly controlled all the illegal gambling, the loan sharks, the drugs and the protection rackets in Detroit. For ten years, Carlo was number three on the FBI's most-wanted list. His own parents were numbers one and two. But he had so many judges, policemen and politicians working for him that nobody could arrest him. He wasn't just above the law. In Detroit, he *was* the law.

Despite their names, the twins were actually American. They had been born in Detroit and grew up in a huge house in Palmer Woods, one of the richest parts of the city. The house was a mansion built in an English style with black timber beams and no fewer than twelve chimneys. Every day they were driven to school by an armed chauffeur and they sat next to each other in every lesson. They never did any work. They understood very little. But their teachers were too nervous to give them a bad report. In fact, they came equal first in every subject. Even so, they left school as soon as they could and didn't bother with college.

They were far more interested in their father's business. Even as teenagers, they loved the idea of becoming gangsters and had actually helped their father on occasion – for example, carrying drugs inside their teddy bears on international flights.

Carlo Grimaldi had recognized his sons' unique talents and when they were sixteen, he promoted them both to capos – short for *caporegime*, a senior commander in a Mafia family. Before they were old enough to get married, both boys were carrying guns – and had used them. Each one of them owned a solid-silver 9mm semi-automatic pistol with ivory hand-grips, made specially for them by the Italian firm, Beretta. They liked to have their initials engraved on the bullets they used. They said it made death more personal.

They worked for their father for nine years but perhaps inevitably they decided, on the same day, that the old man was standing in their way and they could do better without him. A week later, Carlo was gunned down in his Jacuzzi by his own bodyguard, an Italian American called Frankie Stallone, known as "The Flame" because of the tattoo on his right hand. With Carlo gone, the brothers took control of the family and the next few years were bloodier and more violent than any that had gone before.

Unfortunately, they were also less profitable.

The Italian Mafia, also known as the Cosa Nostra, has become a worldwide criminal organization raking in as much as $4.9 billion a year, but it has done so by obeying certain rules. There's the law of *omerta*, for example – the famous code of silence. Families stick together. Women are respected. Giovanni and Eduardo had never even visited their ancestral home in Sicily and understood none of this, and without their father to control them, they soon found themselves hated, isolated and finally almost assassinated. They survived a machine-gun attack on their yacht in Miami simply because they arrived ten minutes late. They also – miraculously – walked out of a hotel in Las Vegas after a bomb had brought all seven storeys crashing to the ground.

They had, however, seen the writing on the wall ... or what was left of it. They knew they had to get out of their family and out of America. That was when they joined Scorpia. The new organization of out-of-work spies and killers which had been formed just after the Cold War was already thriving, specializing in sabotage, corruption, intelligence and assassination – areas that the two brothers knew well. They made contact, managed to get themselves recruited and rose rapidly to the executive committee. They had been there at the meeting when Abdul-Aziz al-Razim had been given the task of blackmailing the British government. They had listened to him as he explained

167

his plans – which involved the assassination of the American Secretary of State and a boy called Alex Rider.

And now, thanks to that boy, Scorpia was finished. Razim was dead. Half of their colleagues had been arrested. Giovanni and Eduardo had managed to get away, one step ahead of the world's security services, but their troubles were far from over. Their main problem was a very simple one: they were running out of money. It was true that they had properties all over the world. Their luxury yacht, *Quicksilver*, was worth millions. They had a dozen superb cars, including two bright-red Alfa Romeos and two silver Rolls Royces. If one brother bought something, the other had to have it too. What they didn't have, though, was cash in the bank. That was why they were planning a new operation and the crucial phase was supposed to be happening in just two days' time.

Operation Steel Claw.

The news they had just received was therefore all the more crushing. Everything had been carefully planned and it had all gone perfectly. Until last night.

"You shot her," Giovanni said.

"The stupid woman got in the way."

Frankie Stallone, the bald man with the flame tattoo, stood in front of the two brothers, wearing a grey suit and a T-shirt. He was still in pain and should have been in hospital. His face was a red and white latticework of burns. His lips were blistered. There was a plaster over the bridge of his nose. And he had lost both his eyebrows. He looked hideous.

"How bad is it?" Eduardo asked, bringing his spoon down hard on his boiled egg.

"Will she be able to fly?" Giovanni asked, doing the same.

"I spoke to the doctors this morning," Frankie replied. He had a New York Bronx accent. "The bone in her shoulder is completely shattered."

There was a lengthy silence. Neither of the brothers ate their eggs. Frankie Stallone stood there, waiting for their response. He was not afraid of them. He had made a mistake, certainly, but he had worked for the Grimaldis for many years – first for their father, now for them. They had sent him to the boat to keep an eye on the Serbian woman who was drunk and unreliable. None of them had been expecting an intruder – and certainly not one who was a teenage boy.

Giovanni put down his spoon. "It's very..."

"...annoying." Eduardo finished the sentence. This was one of their habits. The two of them often shared what had to be said.

"And who was this boy?" Giovanni asked.

"What was he doing?"

Frankie shrugged. The movement hurt him. His shoulder was burned too. "I have no idea. He may have been a thief. He set off a device that distracted our attention and that was how he slipped on board."

The brothers considered. Both of them came to the same decision.

"Well, we're very disappointed," Giovanni began.

"You should have been more careful."

"We'll deal with the situation now. You'd better go and get someone to look at your face."

"Your nose is peeling."

"And your chin!"

Frankie nodded and walked off into the garden, his skin rubbing painfully against his suit, leaving the two brothers alone.

It was perhaps unfortunate that the two of them were identical twins, for it had to be said that both Giovanni and Eduardo were strangely unattractive. They were neat and delicate, almost like schoolboys, with very round heads and black hair that could have been painted on, coming down in cowlicks over their foreheads. Their eyes were also dark and somehow always suspicious, even when they were looking at each other. They were clean-shaven but their cheeks and chin were covered in permanent dark stubble, like sandpaper. They had very small mouths. If the devil had a church, they would sing in his choir. That was the impression they gave.

"So what are we going to do, Gio?"

"I don't know, Eddie."

These were their pet names for each other. Nobody

else ever used them. Not if they wanted to live.

"It shouldn't be too difficult to find someone else but it means we may have to delay Steel Claw," Giovanni said.

"We can't. Everything is set up. That ghastly man, Vosper, is already on his way. He'll be here..."

"...later this morning. Yes. I know. But we have to find someone who can handle the Super Stallion. And it's not an easy manoeuvre, the actual pick-up." He put down his spoon. "We're going to have to use all our contacts..."

"We'll find someone," Eduardo muttered. He had also put down his spoon.

There was another silence. The two brothers sat in the sunshine, looking at their breakfast, neither of them eating.

At last Giovanni muttered the words that both of them were thinking. "This boy..."

"It can't have been..."

"Alex Rider!" Giovanni swore in old Sicilian. It was something that he and Eduardo had learned from their grandmother, an old woman who had been famous for her filthy language. "Who else could it have been?" he went on. "That little snake has caused us enough trouble already. He must have followed us here. And I thought he was finished after Egypt."

"Evidently he's back in business."

"Razim failed completely. I'm telling you, Eddie, we're better off without Scorpia. After Steel Claw, we'll set up a new organization. We'll have money in the bank. We'll have everything we need."

It was a pleasant thought. The two brothers returned to their breakfast. Behind them, one of the gardeners was mowing the lawn while another set to work cleaning the pool. A guard with a sub-machine gun walked past. The villa was patrolled twenty-four hours a day ... more wages to be paid, more money that had to be found.

"What are we going to do about the Serbian woman?" Giovanni asked, touching a napkin against his lips.

"She's in hospital in Saint-Tropez," Eduardo replied, setting his napkin down.

"We should have had her treated on the boat."

"That was the French. They insisted."

"Have they spoken to her?"

"She hasn't told them anything. At least, not yet." Giovanni thought for a moment. "I think we should go and visit her," he said. "One way or another, we really need to take care of her."

"Let's take roses," Eduardo suggested.

Giovanni smiled. "Yes. That's a lovely idea."

Saint-Tropez hospital is a couple of miles outside the city next to a village called Gassin. It's a modern, low, white building, set back from the main road and surrounded by flowers and shrubs. Just before midday, Eduardo and Giovanni Grimaldi pulled up in their open-top Jeep Wrangler and stood for a moment, gazing at the narrow windows and main entrance. The car was a recent purchase and, of course, they both had one. Two Jeep Wranglers had cost them sixty thousand euros, smashing their credit-card limit. But they couldn't resist the chunky off-road vehicles with their four-wheel drive and five-speed automatic transmission. They loved folding the roof down and speeding through the countryside with a blanket over their knees if the weather was cold. This Jeep was Giovanni's. He beamed at it like a proud parent as he left it in the car park, sitting in the sun.

The two brothers walked through the car park and went into the hospital. They were each carrying a single red rose. They asked at the reception for Madame Dragana Novak and were shown to a room on the second floor, where the Serbian pilot was lying in bed, her face grey, her arm in a sling.

Dragana was in a bad mood. First of all, she was in pain. The doctors had operated and removed the bullet and the police had been persuaded that she had been attacked by a thief, trying to break into the boat. But she was angry with herself. She had allowed a boy – a mere child – to get the better of her. She still wasn't sure why the poisoned needle hadn't worked but she knew that somehow she had been tricked and the thought infuriated her. And then there was Operation Steel Claw. She was very well aware that she would be unable to manipulate the Super Stallion with her arm in a sling.

It might well be that her employers would have to cancel the operation altogether. That didn't bother her but the trouble was, she'd only received a small percentage of her fee. For a while now, she'd had her doubts about Eduardo and Giovanni. They might behave like millionaires but they'd been very slow coming forward with the cash.

And here they were, coming into the room, each one carrying a flower as if it were a flag. Why only one flower? That was exactly her point. They could at least have brought a bunch. Dragana straightened herself against the pillows as the brothers sat down, one on each side of the bed.

"How are you feeling, Miss Novak?" Giovanni asked – at least she assumed it was Giovanni. They were dressed identically and she had no way of telling them apart.

"We were so sorry to hear about what happened," Eduardo added.

"It was completely the fault of your guards." Dragana had already rehearsed what she was going to say. "You didn't want me to stay in your house and you said I would be safe on the boat. Instead, I was woken up in the middle of the night and attacked. I could have been killed."

"Can you tell us anything more?" Giovanni asked.

"We understand it was a young boy."

"What exactly did he want?"

"I'm not telling you anything until I've got the rest of my money!" Dragana spat out the words.

She looked from one twin to the other. It really felt strange having them on either side of her, still holding their stupid flowers. "You said you were going to pay me two hundred thousand pounds and so far I've had almost nothing out of you."

"You're no longer capable of doing the job," Eduardo muttered.

"Exactly," Eduardo agreed.

"That's not my fault," Dragana snarled. "You'll have to find someone else." She paused for a moment. Perhaps it wasn't a good idea to be so aggressive. "I've already spoken to my cousin, Slavko," she went on. "He's a qualified helicopter pilot. He works at the Moma Stanojlović air plant and he's highly regarded." She fumbled in her bed-clothes and produced a crumpled sheet of paper. "Don't worry. I telephoned him this morning but I didn't tell him anything about you. He's waiting to hear from you. This is his number."

"Thank you." Giovanni took the paper and handed it to his brother.

"But you still have to pay me something," Dragana went on. "I did what you wanted at the Suffolk Air Show. That was half of the work. I killed two American pilots! Without me, you'd have nothing!" She glared at them.

Eduardo smiled. "We came here because we wanted to take care of you," he said.

"We feel responsible for you," Giovanni agreed. "We bought you flowers."

"Roses. We picked them from our own garden. They have a lovely smell." Eduardo reached out, holding the single flower under Dragana's nose. Almost despite herself, she leaned forward and that was when Eduardo thrust upwards. What Dragana couldn't have known was that there was a very thin, razor-sharp wire concealed inside the flower. The twins had done this before. It was one of their favourite tricks and they would take turns – one watching, one doing the actual work. The wire went straight up her nose and into the *medulla oblongata*, the nerve mass located at the lower base of her brain. Dragana was dead before she knew what had happened. There was a tiny trickle of blood from the corner of her nostril. Otherwise, it would be very difficult to say what had killed her.

The two brothers stood up.

"My turn next time!" Giovanni said as he looked at the piece of paper that Dragana had given them. There was a long number beginning with 381, the international dialling code for Serbia.

"Are we going to call her cousin?"

"I don't see why not, Eddie. She said he was..."

"...highly regarded." Eduardo glanced at his watch. "We'd better get back to the house. Mr Vosper will be here soon."

Taking the roses with them, the brothers left.

It took them half an hour to reach the Villa Siciliana in their Jeep Wrangler. They skirted round the edge of Saint-Tropez and turned off onto the road that wound its way up and up into the hills. Eduardo had driven them to the hospital so Giovanni drove them back. As they approached the gate, an image of the car appeared on a screen inside the guardhouse. The guards immediately recognized the driver and the man sitting next to him and hit the button to open the gate. Without stopping, the jeep rolled past.

Nobody was aware that it was carrying an extra passenger.

The night before, Alex Rider had pulled himself, dripping wet, out of the harbour and crouched in the shadows as the police piled on board *Quicksilver*. He assumed that they would search the boat. He still thought there was a chance they might find Jack. Surely, at the very least, they would arrest Dragana and the two men who had just tried to kill him?

But it seemed that, in France, things didn't work that way. He saw the bald man, standing on the deck, explaining something to a young gendarme. The two of them seemed to be on the very best of terms. A few minutes later, Dragana was carried off on a stretcher and loaded into an ambulance which had also turned up. People were already going back into the restaurants. The fun was over. There was nothing more to see.

Alex felt angry and disappointed as he returned to his hotel. He grabbed his key from the receptionist and ignored her puzzled look as he took the stairs up to his room, his feet squelching on the carpet. He put his trousers, shirt and jacket out on the balcony to dry, showered and went to bed. He already knew what he was going to do the next day. He had planned it even as he had dived into the sea.

Dragana was his only lead. She had more or less admitted that the Grimaldi brothers owned *Quicksilver* but she had said nothing more. He didn't know if they were in Saint-Tropez. He didn't know where they lived. But if he stayed close to her, there was still a chance that she might lead him to them. Alex no longer had his computer but he still had his phone – miraculously it was still working – and he had used it to Google the name and address of the main hospital in Saint-Tropez.

He was up bright and early the next morning. He bought new clothes in the first shop that opened and then took a taxi to the hospital, arriving just before ten o'clock. Since then, he had been in the reception area, hiding behind a French newspaper he had picked up at a kiosk. He wanted to see if anyone asked for Dragana Novak. If she had a visitor, he would follow them. They might lead him to the Grimaldis. And they in turn would lead him to Jack.

He had actually been looking out through the plate-glass windows when the Jeep Wrangler pulled up and he had watched as the two men had got out with their single roses. He had known at once who they were. Colonel Manzour had told him about the Grimaldi brothers and how many other identical twins could there be in Saint-Tropez? Alex couldn't believe his luck. For some reason they had come here themselves. They were exactly the people he wanted to see. He had waited until they had come in, carrying their ridiculous flowers. They had passed within a few metres of him, but neither of them had looked his way. He had heard them ask for Dragana.

While they were upstairs, he had hurried out-side. Again, he was lucky. They had driven an open-top car and had come alone. Making sure that nobody was looking, he had opened the door and slipped inside. There was a blanket lying in the back. He had squeezed himself into the well behind the two front seats and then drawn it over him. It had been about thirty minutes before the brothers had come back.

And now he felt the jeep slow down and stop.

"Vosper is here," he heard one of the brothers say.

"Yes. Let's get this over with," the other replied.

Alex heard the jeep doors close and the crunch of footsteps as the two men walked away. Meanwhile, there was a buzz from somewhere behind him as the guards activated the controls and the gates swung firmly shut.

CEMENT SHOES

Alex remained where he was, under the blanket, listening out for any sound. This was the most dangerous part. He had no way of knowing if anyone was looking at the car – or even where the car was parked. If he moved and somebody saw him, it would all be over. He had heard the two brothers walk off – on their way to a meeting with someone called Vosper. He had heard the gate close and knew that he was effectively trapped inside some sort of compound. He would worry about that later. What else? In the distance, somebody had started a lawnmower. A plane flew overhead. He was well outside Saint-Tropez. He knew that from the length of the journey. This must be somewhere very secluded ... quite possibly one of the villas that were dotted throughout the hills.

He couldn't stay here for ever. Very slowly, an inch at a time, he drew back the blanket, grateful for the fresh air. He saw at once that he was in some kind of carport with wicker screens on each side and branches with leaves and flowers intertwining above to keep the car out of the sun. That was good. He couldn't be seen after all. Gently, he pressed the handle of the back door and opened it. He slithered out.

Crouching down beside the car, he took in his surroundings. In front of him, there was a large house, pink and white, on the other side of a gravel drive. If it had been the home of a Hollywood film star, he wouldn't have been surprised. The gardens that surrounded it could have come straight off the cover of a glossy magazine. He turned round and peered through the wickerwork. The gate was behind him, at the top of a slope. He could just make out the control room next to it, but as far as he could see, he would be out of the sight of any guards who happened to be there. CCTV? He could see a couple of cameras but they were trained on the gate, looking in the other direction. There didn't seem to be anyone around.

He was about to slip out when he heard footsteps crunching on the gravel and he froze as a man walked past, dressed in dark clothes, carrying a machine gun. Alex whistled under his breath. Maybe he had made a mistake coming here. It was certainly going to be harder getting out than it had been coming in. He wondered if Jack Starbright was inside the house. If the Grimaldi brothers had brought her with them to France and she wasn't on the boat, where else could she be? The thought spurred him on.

He made sure there were no more guards in sight and scurried across from the carport, his own feet scuffing the gravel. The front door of the house was open and he was tempted to disappear through it but, at the last minute, he veered off, making for the back of the house. He wasn't going to commit himself to the main entrance – it was much safer to circle round and find a quieter way in.

He ran, crouching, keeping close to the side wall, then skidded to a halt about halfway along. He was certain that nobody had seen him. There was a window close to his head and he peered into a corridor and a flight of steps going down to a basement. There was no sound coming from inside and he couldn't see anyone either. He caught his breath, then continued on his way.

The wall went on for some distance. It really was an enormous villa. Alex guessed it might contain nine or ten bedrooms. Everywhere he looked there were balconies and terraces, each one giving a view over the garden. He came to an archway that opened into a courtyard with a fountain playing at the centre. There were different herbs growing in neat little beds. Alex smelled rosemary and mint in the warm midday air. He saw a closed door which might allow him into the house if it wasn't locked and was about to test it when it suddenly opened and a man in the formal whites of a chef came out carrying a pair of secateurs. Alex drew back, watching him as he cut a few sprigs of rosemary. The chef went back inside without closing the door. Alex waited thirty seconds, then followed him in.

What would he say if he was challenged? Alex might be able to pretend he was a delivery boy or something but he knew it wouldn't work. He wasn't dressed like a delivery boy, and anyway, his accent would give him away. He would simply have to make sure he wasn't caught. He found himself in a long, cool corridor with paving stones and whitewashed walls. The chef had gone through a doorway into a well-equipped kitchen. Alex watched as he set the herbs down and began to carve a chicken that had just come out of the oven. There was a cat watching him, sitting on a windowsill. A telephone rang in the room next door. The chef stopped what he was doing and went to answer it. Alex couldn't have asked for better timing.

But as he went past the kitchen door, he stopped. The smell of the chicken was overwhelming. Alex hadn't eaten since breakfast and that had only been a quickly snatched croissant on the way to the hospital. His stomach growled and although he knew he was taking an unnecessary risk, he couldn't stop himself. He sneaked inside and tore off a drumstick – then, as an afterthought, he threw a second piece at the cat. When the chef saw what had happened, it would take the blame.

The meat was hot and greasy. Alex wolfed it down as fast as he could, then dropped the bone into a plant pot. He came to another half-open door and heard voices on the other side. With his mouth still full of food, he knelt down, trying to fold himself into the shadows, and looked through the crack.

He had reached a living room with floor-to-ceiling windows that opened on to the garden beyond. It was twice as long as any room that Alex had ever seen, filled with expensive furniture that reminded him of *Quicksilver*. Eduardo and Giovanni Grimaldi were sitting next to each other on a low, leather sofa, each of them holding coffee cups; one in his right hand, one in his left.

They were directly facing him but as long as he didn't move too much, it was unlikely that they would see him. He was low down, largely concealed behind the door. There was a third man – presumably Mr Vosper – sitting in an armchair to one side with his legs crossed. Alex could see steel-grey hair and steel glasses, a clean-cut face and cheeks that had gone red in the sun. He wore the classic dress of an Englishman abroad: a white jacket, slacks and loafers. He was holding a panama hat.

"I'm afraid there can be absolutely no question of a delay," he was saying. He had a very clipped way of speaking. "We've got the opportunity, two days from now. If we don't do it then, we may never get another chance." Alex heard the words and knew that, whatever they were planning, he had almost no time to prevent it.

"Why not next week ... or the week after?" one of the brothers asked.

"Because I've seen the names on the list. We're talking solid gold here, gentlemen. It's absolutely perfect for your requirements." He paused. "Do you think I could have some more coffee?"

Alex flinched. If they called the kitchen, someone would come down the very corridor where he was hiding. But it didn't happen. "Help yourself," one of the brothers said.

The man got up and moved closer to the door. He poured himself some coffee from a percolator and Alex was able to see him quite clearly. He must have been about fifty years old. Was he ex-army? There was something regimented about the way he walked and he talked like someone who was used to rapping out orders. At the same time, he was running to fat. His trousers were biting into his stomach, trying to hold it back. "You have a very nice place here," he said.

"Thank you."

"Must cost you quite a bit to keep up."

"Mr Vosper..." The brothers clearly didn't like the way this conversation was going.

"Call me Derek." The man added two lumps of sugar to his cup. "After all, we're in business together now. You know, I'm beginning to think we should have charged more for our services. You two can obviously afford it." He laughed briefly as if to say that he didn't really mean it. "But seriously, gentlemen, let's not have any more talk about postponing. They're seeing Henry at half past three in the afternoon and the rest of it's up to you." He walked back to his chair and sat down again, the cup and saucer rattling in his hand. "I wish I was there to be a witness. It's certainly going to be a dramatic afternoon." He let out another brief bark of laughter. "And now I'm afraid we do have to talk a bit about money," he went on. "It's the reason I've flown all this way."

"We have an agreement, Mr Vosper."

"Precisely. Only you haven't paid up yet. Five hundred grand! That's what we agreed for Steel Claw. Odd name for what you're doing, I'd have said."

"You have received money."

"That's true. But not a great deal of money. That's why I'm here. I'm thinking about my other half..."

Alex never heard him complete the sentence.

He had been so absorbed in the conversation that he hadn't heard the footsteps creeping up behind him. The first thing he knew was a hand grabbing hold of his collar. He turned and looked into the livid eyes and the burned skin of the bald man from the boat. Alex was already searching for a defensive position against the blow that he knew must be coming but it was far, far too late. The bald man was holding something in his right hand. Alex didn't even see what it was. He swung it down through the air, crashing it into the side of Alex's head.

And then there was nothing. It really was as simple as that.

"You've done very well, Mr Stallone."

"Yes. This makes up for what happened on *Quicksilver*..."

"...at least, in part."

Alex woke up to the sound of the Grimaldi brothers talking to a third person. He tried to move. He couldn't. He was sitting on a chair with his hands tied behind him, the rope so tight that it was cutting into his flesh. There was nothing to be gained by pretending he was still unconscious. He opened his eyes.

He was in some sort of basement, a laundry area. It was very warm and he could hear the hum of machinery somewhere behind him. The floor was tiled. There were bare pipes running along one of the walls and over his head. As far as he could see, the room had no windows. The Grimaldi brothers were perched on two laundry baskets, talking to the bald man who had knocked him out. They noticed that he had woken up.

"He's back with us!" one of them exclaimed.

"You get everything ready," the other one said,

addressing the bald man. "We'll talk to him. Then you can deal with him."

"I'll enjoy that." The bald man – Mr Stallone – rubbed his hands together. He got up and left the room.

Alex could only sit there as the two brothers turned to him. His head was pounding and there was the taste of blood in his mouth. But more than anything, he was annoyed with himself. He had behaved like a complete amateur, sneaking into this house without any sort of backup, not checking out the security – and eavesdropping through a half-open door. It was the sort of thing he might have done at school! And he had become so absorbed in the conversation that he hadn't watched his own back. Mrs Jones had been right. *Stay away from us.* He remembered her warning him to go back home. Well, it was too late for that now.

He forced himself to focus. He had been searched while he was unconscious. His passport and phone were on a table in front of him. He could see the hole in the passport cover where the poison needle had penetrated. *We'll talk to him. Then you can deal with him*. He remembered what one of the brothers had just said. He didn't like the sound of it.

"Alex Rider..."

"...we're very pleased to meet you at last."

Alex examined the brothers closely for the first

time. He looked at the black, painted hair, the round heads, the stubble. They reminded him of two ventriloquist's dolls. They weren't just identical. They could have been mass-produced. But there was nothing remotely entertaining about them. They were both looking at him with exactly the same expression: a cold and all-consuming hatred.

"I'm Eduardo," one of them said. "And this is my brother..."

"...Giovanni."

"You've been a real pain in the neck, Alex. I mean, really, thanks to you we've had serious problems."

They could barely wait for each other to finish. This was something they had wanted to say for a long time and the words poured out.

"Razim!"

"Julia Rothman!"

"Scorpia ... the whole organization!"

"I have to say that, looking at you, I'm frankly surprised," Eduardo went on. "You're just a kid..."

"...and a stupid one at that. Did you really think you could just walk in here? What do you take us for?"

"But we're very glad to see you. Really we are." Eduardo beamed at him. "We need to know who you're working for, how you found us and what you're doing here."

Giovanni nodded. "Of course, you won't tell us to begin with. We understand that. I'm sure you're very brave. So we'll have to torture you."

Eduardo turned to his brother. There was something very unpleasant in his eyes. "Can I go first?"

"It's my turn first, Eddie. You went first last time."

"No, I didn't."

"Yes, you did. And you got to kill Dragana Novak this morning. It's definitely my turn."

Alex filed that piece of information away. So the woman on the boat was dead. That was interesting ... and it might be useful. "You don't have to torture me," he said. "I'll tell you everything you want to know."

"Really?" The brothers looked disappointed.

"I don't have anything to hide. And I'm not working for anyone. It's very simple: I'm looking for Jack Starbright."

Giovanni and Eduardo exchanged a look. "Is that why you were on *Quicksilver*?"

"Yes. She wasn't there so I came here."

As Alex spoke, he was waiting for his head to clear. At the same time he was testing the rope around his wrists. There was always a chance that some sort of opportunity would present itself and he had to be ready to take it. But whoever had tied the rope had done a professional job. It wouldn't move. He could no longer feel his fingers.

"You're lying!" Eduardo scowled. "If you're not working for anybody, what made you think that Miss Starbright might be with us? And how did you find your way here?"

Alex knew he had to be careful what answer he

gave. The two men probably didn't know that Jack had managed to send him an email. If they were holding her, and he told them the truth, he might cause her difficulties. "I went back to Siwa," he said. "I found your name scratched into the wall of her cell."

"That's all very well but what about our address? Was that scratched on the wall too?" This time it was Giovanni who had asked.

"I was helped by the Egyptian secret service. Colonel Ali Manzour. He knew you were in Saint-Tropez and he's looking for you now. If anything happens to me he'll come after you, I promise you." Alex was carefully mixing fact and fiction. It was the best way to create a believable story. "He sent me here and when I arrived, I checked out all the boats in the harbour. I guessed you might have sailed from Alexandria and I thought one of them might lead me to you. *Quicksilver* is registered to a company called Draco d'Olivo. It belongs to you."

"OK. So you found the boat..."

"...but how did you find this house?"

"Dragana told me where you lived. I broke into her cabin and she gave me your address." This was a complete lie. But Alex knew there was no way they could check it out. Dragana Novak wasn't going to tell them anything.

The two brothers thought for a moment, questioning what they had just heard. But they came to the same conclusion at the same time. The story made sense. As much as they might want to hurt him, they had to believe it.

"Where is Jack?" Alex asked.

Giovanni glanced at his brother as if asking permission. Eduardo nodded and Giovanni leaned forward and slapped Alex on the side of the head. It wasn't a hard blow but Alex reeled back and the chair rocked beneath him. "You don't ask us questions," he said.

"You don't say anything," Eduardo agreed.

The two of them gazed at him and, despite everything, Alex understood how they felt. He had defeated Scorpia three times before he had allowed himself to fall into their hands. They had been part of what was supposed to be the greatest criminal organization in the world and he had humiliated them over and over again. He had also followed them from Egypt to France. He had found their superyacht and their home, walking through all their security systems. More humiliation. No wonder they hated him. He waited, uneasily, for what was to come.

"We're going to finish this," Eduardo said. "We're going to kill you. Scorpia should have done it a long time ago. But we're going to make you pay."

Alex didn't answer. He was trying to pretend he didn't care.

"We could just shoot you," Giovanni said.

"We could do it now."

"It would be very easy. But we're not going to do that, are we, Eddie!"

Eduardo smiled. "As it happens, Gio and I were brought up in a proper Mafia family. Our father..."

"...our grandmother..."

"...she very much liked the old methods. Grandma always used to tell us to respect the old traditions."

"Cement shoes," Giovanni said.

"I don't suppose that means anything to you – so let us explain." Eduardo glanced at his brother as if for approval, then began. "In the old days, the Mafia had a very unusual way of getting rid of their enemies. They would make them sit with their legs in a large bucket. They would fill the bucket with quick-drying cement – and then, when it had set, they would throw them in a river."

"They drowned," Giovanni added, unnecessarily.

"The whole point was that everyone knew this was a Mafia punishment. There was something about it that caught the imagination. It was such a horrible way to die!"

"We're going to do the same to you," Giovanni said.

"Yes. It's a shame we don't have time for the full works – but fortunately there's a variation."

"Concrete blocks!"

Eduardo nodded. "Same idea. Same result. But a little easier – and certainly less mess."

As if on cue, the door of the basement opened

and the bald man came back in, carrying a length of chain. "Everything's ready," he said – and Alex was surprised how much venom he managed to inject into his voice.

"We're not going to be able to come," Giovanni said. "We have to leave straight away."

"So make sure you take your phone," Eduardo instructed. "Record the whole thing. We'll watch it a few times and then we'll send it to the Egyptian State Security Service. I'm sure they'll find it all very entertaining."

The two brothers stood up and rounded on Alex.

"There's a van waiting for you outside," Giovanni explained, his eyes glinting. "It's going to take you to a part of the coast about a mile from here called *Point d'Aiguille*."

"It translates as 'Needle Point'."

"There is nobody there. Nobody will see you arrive. You will be taken out of the van and Mr Stallone will attach your feet to two concrete blocks…"

"…and then he will drop you into the Mediterranean."

"Splash! Can you imagine what it will be like, being dragged feet first to the bottom of the sea?"

"*Au revoir*, Alex," Eduardo said

"I think the word is *adieu*," Giovanni corrected him. "It's more permanent."

For a moment Alex went berserk, struggling with the chair, trying to smash the wood. But it was too thick. There was nothing he could do as the twin brothers walked out of the room. The bald man with the crumpled head and the mad eyes waited until they had gone, then came over to him, holding out the chains.

"Cement shoes," he muttered. "I think I have a pair that fits."

NEEDLE POINT

The white van was following a minor road that twisted its way past vineyards and olive groves, climbing ever further uphill. It came to a rough track and turned off, now forking back down towards the sea. Frankie "The Flame" Stallone was driving, his tattooed hand resting on the steering wheel, a glowing cigarette between his lips. The younger man who had been with him on *Quicksilver* was in the passenger seat beside him. He was known as Skunk – which was the street name of the drug he had been smoking since he was twelve years old. It had caused him a certain amount of brain damage as well as the very bad skin around his eyes and mouth. His appearance hadn't been helped by the fact that his clothes had caught alight in the explosion. Underneath his baggy shirt and cargo trousers he looked as if he ought to be in intensive care. One of his eyes was swollen shut. His lips were so blistered he could hardly talk.

"Arex Ryer," he said.

"What about him?" Stallone glared at him.

"Make it slow. I wan' him to suffer!"

Alex Rider was in the back of the van, which was effectively a metal box. The door was locked and there were no windows. He felt every bump and vibration of the journey but he could see nothing. The Grimaldis had described exactly what they were going to do to him and he had to use all his mental reserves to hold himself together, to stop himself panicking. The chains that the bald man had carried into the basement were in front of Alex and but the blocks of concrete were beside him. Each one weighed about ten kilograms. Alex had already tested them, in case he could use them as weapons. But it was hopeless. He could barely pick them up and they would be impossible to throw. Even looking at them filled him with horror. The men were going to attach them to his feet and throw him into the sea. He would be dragged down instantly and he would drown. That was how the Mafia got rid of its enemies.

The van bumped over a particularly rough piece of ground and Alex heard the chains rattle. It was a reminder – if he needed one – of what lay ahead, but he was determined they weren't going to kill him without a fight. When they opened the doors, that would be the time to make his move. If they were close to the sea, he would dive in. They might shoot at him but at least a bullet would be fast ... better than the alternative.

They came to a halt. The engine was turned off. Alex heard the two men get out and a moment later the back doors opened, allowing the light to flood in. He had grabbed hold of one of the chains but he knew at once that they weren't taking any chances. The bald man was standing well back, holding a gun. The younger man leaned in and snatched the chains away. Alex let them go. He could only watch as first the chains and then the concrete blocks were removed.

"We'll be right back," the bald man said.

The doors were closed and locked again.

Alex was left alone in almost pitch darkness. Just a few chinks of light were able to leak in through the side of the doors. He had nothing on him. All his possessions, including his passport and mobile phone, had been taken from him at the Villa Siciliana. He had already searched the back of the van but he decided to do it again. He had to keep his mind occupied, to stop thinking about what lay ahead. Carefully, he ran his fingers over the floor, feeling the surface around him. He had found nothing before. He was sure he would be unsuccessful again. But this time there was something. His probing fingers discovered a single loose nail. There was a ridge running around the interior and it must have got stuck in there. The last big bump had jostled it free. Alex rolled it in the palm of his hand. The nail was about five centimetres long. He wasn't sure how he was going to use it but just having it made him feel better about the situation. These people weren't as clever as they thought. They made mistakes.

The handle turned and the door opened a second time. The bald man, Frankie Stallone, stood there, the sunlight streaming over his shoulders. He still had his gun and it was aimed directly at Alex's head. "Get out!" he said.

"I've got an idea," Alex said. "Why don't you just drive me back to Saint-Tropez and pretend this never happened. That way, the British secret service won't come looking for you and there's just a chance that you won't spend the rest of your life in jail."

"They'd have to find me first," the bald man sneered.

"That won't be difficult. You've got no eyebrows. You look hideous."

"Get out!" The bald man repeated the words. "If I have to tell you a third time, I will shoot you in the knee. I would like to do that."

Alex saw that he had annoyed the man and he was glad about that. It might make him careless. But for the moment he had no choice but to obey. Hiding the nail in the palm of his hand, he climbed down.

He took in his surroundings.

They were in a place so remote, so desolate that he knew at once that there was no chance of any farmer or tourist happening to come along. There was no track. They had driven over clumps of wild grass and thistles to a strip of land that formed a narrow corridor between a tangle of ugly-looking shrubs. These were dotted with bright red berries that hung in clusters, probably poisonous, surrounded by spiky leaves.

The sea was directly in front of him, a long drop down. Alex looked in vain for a passing boat, perhaps a fisherman. He understood now how this place had got its name. There was a long, narrow overhang, which stretched out over the water like a needle tapering to a point. The two blocks were waiting for him, quite close to the edge, with the lengths of chain already connected. There were also two padlocks. Alex would stand with one foot beside each block. The chains would be locked around his ankles. He would be thrown in. His own weight would drag the blocks with him. And then it would all be over.

The younger man was standing to one side. He was holding up his mobile phone, squinting in the sunshine and Alex noticed him swing round to capture him as he stepped down from the van, recording his every move. He also carried a gun in a holster that hung from his shoulder. That was bad news. One armed man Alex might be able to deal with. Two was going to be difficult.

"Move it!" Stallone snarled.

"How about a close-up?" Alex asked. He turned to the camera phone and lifted a single finger.

A final message to the Grimaldi twins.

The bald man was still being careful to keep plenty of distance between the two of them. Alex couldn't initiate an attack. His only chance would come when Stallone tried to attach him to the weights. He knew that whatever happened, he had to make his move before the two locks clicked shut. Once he was chained to the concrete, he would be finished.

But he had worked out a plan. His hand was dangling by his side with the nail jutting out of his palm like a miniature knife. First, he would take out the bald man. Then he would dive into the sea. That was the simplest way. He could swim ten strokes underwater and by the time he came to the surface he would be well out of the range of both of them. Moving slowly, he walked forward, the path narrowing with every step he took. The bald man followed three or four steps behind. His partner stood where he was, holding the phone.

Alex prepared to make his move – but suddenly everything happened very quickly. The bald man had run forward without making a sound. Before Alex could do anything, he felt himself grabbed by the shoulders and pulled backwards. He cried out but it was too late. He fell heavily, crashing into the soft grass, and for a brief moment he was dazed. It gave Stallone enough time to slip the first chain around one of his ankles and, to his horror, Alex heard the padlock snap shut. He was lying on his back at the very end of Needle Point, with the sea below on both sides of him. Stallone was stooping over him, smiling, reaching for the second chain. Alex wasn't going to let that happen. He slashed upwards with his hand balled into a fist, the nail jutting out. He smiled with satisfaction as the point drove into Stallone's neck. Stallone howled and fell back, blood spurting out between his fingers.

Alex scrambled to his feet. He was pinned to the spot, one foot chained to a ten-kilogram block of concrete. He couldn't run. Certainly he couldn't dive into the water. But he wasn't finished yet. He still had the nail. He was ready to use it.

But then Stallone surprised him a second time. Alex had thought he would try to close the second padlock, but instead he rushed forward, still howling in pain. He was like a stampeding bull. He slammed into Alex, forcing him backwards, and at that moment Alex realized with a mixture of terror and despair that there was no longer anything beneath his feet. He had been bludgeoned off the end. His hands flailed in the air as he fell.

The whole world spun around him. He felt his left leg jerk up as the chain, attached to his ankle, became taut. But then, as he continued to plummet down, he dragged the concrete weight off the edge and he could actually see it, out of the corner of his eye, following him down – a huge grey bullet that wouldn't need to hit him. The two of them crashed into the water at the same time, a tangled mess of steel, concrete and flesh that disappeared immediately beneath the surface.

Alex just had the presence of mind to take a deep breath before he went under, passing from bright sunlight to the darkness and iciness of certain death. The block was too far away for him to reach but he could feel the chain pulling him down irresistibly. The water swirled past him, twisting over his shoulders and through his hair as he was swallowed up by the sea.

On the edge of the overhang, at Needle Point, Frankie "The Flame" Stallone took his hand away from his neck and swore. He was bleeding badly. He still didn't quite believe what had happened. He moved towards the edge and looked down. The boy had disappeared into the Mediterranean. It was all over very quickly. A few ripples showed where he had hit the water but then they closed in on themselves and disappeared. No bubbles rose to the surface.

He turned to Skunk, who was standing next to him with his phone. The other man didn't look happy. "Did you get that?" he asked.

"No!" Skunk shook his head. He had difficulty forming the words with his burnt lips. "You were inner way."

"Did you get anything?"

"I got th' bi' when he stab you wibber nail."

Stallone thought for a moment. The blood was

still trickling down his neck. He knew that the nail had only missed his carotid artery by a fraction. He wondered where the boy had found it. "Let's get out of here," he said.

Skunk was filming the surface of the water. Apart from the breaking waves, there was no movement. Alex had already been under for a minute. There was no way he was coming back up.

The two of them walked away and climbed into the van. Stallone sat in the driver's seat and a moment later they set off. This was their last day in the South of France. That afternoon, they had a flight to Heathrow, London.

The last phase of Operation Steel Claw was about to begin.

Alex would never forget the moment his feet hit the surface, the terrible impact and the rush of freezing water as he was dragged down, his body tilting to one side. His legs were slightly apart, the concrete slab far below him. His eyes were closed. He could feel the water rippling through his hair. He was still holding his breath, flailing with his arms as if he could somehow slow himself down. The sea was icy cold. He was surprised his heart hadn't already stopped.

And then he felt the weight hit the bottom and settle in the sand. He was left floating above it, his left foot slightly lower than his right. He was deep down. He could tell from the pressure in his ears.

The nail.

He was still holding it. He could use it to pick the lock. It was his only hope. Alex guessed that he had, at most, two minutes before he drowned. He reached down and found the chain, then used it to pull himself towards the padlock that had snapped shut next to his ankle. He still couldn't see. Somehow his fingers – almost numb – found the keyhole. It took him three tries before he was able to push the nail inside, forcing it into the lock. Finally, when he was sure it was in place, he rotated it.

Nothing happened.

He tried again and this time he fumbled it. Before he realized what had happened, he had let go of the nail and he knew he would have no chance of finding it in the darkness.

Alex's lungs were already feeling the strain. Desperately, he grabbed the chain and pulled with all his strength, trying to free his foot. He felt the chain biting into his flesh. It was too tight. His foot wouldn't move. How long had he been underwater? He knew he couldn't survive any longer. It was over. He opened his mouth to scream.

Something clamped against his lips.

A hand.

He felt a second hand resting on his shoulder and became aware of a body pressing against him. The shock of it almost made him choke. There was a man – or perhaps a woman – holding on to him, reassuring him. Alex opened his eyes. The first thing he saw was the ceiling of light, the surface about twenty metres above him. He twisted round and through the blur of the water he made out a scuba-diver, masked and wearing a black neoprene wetsuit with an oxygen tank on his back and a spare one clipped to his belt. The face behind the mask was indistinct. It was a man. That was all he could say. And the diver was signalling to him. *Relax. Stay still. Try not to panic.*

Alex had already been underwater for two minutes. He knew it was impossible to keep holding his breath. His whole system was in shock. The man reached down and Alex felt something being pressed against his lips. Bubbles rose up in front of his face. It was a spare respirator. Alex took hold of it and pressed it onto his mouth, pushing the purge button to expel any water. Then he took a breath. The air might be canned but he had never tasted anything more delicious.

He was going to live after all. It took him a minute to accept that, still hanging in the water, chained to the weight. His whole body was shaking. He had to force himself not to gulp the air. The man must have understood what he was going through. He didn't move but just hung on to him until he had recovered a little. Then he swum round and signalled again. *You have to wait here. A couple more minutes. It's going to be OK.* He had detached his spare oxygen tank and gave it to Alex to hold. Alex had the respirator clamped between his teeth. He nodded his head weakly. What else could he do?

The man swam away and for the next five minutes, Alex was on his own. That was worse than anything that had happened so far. Suppose the whole thing had been a trick? Suppose he had been given false hope simply to make his death even worse? Suppose the man couldn't find him again? Alex had no idea how much oxygen he had been given nor how long he was going to have to wait. He stared into the emptiness of the Mediterranean until it hurt his eyes. He had never felt more horribly alone.

At last the scuba-diver reappeared, carrying some sort of equipment. He checked the gauge on Alex's oxygen tank and made a circle with his index finger curving round to touch his thumb: the universal sign that everything was OK. He showed Alex the equipment he was carrying. It consisted of a complicated-looking cylinder, a long, silver pipe and a series of curving tubes. Again, using sign language, he warned Alex not to look. He turned away and swam down and a moment later the sea was lit up by an intense white light that burst out of the end of the pipe. Alex understood. The man had ignited some sort of oxo-acetylene torch, one designed to burn underwater.

Things happened very quickly after that. The man worked on the chain close to the concrete blocks, as far away from Alex's foot as possible.

Alex squinted down and saw the glare of the flame lost behind a cloud of bubbles. The man was kicking gently with his fins, keeping himself steady while he cut through the chain. At last it came free. Alex's immediate instinct was to swim for the surface but the man was well ahead of him. He felt a hand clamp down on his ankle. Of course. He risked decompression sickness – "the bends" – if he rose too quickly. He let the man work out the rate of ascent for both of them. Taking their time, locked in an embrace, they rose to the surface.

They broke through together. Alex saw Needle Point above him, empty now. He guessed that Frankie Stallone and the other man must have gone. He wondered if they were going to swim ashore, but before he could say anything, he heard the sound of an engine and a small dinghy came cruising towards them with another man at the stern. It was a grey Inflatable Raiding Craft, an IRC similar to the ones used by the Navy; sleek, fast and low in the water.

The man who had saved him had lifted his mask and Alex recognized him at once. A black face. Watchful eyes. In his late twenties. It was almost the last person in the world he had expected to see. "Wolf!" he exclaimed.

"That was cutting it a bit fine, Cub," Wolf said.

Wolf and Cub. They were names by which they had known each other when Alex had trained in the SAS. The man's real name was Ben Daniels.

Alex had learned that when the two of them had joined forces in northern Australia, taking on the gang known as Snakehead.

"What the hell are you doing here?" Alex demanded, spluttering water. "How did you find me?"

"Not now, Alex." Ben was still holding on to him. "We've got a mother ship about a mile away. We need to get you on board."

The two of them were treading water together. Alex was beginning to shiver. But still he had to know. "Did Mrs Jones send you?"

Ben smiled. "Of course she did. She told you to go back to America but she knew you wouldn't listen to her." He glanced ruefully at Alex as the IRC drew up. "I'm afraid she's not going to be at all pleased."

The IRC took them to an old fishing trawler that was anchored around the corner, a short way up the coast. It was eighteen metres in length, painted white and blue, beaten about by the years it had spent at sea. There was a main mast with a seemingly impossible tangle of rigging, a bulky wheelhouse with a funnel, half a dozen portholes and a deck strewn with nets and cables. Only the sophisticated radio masts – there were three of them – and the single satellite dish hinted that it might be more than it seemed. Alex saw its name: *Liverpool Lady*. He had to smile. MI6 Special

Operations had offices in Liverpool Street, London and Mrs Jones was very much their lady.

Ben Daniels and the other man barely spoke during the brief journey and Alex was grateful to them. His teeth were chattering – partly because of the shock of what he had been through, partly because he was cold. A third man was waiting for them and took Alex below. The galley was filled with sophisticated equipment: computers, radar and solar monitoring systems, satellite communications and the rest of it. *Liverpool Lady* was a spy ship – nothing more, nothing less. He wondered what it had been doing in the South of France.

He was shown into a cabin where he was able to take a hot shower. A pair of trousers and a jersey had been left out for him. They were both too big but Alex didn't complain. He still had a ring of steel and a padlock attached to his ankle but he struggled into the clothes. After he had got dressed there was a knock at the door and one of the men came in. He was young, fair-haired, very tanned. "I'm Pete," he said. "Nice to meet you, Alex. Can I get rid of that for you?" He was holding a picklock – a proper one rather than a loose nail – and set to work at once.

Ten minutes later, Alex was sitting on one side of a table in the galley with a cup of hot chocolate. Ben Daniels was opposite him. He had changed out of scuba gear and wore a polo shirt and shorts. All the men on the boat were informally dressed. Ben was smiling at him but Alex could see how worried he had been. It had all been perilously close. Another few seconds and he wouldn't have made it.

"How are you, Ben?" Alex asked. "You got shot. I heard you were in hospital."

"That's right." Ben tapped his own stomach gently. "I've still got the souvenirs of my last outing with you. Fortunately, Winston Yu was a rotten shot."

"Are you still with the SAS?"

"No. I've moved over to Special Operations now." He paused and once again the concern was there in his eyes. "I'm sure you've got a thousand questions, Alex, and you need to rest. So I might as well spit it all out and if there's anything else you want to know, you can ask me then. OK?"

"Fine."

Alex sipped his hot chocolate. It was thick and sweet. He couldn't think of anything he would rather be drinking.

"All right. Mrs Jones saw you in Saint-Tropez yesterday. As I understand it, she gave you a ticket back to San Francisco. Of course you didn't use it. She guessed you wouldn't – but she checked out the plane just to be sure. She'd already told me to come down here. We keep a few boats in the Med just like this one. You never know when they're going to be needed.

"I've been keeping an eye on you as best I can.

We know you were on *Quicksilver*. And I was able to track you to the hospital..."

"Have you bugged me?" Alex asked.

"There was no need." Ben grinned. "We simply hacked into your mobile and used it against you. I'm sure you know, Alex, the software's not that complicated. We can turn anyone's phone into a tracking device. It'll tell us exactly where they are. We can activate the camera and watch you. We can listen to everything you say, even across the room."

Alex remembered Mrs Jones asking him if he had his mobile phone. He had thought it odd at the time. *Make sure it's on and keep it with you*. That was what she had said. Now he understood what had been on her mind.

"We were always just a few steps behind you," Ben went on. "We tracked you down to the Villa Siciliana and we were able to hear everything that those two creeps said when they captured you. It was lucky they told you what they were planning. As soon as we heard Needle Point get a mention, we shot round in *Liverpool Lady*. I slipped into my scuba gear and I was waiting for you when they threw you in."

"I'm very grateful," Alex said, but at the same time he wondered why they had waited so long. Why hadn't they simply arrested Frankie Stallone and the man with the phone while they were on land?

Ben knew what he was thinking. "I decided it

was better, all in all, if they thought you were dead," he said. "And it was safer for you. If we'd started a gunfight at the villa or up at Needle Point, you might have been killed."

"What about the Grimaldi brothers?"

"They've already gone." Ben frowned. "We tipped off the French police but I'm afraid they were completely incompetent. It took them ages to get round to the villa and by the time they arrived, the birds had flown. It's very annoying. We still don't know exactly what they're up to ... this operation of theirs. But we're fairly certain it's taking place on our own turf, in England. That's why Mrs Jones wants you back for a debrief – immediately."

"You said she wasn't pleased."

"Well, she's glad you're still alive. But she had rather hoped you'd stay out of all this and go back to America. Speaking personally, I'm delighted we're together again. That was quite an adventure, wasn't it, that oil rig out in the Timor Sea. With a bit of luck, Mrs Jones will change her mind and let us go after Giovanni and Eduardo together. Another bit of Scorpia bites the dust!"

"There's one thing I have to ask," Alex said. "Have you heard anything about Jack Starbright?"

Ben Daniels shook his head, the smile fading from his face. "Didn't the brothers tell you anything?"

"No. They didn't even say if she's dead or alive."

"If they've got her, we'll find her, Alex. They

think you're dead. They have no idea we're on their tail. We could only hear part of the conversation at the Villa Siciliana. You're going to have to remember the rest of it."

There was the sound of feet coming down the steps from the main deck and the man called Pete appeared, leaning into the galley. "Where to, sir?" he asked, addressing Daniels.

"Back to Nice Airport," Daniels replied. He rested a hand on Alex's shoulder. "We're heading home."

BACK HOME

"It's a beautiful house. I'm sure you'll be very happy here."

The estate agent spoke over her shoulder as she came down the stairs. This was the third family she'd shown round the house in Chelsea but this time she'd known at once that they were going to buy it. Mr and Mrs Bogdanov were from Moscow. They were moving to London for business reasons, they'd said, although they had been careful not to tell her what that business was. They had hardly talked at all. Mr Bogdanov was not a friendly man. In fact he seemed to go out of his way to be actively unfriendly, grim and unsmiling, looking around the house as if it were some kind of slum. His wife was a great deal younger than him, far too thin and wearing too much make-up. She was clearly nervous of her husband, gabbling in a high-pitched voice to cover his silences.

But they were cash buyers. They had made that clear from the start. Mr Bogdanov hadn't been in the house five minutes before he had nodded and muttered the single word, "Da!" The Russian for yes.

It was excellent news. The property market in London was very quiet at the moment and the estate agent had monthly targets she was supposed to meet. This house had come up for sale quite suddenly when the owner had moved to America, following a death in the family. She had heard some very strange stories about him. Apparently, he had worked for some secret department of the government and everything had to be very hush-hush. Nobody was allowed to mention his name, certainly not to prospective buyers. And there were even rumours that a specialist team from Scotland Yard had gone in to disconnect the telephone system and remove certain security devices from inside the house ... things that weren't available to the general public.

Of course, the estate agent hadn't mentioned anything about this to her clients. The house was in a quiet street, just a short walk from the famous King's Road. It was also close to Chelsea Football Club, if you happened to be a supporter. There were three spacious bedrooms and two bathrooms. The ground floor had an open-plan kitchen and living room with double doors opening onto a pretty garden. Another staircase led down to a basement, which had been converted into a work area. Mrs Bogdanov, who worked as a designer, had taken dozens of photographs on her mobile phone. She had explained that she was going to strip the place bare. She liked very bright colours and chandeliers. This room was going to be turned into a home cinema with a full-sized snooker table going over there. The bar would go in that corner. A Jacuzzi on the roof. "Da!" Mr Bogdanov had agreed, although he hadn't looked pleased. But then, of course, he was paying for it all.

"How quick we get our builders in?" Mrs Bogdanov asked. She had a heavy Russian accent. Her English was not good.

"Well, it will have to be a few weeks."

"But we pay cash!"

"Even so..."

She stopped. They had reached the entrance hall and a boy was standing there, looking at them with tired, watchful eyes. His clothes looked crumpled, as if he had slept in them, and there was a backpack on the floor beside his feet. How had he got in? The estate agent was certain she had locked the front door before she had started the tour of the house. "Excuse me..." she began.

"Who are you?" the boy asked.

"I'm Corinne Turner from Fleming Estates." The boy said nothing so she went on. "We're selling the house."

"I'm afraid it's not for sale."

"I'm sorry?" The estate agent was confused. "It's been on the market now for quite some time..."

"You leave!" Mr Bogdanov pushed her out of the

way. He jabbed a stubby finger in the direction of the intruder. "This my house. We agree sale."

"It's *my* house," the boy replied and there was something dangerous in his voice. "And I've decided not to sell it. Do you mind leaving now?" He glanced apologetically at the estate agent. "I'll call your office this afternoon. I'm sorry to have wasted your time."

"Are you Alex?" the estate agent asked. She had seen the name on the deeds.

"That's right."

"We'll leave at once."

The strange thing was that, despite what she had been thinking a moment ago, Corinne Turner was quite glad that the boy had returned. She had taken an immediate liking to him. And even though she had just lost the sale, it also seemed to her that he belonged here in a way that Mr and Mrs Bogdanov didn't – and never would. With a smile, she went over to the front door and opened it. The two Russians scowled but said nothing. A moment later, all three of them had gone.

Alex stood where he was. He was holding the spare key that he had taken out of its hiding place: a fake brick, which rotated if you pressed it in the right place. It felt so strange to be back in a house he had thought he would never see again. He was just glad that it had remained untouched. The estate agents had thought it would sell more easily if it looked as if someone was still living there so all the furniture was still in place; the pots and pans stacked up in the kitchen, the beds made. Even his clothes would still be hanging in the wardrobe. And yet he felt that the house hadn't quite welcomed him back. It was unnaturally quiet, as if it was annoyed that it had been abandoned. Alex realized that it would take both of them a while to get used to each other again.

He went upstairs and into his old room. There were just a few thing missing: a couple of photographs and a football signed by the Chelsea squad, which he had taken with him to America. Maybe Edward Pleasure would send them back one day ... if he stayed in London. Right now his entire future looked uncertain. Part of it depended on what MI6 had in mind. But at the end of the day, he still didn't know if Jack Starbright was alive or not – and that was what mattered to him most.

He threw off his clothes, padded into the bathroom and took a long shower. The hot water was still on automatic timer and it felt good, standing there with the water hammering down on him, washing away some of the memories of the last few days. He got out, dried, then opened a drawer to reveal all his T-shirts neatly ironed and folded. Jack would have done that for him before she left for Egypt.

He got dressed and then, on an impulse, went into Jack's room, which was at the far end of the corridor, overlooking the garden. Usually, he never came in here. It was her space and the two of them had an unwritten rule that they would respect each other's privacy. The room was strangely unfamiliar to him. Jack had a double bed with a brightly-coloured duvet and a one-eyed teddy bear sprawling limply on the pillow. Everything was very neat and tidy. There were a lot of books in the room. She was always reading something. Every surface was covered with photographs. Alex looked at all the pictures in a variety of frames. There was an elderly couple, her parents, and next to them a woman with three children. This was her sister. The two of them looked similar.

Alex hadn't spoken to any of Jack's family after he had lost her in Siwa. Edward Pleasure had done all that for him. But looking at the photographs, he felt ashamed. He should have got in touch.

Many of the photographs were of him, starting at the age of seven and continuing all the way to just a few months ago. Here he was with Ian Rider, on a skiing holiday at Gunpoint, Colorado. He remembered it well. And here he was again, standing with Jack outside the Old Vic theatre in London. They'd gone to see a Christmas show. Suddenly he felt uncomfortable being in her room. He went out, closing the door behind him.

It had been a short journey from the South of France but he wouldn't have been able to travel at all without the help of MI6, as he had lost his passport along with everything else. The clothes he was wearing and the new backpack he was carrying had been bought for him in Nice. Ben Daniels had flown with him – a commercial flight – but they had parted company at Heathrow Airport where two cars had been waiting to take them their separate ways. Alex had felt a mix of emotions, driving into west London along the M4, past the huge advertising hoardings and the new buildings around Hammersmith. He was back home. Part of him was excited by that. But despite everything that had happened, he still hadn't found Jack.

The car was waiting outside. He had been given just thirty minutes to get ready before he was driven to a crisis meeting at MI6. Mrs Jones would be there. She was insisting on a full debrief. Alex was hungry but he knew there would be no food in the house. There was no point hanging around. He glanced at himself in the mirror, then let himself out again. He wondered if he could persuade the driver to stop at a McDonald's on the way.

They met, not in Mrs Jones's office but in a conference room on the twelfth floor. It was a very ordinary room – but then every room in the building was designed to look ordinary. It suited the secret work that was being done. There were no pictures on the walls, only a seventy-inch television screen built into the wall. A large window looked out on Liverpool Street with hundreds of people pouring in and out of the station far below. Alex knew that the glass would have been treated so that no camera or listening device could penetrate. It was probably bulletproof too.

He was sitting at the end of a long, polished table. His voice was hoarse from talking so much. He had already told Ben Daniels everything he knew when they were together on *Liverpool Lady*, but Mrs Jones had insisted on hearing it a second time and then a third, as if she might snatch some new clue from what he was saying. She was sitting opposite him at the other end of the table, a notepad in front of her and a pen in her hand. Daniels was next to her. John Crawley was on the other side. Alex knew the "Head of Personnel" quite well. That was how he had described himself when he had first come to Alex's home after Ian Rider had died. "Very good to see you, Alex," he had muttered when he had entered the conference room. "How was France?" The way he asked, Alex could have just come back from a short holiday.

There were two other men he hadn't met before, both of them in uniform. One had been introduced as Chief Marshal Sir Norman Clarke. He had as many titles as he had medals across his chest. He was gruff and clearly uncomfortable addressing a fifteen-year-old. The other man's name was Chichester. He was from naval intelligence and seemed to be the more pleasant of the two.

"Let me sum up, then," Mrs Jones was saying,

finally giving Alex a chance to rest his voice. "We now know that the Super Stallion helicopter was stolen by Dragana Novak, acting on the instructions of the two brothers, Giovanni and Eduardo Grimaldi. She also murdered the American pilots. You've received my security briefing on Ms Novak. She was formerly a pilot with the Serbian Air Force but was court-martialled following a bar-room brawl. She is now deceased. The Grimaldi brothers are well known to us through their association with Scorpia. It's a great shame that we were unable to pick them up in the South of France."

"How did that happen?" Sir Norman demanded. From the tone of his voice, it could have been Mrs Jones who was to blame.

"We tipped off the French police as soon as we had the information," Ben Daniels said. "But they were too slow. By the time they got to the Villa Siciliana, the brothers had gone."

"Thanks to Alex, we now know that they are planning an operation that they call Steel Claw," Mrs Jones continued. "Presumably, this involves the helicopter but we have no way of knowing in what way. However, it would seem likely that – as I first suggested – terrorism is not their goal." She was addressing the Air Marshal in particular. "They need money, pure and simple. They're planning some sort of theft. Something heavy. They need the helicopter to take it away."

"A lot of people can still get killed during a

theft, Mrs Jones. These people have already dem-
onstrated that they are utterly ruthless."

"Of course, Sir Norman. We also know that this
event, Steel Claw, is going to take place some time
tomorrow afternoon, possibly at half past three.
The question is – what are we going to do?"

Alex had been listening to all this with a sense
of disbelief. It seemed incredible to him that a
single email received just days ago had catapulted
him back into another adventure with MI6. And
what was Jack doing mixed up in it all? Nobody
in the room had mentioned her yet but surely
she must have some part to play. The Grimaldis
wouldn't have taken her otherwise.

Chichester was the next to speak. "It seems
to me that we should be focusing on this man,
Vosper."

"Yes. We have some intel on him," Crawley said.
He had a laptop in front of him and punched a few
keys. It had a wireless connection to the screen on
the wall. A face flashed up. "Recognize him?"

Alex looked across to a photograph of a grey-
haired man with thin lips, wearing spectacles. He
felt a stirring of excitement. "That's him!" he said.
"He was at the villa…"

"Derek Vosper," Crawley continued. "It wasn't
that difficult to pin him down. We checked every
flight into Nice Airport over the last three days. As
a matter of fact, there was only one person called
Vosper – it's quite an unusual name – and we could

see at once that he fitted the description Alex gave us."

"Who is he?" Sir Norman demanded.

"Derek Vosper is forty-six years old and lives in Oxford—" Crawley began.

"Dragana had a map showing Oxford in her cabin," Alex interrupted. He had already told them what he had found, but he thought it was worth reminding them.

"He's married. He has no children. His wife is Jane Vosper. She's a coach driver and works for a private school. As a matter of fact, she was checked out by the police a few years ago. It was a routine security clearance. She has no criminal record. Neither of them do."

"What about the husband?" Mrs Jones asked.

"Well, that's where it gets quite interesting." Crawley clicked with his mouse, changing the image on the screen. This time it showed a classical building with tall, white columns. "Derek Vosper is an assistant curator at the Ashmolean Museum in Oxford. He helps organize exhibitions. And this is what they've got on at the moment."

Another click and the image changed to a golden statue of a completely naked man, crouching with his legs crossed. It was the front cover of a brochure and there was a caption in bright red letters: SOUTH AMERICAN GOLD.

"I read about this..." Ben Daniels muttered.

"That's right. It's been in all the newspapers.

Inca, Aztec and Mayan gold. They say there's never been an exhibition like it – so many treasures in one place. I understand that the collection is insured for forty million pounds."

"That's it, then!" Sir Norman brought his hand crashing down onto the table. "That's what they're planning to steal!"

Mrs Jones turned to Alex. "When you were in the Villa Siciliana, Vosper said something about solid gold."

Alex thought back, trying to remember the exact words he'd heard. "That's right," he said. "But it wasn't quite like that. He said he'd seen the names on the list and that they were solid gold."

"He must have been talking about the statues on show!" Crawley said.

"Did he definitely use those words?" Mrs Jones wanted to be sure.

"Yes. Definitely." But even as he spoke, Alex knew there was something wrong. Had Eduardo and Giovanni really stolen a multi-million pound helicopter to attack a museum in Oxford? Surely it couldn't be as simple as that.

"There's something else!" Crawley was pleased with himself. "Alex said he heard the name Henry mentioned. 'They're seeing Henry at half past three in the afternoon.' Is that right, Alex?"

Alex nodded.

Crawley flashed another image onto the screen; this time a middle-aged, severe-looking woman standing outside the House of Commons. Alex thought he recognized her.

"This is Susan Hendrix, the Minister for Culture," Crawley explained. "As it happens, she's visiting the museum tomorrow afternoon. Do you see? You were listening to the conversation from the other side of a door and you didn't get it quite right. It wasn't Henry you heard. It was Hendrix."

"No." Alex shook his head. "It was definitely Henry, Mr Crawley. I heard it distinctly."

"Henry who?"

"They didn't say. But it wasn't Hendrix. I'm sure of it." Alex stopped. Nobody in the room looked convinced. They had already made up their minds.

"The minister must cancel her visit," Chichester said. "We can't risk putting her in any danger."

"There is no danger!" Sir Norman cut in. "We now know what Operation Steel Claw means and we can prevent it from going ahead. All we have to do is arrest this Derek Vosper character. He'll lead us to his employers and we can get the helicopter back too." He got to his feet. As far as he was concerned, the meeting was over. "Very good work, Mrs Jones." He nodded at Alex. "And congratulations to you, young man. You should have listened more carefully but otherwise you've done very well too."

He left the room. The man called Chichester muttered a few words of thanks and followed him. Alex was left alone with the three people he knew.

"Vosper will be at the museum now," Crawley said. "Do you want me to pick him up?"

"I don't think so," Mrs Jones said. "Despite what Sir Norman said, I'm not sure it's quite such a good idea." She paused, collecting her thoughts. "We want the helicopter but, more than that, we want the Grimaldi brothers," she went on. "If we arrest Vosper, they'll know we're onto them. They'll simply disappear. But we can take advantage of this situation. We can use the museum as a trap!"

It was the first time that Alex had seen Mrs Jones in action, working as the new head of Special Operations. It seemed to him that the more she spoke, the more she convinced herself she was right. "I want the museum surrounded," she said. "Armed response officers! Our first priority must be to keep the public safe. Daniels – you'll follow Vosper. I want you to keep him in your sight from the moment he wakes up until the moment he goes to bed. You can select a team for backup. Anyone you like."

"Anyone?"

"Yes."

"In that case, I'd quite like Alex to come along."

"Why?" Mrs Jones looked at him with a spark of annoyance in her eyes.

"Because without Alex, we'd never have known that Derek Vosper existed. And it's still possible we're making a mistake." He sighed. "Forgive me, ma'am. I know it seems to make sense. The gold. Hendrix. But if you ask me, it all feels a bit small-time for a Scorpia operation."

"The Grimaldis aren't with Scorpia any more."

"I know. But forty million pounds? They could have made thirty million for just selling the Super Stallion. It must have cost twice that. And I bet you they spent quite a few million setting this whole thing up. They've murdered at least three people. You really would have thought they'd be a bit more ambitious."

"And Alex?"

"He may see something or hear something. He may remember something. I don't know. I'd just like to have him with me."

Mrs Jones didn't speak. Next to her, John Crawley was looking uncomfortable. Finally she glanced at Alex. "When we met in Saint-Tropez, I told you to go back to America," she said. "I even paid for your flight. You disobeyed me and as a result you were very nearly killed. If you're going to work for me, you're going to have to learn to obey orders."

"You don't want me to work for you," Alex said.

"I know. That's what I said. I still remember what happened to Ian Rider. I don't want to be the one sitting here being told that the same thing has happened to you." She fell silent for a moment. "Do you want to do this, Alex?"

"I want to find Jack," Alex said simply.

"All right." She nodded at Daniels. "Take him with you. But if anything happens to him, I promise you, you're fired!"

UNDER SURVEILLANCE

The alarm clock went off at exactly seven o'clock.

Derek Vosper woke up next to his wife in the small, end-of-terrace house that they occupied in Headington, a village about three miles outside Oxford. He swung himself out of bed and sat there for a moment in his striped pyjamas. He reached for his glasses, put them on, then headed into the bathroom. Meanwhile, Jane Vosper went downstairs to make the breakfast. She was overweight with dark brown hair that hung limply after a night's sleep and that wouldn't look any better when she'd brushed it. Her face was blank. She put the kettle on, sliced some bread for toast and took some eggs out of the fridge.

Neither of them was aware that they were being watched, that no fewer than twenty-eight cameras had been concealed around their home, picking up their every movement. A team from MI6 Special Operations had arrived just hours after the meeting at Liverpool Street had ended. Both the Vospers were at work and if there had been any neighbours around, they would have paid no attention to the Waitrose van which had pulled up outside the front door, nor to the three men who seemed to be making a perfectly ordinary delivery, carrying supermarket bags through the front door.

When they left, one hour later, there were cameras in the skirting board and in holes that had been specially drilled into the brickwork. More cameras had been concealed behind mirrors, on the edge of a lampshade and behind the screen of the TV. Each one had a lens which measured just 3.7 millimetres but which gave an 86-degree field of vision. This meant that there wasn't a single square millimetre of the house that wasn't in view. If the Vospers had chosen to go out into the garden, they might have noticed a bee hovering over the lawn. It was actually a miniature camera drone, operating under remote control and it was watching them through the windows.

There were also bugging devices scattered throughout the house. These were so sensitive that they had picked up the sound of Derek Vosper unscrewing his toothpaste tube. An unmarked white van was parked a short way down the road. Two men were sitting in the back, both wearing headphones, gazing at a bank of television monitors. They had been in position for three hours, replacing the team that had stayed there throughout the night.

"How do you want your eggs, dear?"

"I don't think I fancy an egg today."

"How about a yoghurt?"

"Thanks..."

Every word that the Vospers spoke was recorded, transcribed and sent over a secure line to the seventh floor – the Communications division – of MI6. But as they got dressed, made the bed and then sat at the kitchen table for breakfast, the husband and wife said nothing of any interest. There was no mention of the Grimaldis, nothing about Steel Claw. Perhaps they had been warned or perhaps they were just too nervous to talk about the day ahead. It was easier to pretend that they were an ordinary couple, setting off to their different jobs.

"Well, I'd best be on my way then."

"Have you got your tea?"

"Yes. It's here."

They kissed each other goodbye and seventy-one seconds later, Jane came out of the front door carrying a handbag in one hand and a large, silver Thermos in the other. She was wearing a light raincoat over an olive-green jersey and dress. The bee briefly hovered over her as she walked down the path and got into the second-hand Mazda which was parked in the main road. It filmed her as she drove away. Derek Vosper was left behind. He didn't seem to be in any hurry to leave.

In fact it was twenty past nine when he finally emerged, wearing a cheap suit and carrying a briefcase. As he walked the short distance to his own car, he was overtaken by an ice cream van and although he was completely unaware of it, he was briefly bathed in X-rays which not only showed him naked but revealed the contents of his pockets and briefcase. He had a telephone, an iPad, a book, some papers and pens, a packet of chewing gum. There was absolutely nothing to suggest that he might be involved in the theft of forty million pounds' worth of gold. Derek Vosper had a slightly better car than his wife: a VW Golf. He opened the doors with a remote control and got in.

Thirty metres away, Alex Rider was sitting in the front seat of a Vauxhall Astra Sports Tourer, the same car that is used by many of the emergency services throughout the UK. This one, however, was anonymous, with no identification number or siren. It was oyster grey with a sunroof. Ben Daniels was next to him, behind the wheel. They had been outside the house since half past six.

Alex had watched Derek Vosper having his breakfast. The car had a satnav screen mounted in the front dashboard but, of course, it was much more than that. Ben Daniels had touched a switch on the car music system, which had silently pivoted around to reveal a state-of-the-art control panel with a dozen different dials and buttons. The Vauxhall had a sophisticated communications system that allowed him to tune in to the data flow coming from the house, channelling the same images as MI6. If the Vospers sent or received a text or an email, he would be able to read the contents. If they dialled a number on their mobile phone, he would have the name, the address and the life history of the person they were calling before they had even been connected. Alex wondered what other secrets were concealed within the car.

Ben started the engine. "It looks like we're on the way," he said.

"About time." Alex had been grateful when Ben had asked for him to join the team but he was tired after his early start and even a bit bored. Watching a very ordinary couple having their breakfast wasn't going to help him find Jack. And he was still unsure about the whole plan. Without knowing what it was, he was certain that something was wrong and he was worried that it was his fault. What was it that he had missed?

Derek Vosper's VW overtook them and they set off after it, keeping a good distance behind.

"He's heading into Oxford," Ben muttered.

"To the museum?"

"I suppose so."

"Here's something I don't understand," Alex said as they continued forward at a steady thirty miles an hour. "There's forty million pounds' worth of gold statues inside the building. You think he's going to steal it, using the helicopter. But he's got to get it all outside first. How's that going to work?"

"You said he wasn't working alone."

It was true. When Alex was at the Villa Siciliana, he had heard Vosper talking about money. "We should have charged more..." It was definitely "we". Did he have other people working with him inside the museum? "Where's the helicopter going to land?" he asked. "It's the middle of Oxford."

Ben Daniels shrugged. "On the roof?"

They had come in on the London Road. Now they crossed the River Cherwell with the great tower of Magdalen College over to the right. The road was very wide here with trees on either side. Derek Vosper was three cars ahead of them, heading towards a junction with traffic lights. He went through on green but before Ben could reach them, the lights suddenly changed to red. Alex felt a twitch of annoyance. They hadn't even entered the town and already they might have lost their target. Sitting next to him, though, Ben didn't seem concerned. He reached out and flicked another switch in the control panel. At once, like a magic trick, the lights changed back to green. The rest of the traffic was confused. Cars that had started moving forward jerked to a halt. Other drivers just sat there, unable to work out what had happened. Somebody hooted. Ben swerved round them and steered his way through a gap. At the end of the manoeuvre he was just one car behind Vosper.

"I sent out an electromagnetic pulse," he said, before Alex could ask what had happened. "It interfered with the control box inside the traffic light. Very useful for getting round cities."

Typical Smithers! Alex was sorry that the gadget master had left MI6. He would have liked to have seen him again.

They were heading down the High Street with more old and attractive buildings on either side. They passed a church with a homeless person – a very large black woman – sitting on a bench, surrounded by shopping bags. Neither of them saw the woman lean forward and speak into a microphone concealed in her sleeve.

"Target and pursuit vehicle have just gone past, heading for next junction. Vehicle 7K in close pursuit."

They were forced into a one-way system and followed the VW past more colleges, parks and very neat, pastel-coloured houses. A few students went by on bicycles and Alex wondered what it must be like to study here, in this famous town. His education had been interrupted so frequently that he sometimes wondered if he would even get his A-levels, let alone a place at university. He made a mental decision. When this was all over, when he had found Jack, he would get himself a tutor and work day and night to catch up. Maybe one day it would be him on one of these bicycles, preparing himself for a real life.

"Target has turned into Walton Street, heading south."

The speaker was a street cleaner in a yellow fluorescent jacket, standing behind a plastic bin and speaking into the microphone concealed in his broom. Ben and Alex passed him a few moments later, then turned left, following Vosper round a corner and past a theatre – the Oxford Playhouse. Alex saw him pull in ahead of them and instinctively looked for somewhere to park. The road was crowded. There seemed to be nowhere for them to stop and wait, apart from a narrow gap between a parked car and a builder's skip. Ben slowed down and stopped so that the space was right beside him. It was barely five centimetres longer than the car, making it impossible to fit in. Alex saw him flip up the top of the gear handle. There was a tiny joystick inside. Ben glanced out of the window, then used his thumb to slide the joystick to the right. To Alex's astonishment, the car, instead of moving forwards or backwards, suddenly slid sideways, neatly fitting into the gap.

"Omnidirectional wheels," Ben explained. "Smithers was very pleased with them. They're actually quite similar to what you'd find on a supermarket trolley. Very useful, occasionally."

Alex looked out of the window. The Ashmolean Museum was just across the road, a very handsome, classical building built in the Greek style, with two wings and a massive portico at the front that could have been the entrance to a temple. It reminded Alex of the British Museum in London, except that it was smaller and somehow more welcoming. A long balustrade separated it from the street with steps leading into a courtyard. Two banners fluttered in the breeze. Each one showed a solid gold figure with the legend: SOUTH AMERICAN GOLD. There were no visitors yet. The museum opened at ten.

"What do we do now?" Alex asked.

"We wait."

Ben leaned forward and dragged his finger across the satnav screen. It was touch-sensitive. The map of Oxford swiped across to be replaced by a moving film: the unmistakable shape of the assistant curator, walking down a corridor inside. Alex realized that MI6 technicians had been in the museum too. The camera was hidden somewhere above him, watching from behind. A girl came out of a doorway.

"Oh – Mr Vosper! I didn't know you were in today."

"Just come to catch up with some research."

"Right."

The image changed as Vosper went into his office and sat down at his desk. A second camera had taken over. Alex watched as he opened a laptop, booted it up and, a few minutes later, began to read a document on the screen.

"Let's have a look," Ben muttered.

Alex wasn't at all surprised that MI6 had access to Vosper's computer. After all, they'd found it easy enough to hack into his own mobile phone – as he'd discovered in Saint-Tropez. Briefly, he wondered about the sort of society he was living in, where everyone – innocent or guilty – could be watched. Ben tapped the screen a couple of times and the first page of a report appeared. It was headed: CELTIC ARTEFACTS: COLLECTION & INTERPRETATION. This was what Vosper was reading...

...and continued to read for the next hour and a half. The picture on the screen was now completely silent. There were just words, thousands of them, about Celtic jewellery and coins.

Meanwhile, the museum was now open and the day's visitors had begun to arrive. The exhibition had been on for a while so it wasn't quite as busy as it had been earlier in the summer. Even so, by eleven o'clock, two hundred people had bought tickets, unaware that they had all been photographed and scanned by facial recognition software and that MI6 knew everything about them before they had passed through the main entrance. Nor could they have known that the museum's usual security staff had all been sent home for the day. They had been replaced by armed field agents. All bags were being thoroughly examined. More agents – in radio contact with one another – had joined the queue, pretending to be visitors and listening in on every word that was said. Mrs Jones had thrown a huge security net around the museum. Every street leading to and from the building was guarded by dozens more men and women. If the order was given, the museum – indeed, the entire area – could be cordoned off and isolated at a moment's notice.

Alex stared at the screen as another page of type appeared. Vosper had reached a section entitled: IRON AGE BURIAL SITES. He was reading in silence. Nobody had come into his office. The telephone hadn't rung. He had told his assistant that he had come to catch up with some research and that seemed to be exactly what he was doing. Alex had been in the car for several hours now. He was cramped and frustrated. Worse still, he was increasingly certain that this was a mistake. They'd all overlooked something. What was it?

He let his mind drift back to the Villa Siciliana and played over the conversation – although he had already done it many times before. He saw himself crouching at the door, watching Derek Vosper with the two brothers.

I've seen the names on the list.

It's certainly going to be a dramatic afternoon.

I'm thinking about my other half...

They're seeing Henry at half past three.

It was definitely Henry – not Hendrix. But Henry who? Alex had persuaded Ben to search the list of museum staff. There were three men called Henry but two of them worked in maintenance and one, a cloakroom attendant, was eighty-five. The name

Henry didn't seem to have any connection with South America or the gold. And there was something else that puzzled him. Who exactly were "they", the people who were seeing Henry? Why was the time significant?

He'd gone over what he'd heard with both Ben Daniels and Mrs Jones. Alex had a good memory and all the work he had done for MI6 had helped to train him: he didn't miss details. But this time there *was* something. Could it be something he'd seen on the boat? He remembered the map that he had found in Dragana Novak's cabin. It hadn't shown the Ashmolean Museum. The scale had been too big. In fact, it had shown Oxford and two other towns.

No. Alex tried to remember what John Crawley had said during the debrief. For some reason, he was sure that he'd said something that was a clue. He'd meant to ask Crawley about it at the time but everyone had moved on so quickly that he hadn't had opportunity. And now he had forgotten! The one piece of information that would make everything else make sense.

"Here we go!" Ben muttered. "He's moving again."

Alex was miles away. He glanced at the screen to see that, at last, Derek Vosper had closed the document and got to his feet. He had been picked up by the hidden cameras, leaving his office.

"Where do you think he's going?" Alex asked.

Ben looked at his watch. "It's after one o'clock,"

he said. "He's probably going for lunch."

Two minutes later, Vosper appeared in real life, coming out of the museum. Ben started the engine. "Once more unto the breach..." he muttered.

"What did you say?" Alex asked.

"Once more..."

"...unto the breach. Yes. It means let's get moving! It's from a play!"

And suddenly, Alex knew. The play was *Henry V* by William Shakespeare. He had studied it at school – when he was at school. It was Henry talking just before the Battle of Agincourt.

Once more unto the breach, dear friends, once more;

Or close the wall up with our English dead.

The pieces had been in front of him all the time. It was only now, with no particular reason, that they had all come together to make sense. The key was the map. Oxford. Cheltenham.

And Stratford-upon-Avon.

Alex turned to Ben. "Quickly," he said. "I want to know what's on at the theatre."

"Alex, I don't think we have time..."

"Today. There's a theatre in Stratford. The Royal Shakespeare Theatre." Alex remembered going there once. It had been a lifetime ago.

Ben could hear the seriousness in Alex's voice. Ahead of him, Vosper was coming down the main steps, on his way to his car. He stabbed at the dashboard screen, searching out the information.

"Henry V," he said. "It starts at half past three."

It was what Alex had been expecting. It made complete sense. "That's the Henry they're going to see! Not Hendrix. I was right about what I heard. But it's not a person. It's a play! And the map I saw in Dragana's cabin ... it didn't just show Oxford. It showed Stratford-upon-Avon. That's where they're heading."

"That's where who are going? What are you talking about?"

"I don't know..."

In front of them, Derek Vosper had reached his car and was just getting in. They watched him start the engine.

"We've got to get after him," Ben said. He reached for the little joystick, to guide them out of the space.

"No." Alex stopped him. "That's the mistake we've been making. Vosper was there at the villa in France but this has got nothing to do with him. It's his wife!"

"Jane Vosper?"

"Yes!" Alex knew he was right. "I actually heard him talking about her. He said he had to think about his other half – and I thought he meant the other half of the money he was owed. But he was talking about his wife!"

"But why? She's just a coach driver." Ben remembered what Crawley had said about her. "She works for a school."

"Yes," Alex agreed. "But he also said that she'd had a security check done by the police. Everyone in the room just accepted that because it didn't show anything – she had no criminal record. But that was what I was meaning to ask! Why did they need to check on her in the first place? It must be because she works somewhere important, with lots of security. Maybe that's the real target. Something's going to happen between now and half past three and she's involved!"

Ben hesitated, but only for a moment. He jabbed at the control panel and spoke urgently into a microphone somewhere in the dashboard. "This is Daniels – calling from Vehicle 7K. I need immediate intel on Jane Vosper. Repeat, Jane Vosper. We need to locate her at once!"

A few metres further down the road, Derek Vosper was about to pull out when he heard a squeal of tyres and looked in the mirror just in time to see a silver Vauxhall Astra, which had appeared from nowhere and which was overtaking him at high speed. He jammed his foot on the brake and stopped. It seemed to him that he had only avoided a collision by a matter of inches ... and that was something he wouldn't have wanted today of all days. He sat there for a moment watching the car as it tore into the distance. A traffic light which had been red instantly flicked back to green as it approached. And then it was gone.

STEEL CLAW

One hour earlier, about forty miles east of Oxford, a school bus was preparing to leave. It was no ordinary school bus, but then Linton Hall was definitely no ordinary school.

To begin with, it was by far the most expensive prep school in the country. Its boarding fees began at £12,550 a term ... but these could easily rise up to as much as £15,000 once parents had paid for all the extras, which might include piano lessons, judo, horse riding, mountaineering, hot-air ballooning, real tennis, classical ballet and golf. It was, of course, extremely exclusive. There were just three hundred boys and girls aged 8–13 and every one of them had had to pass three days of intensive interviews and exams before they were accepted. Linton Hall's record spoke for itself. Eighty-five per cent of the students went on to one of the country's top private secondary schools, with Eton, Westminster and Benenden high on the list. They would all have studied Latin and ancient

Greek and would have a grasp of at least three modern languages, including Chinese. They would play a musical instrument. They would be able to recite hundreds of lines of poetry off by heart.

The main body of the school was an Elizabethan manor house, a gorgeous building four storeys high, with chimneys and slanting roofs. It had once been the home of Sir Christopher Linton, a close friend of King Henry VIII and, briefly, Master of the Hunt. That was almost five hundred years ago. Now the house contained several classrooms, a very well stocked library and a dining hall – candlelit at night. It was surrounded by a low balustrade and a series of hedges perfectly cut into the shapes of animals. Real peacocks wandered over the lawns.

There were a dozen other more modern buildings in the grounds. These included a state-of-the-art gymnasium, an arts and leisure complex, a science block and five boarding houses named after British poets. The grounds also boasted a heated swimming pool, squash courts and an Olympic-standard athletic track. Less visible, set on the edge of the main school area and low in the ground, was a circular building made of brick with blacked-out windows. It was known as the Hub, and it was the school's security centre, manned twenty-four hours a day, the whole year round ... even during the holidays.

Linton Hall was not easy to find. It was buried in the Chilterns, at the end of a long track that ran through farmland and over a humpbacked bridge. There was no signpost. The school had no website and entering the name into a satnav system would produce no result at all. The nearest village was called Great Kimble and, despite its name, it was actually very small indeed. None of the villagers ever talked about the school. If anyone asked for directions, they had been warned to call the police.

We want our students to have a happy, normal, carefree time while they are with us.

The words were written on the first page of the school brochure (although the brochure was only sent to a tiny number of people and each copy had to be returned as soon as it had been read). This was the whole point of Linton Hall. The children who went there were the sons and daughters of some of the richest and most powerful people on the planet. In the past, they might have been able to fit into ordinary schools. But modern-day terrorism and the threat of international crime had made that too risky, and at the start of the twenty-first century, a Swiss business group had the bright idea of creating a single location where they might all be brought together and given a first-class education in complete safety.

Two prime ministers – and many senior politicians – had sent their children to Linton Hall. Several members of the royal family had been there and it was rumoured that the future king of

England would be starting as soon as he was old enough. But most of the parents could be simply described as "the super-rich". They were entrepreneurs, the top executives in companies like Apple, Google, Amazon and Shell. The Head Girl was the daughter of one of the world's best-selling authors. The captain of the first eleven was the adopted son of a pop singer who had sold over two hundred million records worldwide. Many of the children had come from abroad, with parents who included Russian oligarchs, Chinese businessmen, Hollywood stars, Saudi Arabian sheikhs. There was barely a parent in the school who had not been mentioned at some time or other in the press.

While Derek Vosper was reading his report on Celtic artefacts and Alex was kicking his heels in a car outside the Ashmolean Museum, fifty-two children from Years Five and Six were assembling outside the Manor House. At school they wore a distinctive uniform – two shades of blue with the word *Virtus* and a crest with a golden key on the top pocket. *Virtus* was the Latin for "excellence" and it was the school's one-word motto. However, it was the school policy that they should wear nothing that might identify them when they went on trips outside the grounds, so they were in their own clothes, smart but casually dressed.

They were being driven to Stratford-upon-Avon for an afternoon performance of *Henry V*. At some schools, it might be thought that children in Years

Five and Six were too young for Shakespeare, but at Linton Hall, the opposite was true. Children read their first play when they were nine and at the end of the previous term, quite a few of them had appeared in *A Midsummer Night's Dream*, performed in the open air with the school jazz band providing the music.

The coach that was waiting for them was a fifty-five-seater Mercedes-Benz Tourismo, painted in the school colours but with no other identification. The driver was standing waiting at the front door.

Jane Vosper had once driven buses for National Express but had joined Linton Hall four years ago. Like all the other teachers and support staff, she had been interviewed several times and had undergone a thorough police security check. She was not particularly popular with the children, as she hardly spoke and never smiled. But the school saw her as a safe pair of hands. With her solid shoulders and her muscular arms, she looked completely comfortable behind the steering wheel of a vehicle that measured thirteen metres in length and which weighed twenty-four tonnes. The children referred to her as Mrs T because she never went anywhere without her silver tea flask. She would sip tea while they were at the theatre, the museum, on a field trip ... wherever.

Of course, they were not travelling alone. The head of drama at Linton Hall was a slight, nervous-looking man in his early fifties. Jason

Green had been a successful actor and writer until he had been wooed by a generous salary and the promise of long holidays, which would allow him to travel and write plays. He had been at Linton Hall for twenty years, during which time he had seen many of his boys go on to become stars. He was in charge of the expedition.

Also in the coach was a well-built, watchful man with a blank face and a crew cut. His name was Ted Philby, an American recruited from the FBI. He was wearing a suit, a white shirt and dark glasses and there was a wire trailing down from his ear to a microphone next to his mouth. All in all, he could hardly have done more to advertise himself as a hired bodyguard ... which is exactly what he was. The school was looked after by a private security firm that consisted of seven full-time operatives: five men and two women. Most of the time, they based themselves at the Hub but whenever there was a school trip, they went too. Very unusually, they were allowed to carry guns. The firm had lobbied the government to make this possible – although it probably helped that one of the students was the son of the minister of defence.

When the coach left, Philby would be on board and it would be sandwiched between two identical Land Rovers with four more armed operatives, travelling in pairs. The cars would be parked outside the theatre throughout the play and the drivers would be in constant communication with the police. If anything happened, they could call for help on a special channel reserved for them. Armed backup would arrive within three minutes.

It wasn't surprising that everything was done to a tight schedule at Linton Hall and at exactly five past one, the children – who had formed an orderly line – climbed onto the bus and took their places behind each other, rows of two plush seats on either side of a long corridor. The coach had a toilet about halfway down and every seat had a television screen. Normally, the school would transmit classic films or documentaries during long journeys but Stratford-upon-Avon was only an hour away so this time they were blank. Jane Vosper took her place with Philby beside her. As the children settled down and Jason Green began a final headcount, she drew a packet of red and yellow sweets from her handbag.

"It's my birthday today," she announced.

"Is that so?" The security man wasn't interested. He didn't much care for the school, the children or anyone who worked there. He did this job for the money. He was well paid.

"Yes. Would you like one?" She held out the packet.

"All right." It was the fastest way to get her off his back. Philby took out a sweet and slid it into his mouth.

Jane had made sure that the red sweets were

at the top of the packet. He had taken one. She watched him eat it, then chose a yellow one, just as she had been instructed. Beneath her coat, her heart was beating rapidly. It had begun.

The other security people climbed into their cars, in front of the coach and behind it. The time was ten past one. They set off.

Jason Green was at the end of the aisle, studying a text of the play they were about to see. Ted Philby stayed at the front, chewing the sweet he had been given, occasionally glancing back to look at the passengers. When he had started working there, Philby had been surprised that, despite their extraordinary backgrounds, the children who went to Linton Hall were no different from any other children he had ever met. "Brats are brats no matter how much money they've got." That was what he had told his wife. Looking at them now, he saw that they were bored and excited at the same time. Mobile phones and computer games weren't allowed on school trips but one or two of them had brought books and were reading quietly while the others chatted noisily to their neighbours and to the people around them. They were black, white, Asian – and they were wearing exactly the sort of brands of jeans and trainers as other children of their age. The girls weren't allowed to wear jewellery and expensive watches were discouraged. They might be sitting in a very smart two-hundred thousand pound coach but to look at them, they could have come from any comprehensive school anywhere in the UK. Which was, of course, what they wanted everyone to think.

Philby glanced out of the window as they made their way down the first of several narrow, country lanes. Jane Vosper handled the coach expertly, steering it round some of the tighter corners with a sense of ease. Her silver Thermos was wedged beside her, a big, heavy thing that must have contained several pints of tea. She changed up a gear as they hit the A41, the main road that would take them all the way to the motorway. From there it was a straight run to Stratford-upon-Avon. Philby settled back in his seat. He had only ever been to one Shakespeare play and he had slept the whole way through it. He wondered why anyone bothered. It was all old stuff with no guns or car chases. He couldn't understand half the words. He wiped a hand across his brow. He was sweating. It was unusually warm inside the coach and he was getting tired. He leaned over to Jane. "Can you turn up the air conditioning?"

"It's on full," Jane replied. "Is there something the matter?"

"I don't know. I..." Ted Philby's head fell forward. He didn't say anything more.

Jane Vosper stared straight out of the window. The first Land Rover was right in front of her and she knew without looking that the other one would be directly behind. None of the men from the Hub would communicate with each other during the journey. They never had before. So they wouldn't know that anything was wrong. And they would be completely relaxed. After all, they were armed. They were in contact with the police. They were on their way to a play. They weren't expecting any trouble.

And as they turned onto the M40 motorway at Junction 9, near Bicester, not one of them even noticed the oversized helicopter that had suddenly appeared in the sky about a mile behind, like some strange, primeval monster. They didn't see how almost at once, it began to swoop down towards them, trailing something that looked, at least from a distance, like a huge claw...

Strapped into his seat in the Vauxhall Astra, Alex Rider felt like a player in an insane computer game with the world flashing past, the houses almost blurring into each other on either side. Ben Daniels was sitting next to him, hunched forward, his hands gripping the steering wheel as if it was the car that was in control, and it was all he could do to avoid the obstacles hurtling towards him. A taxi came out of a turning and he twisted to the right, then spun back to avoid the lorry that loomed up in front of them, headlights blazing. The needle on the speedometer was touching ninety ... on the wrong side of it. This was a residential area. One mistake, one lapse of concentration and innocent people would die. Alex would almost certainly be one of them.

They tore through a traffic light and, with a sense of relief, Alex saw that they had finally left the city and its suburbs behind them. The shops and the houses thinned out and suddenly they were heading north along a dual carriageway with fields on either side. While Ben drove, it was Alex's job to read out the route that was being sent to them via the satnav screen. They were being directed towards Junction 10 of the motorway – it seemed the most likely point where they might intercept the school coach. Nobody knew quite where it was. Jane Vosper had not yet been located and the security man, Ted Philby, wasn't answering his phone. But the route was known. Other cars were racing in the same direction, although it looked as if Alex and Ben would get there first.

"Right at the next roundabout!" Alex called out. "You want to get onto the A34."

The roundabout was ahead of them. The M40 was signposted to the right. But Alex saw that two huge lorries had arrived at the same time, slowing down to take the turn, and they were blocking both lanes. There was no way past. Ben would have to stop, losing precious seconds. Alex watched him as he worked out the angles and made up his mind. He stamped his foot on the accelerator and wrenched the wheel to the left, mounting the pavement and skidding over the grass verge, narrowly missing a lamp post. Now the car was off the road, parallel with the other traffic. He spun round and suddenly he was shooting towards a narrow gap between two cars. He cut through with inches to spare and hit the roundabout, ahead of the two lorries now. Other cars blasted their horns as they slammed on their brakes to avoid him. The car tore round the roundabout and exited on the other side. Throughout the entire manoeuvre they had never dropped below eighty.

Ben was angry with himself. "We should have listened to you," he muttered, as he changed up a gear. He didn't look at Alex. His eyes were still fixed on the road ahead. "That bloody museum! We convinced ourselves that was what they were after and we didn't think."

"I should have worked it out," Alex said.

"No. You'd already given us all the clues. We had the whole thing handed to us, gift-wrapped and tied with ribbon."

"But schoolchildren...?" Everything had happened too quickly. Alex still hadn't completely worked out what the Grimaldis were planning.

"Fifty-two insanely rich schoolchildren, Alex." MI6 had already sent Ben a complete briefing on Linton Hall. "Don't you see—?" Before he could explain anymore, he swore and jerked the wheel to overtake a camper van, the tyres protesting as they cut across the asphalt. After that, the traffic was heavier and he fell silent as he steered the car in and out of the gaps.

"Next left," Alex said.

They were on a single track road now, almost empty and cutting dead straight through the Oxfordshire countryside. For the next five minutes, they travelled at one hundred miles an hour but just when Alex thought they were home and dry, Ben was forced to slow down. There was a major traffic jam ahead of them and this time there was no way to avoid it. Ben hit the brakes and a moment later they were hemmed in with cars and lorries on all sides. Alex realized that they had arrived at the junction with the motorway. The only trouble was that there was no way of reaching it.

The satnav gave him an overview. They had come to the first of three interconnecting roundabouts, a complicated system that would eventually allow them to access the slip road onto the M40. But it would take them at least fifteen minutes to get there. It was as if the whole of Oxfordshire had decided to go the same way, arriving at the same time. There were cars everywhere, the drivers staring blankly out of the front windows, the passengers bored and silent. They crawled forward and reached a wide, concrete bridge crossing the motorway with four lanes of traffic moving in two directions. He turned to say something to Ben and gasped. Without meaning to, he had looked out of the window – and there it was, in front of his eyes.

It was one of the most extraordinary things he had ever seen.

A huge coach painted in two shades of blue was thundering towards them along the motorway, with one Land Rover in front of it and another behind. That in itself was unusual. But the three vehicles were being pursued by the biggest helicopter Alex had ever seen, a huge piece of machinery that looked even more monstrous and dangerous because it was so close to the ground. It was trailing a gigantic metal hoist underneath it, the chains and cables disappearing into its belly. A circular disc with five metal bands stretched out like fingers. In that instant, Alex understood the meaning of Steel Claw. The disc was magnetic. The helicopter was going to pluck the coach off the motorway. That was the plan. In one swoop, quite literally, the Grimaldi brothers were going to kidnap fifty-two children from the wealthiest families in the world.

That was what Ben had been trying to tell him. Fifty-two ransoms. They would add up to far more than forty million pounds' worth of gold. How much would the Grimaldis demand? The sky really was the limit.

And there was nothing they could do about it! They had arrived too late. Ben and Alex were trapped on the bridge above the motorway in traffic that had come to a complete standstill. Perhaps the other drivers had stopped to see what was happening. The giant helicopter was an amazing sight. What was it doing flying so low?

Once again, Alex saw Ben make his decision. He was in the left-hand lane. Next to him were the railings that ran along the side of the bridge and, on the other side, a long drop down to the motorway below. The coach rushed past, passing underneath them, and the sun was briefly blotted out as the helicopter followed, flying above their heads, getting lower all the time. The magnetic hoist came so close to the car that Alex almost felt it as it swooshed past. Ben's hand shot out and he gripped the joystick concealed in the gear-stick. He twisted it and the Vauxhall Astra swung round like the needle in a compass, spinning on its omnidirectional wheels so that it was facing the railings with the motorway stretching out below. Ben pressed a button on the control panel and a second later a great tongue of fire leapt out of the front of the car causing the railings to melt and fall away.

"Flame-thrower behind the radiator grille," he muttered. "Smithers always said it would come in useful." He gripped the wheel tighter. "Hold on, Alex," he warned. "This may hurt." For perhaps half a second, Alex wondered what he was going to do. Then he got the answer. Ben accelerated. The engine roared and the car leapt forward, shooting through the burnt-out railings, launching itself into the air.

They seemed to hang there for an impossibly long time. Alex saw the motorway below them, the cars speeding towards them, the whole world slanting diagonally across the windscreen. Then the surface of the road was rushing towards them. Alex wanted to cover his eyes. It seemed almost certain that they were going to be killed.

The car hit the ground. There was a terrible sound of tearing metal and a great burst of brilliant, crimson sparks. Alex felt his throat tighten as he shrank into his seat. They had fallen an incredible distance from the bridge to the motorway below and he was certain that the Vauxhall Astra had been ripped apart. The wheels screeched. The entire bonnet crumpled and a huge crack appeared in the windscreen, dividing it in two. And yet somehow the car righted itself and kept going. Ben Daniels fought for control, wrenching the steering wheel to find a gap in the traffic. Incredibly, he managed to weave his way between a caravan and a car transporter. The bridge slipped away behind them. They had survived.

They were on the motorway, racing forward with the engine screaming. The car was a wreck. The whole thing was shuddering. Thick smoke was pouring out of the exhaust.

And it was all for nothing.

As Alex straightened in his seat, his neck aching, his heart pounding, he saw that they had fallen behind. The Linton Hall coach was about a quarter of a mile in front of them and the helicopter had moved forward so that it was directly above it. Worse than that, the magnetic hoist had found its target. It was a massive, circular block of steel, suspended on a chain with several cables feeding into it. The pilot manoeuvred the hoist precisely so that it came to rest in the very centre of the roof, clamping itself to the metal surface. Even as Alex watched, the helicopter began to rise into the air, the huge blades beating down, dust billowing all around. The coach struggled briefly, as if there was really any chance of it continuing its journey. Then – it was something Alex would never forget – its wheels left the tarmac. For a few seconds it hung there, rushing forward at seventy miles an hour like all the other cars except that it was no longer in contact with the road. Inch by inch, it was jerked upwards. The two Land Rovers were still trying to protect it but there was nothing they could do. Suddenly they were on their own, on either side of an empty space. The coach was above them.

At first, Alex couldn't take it in. It was like some elaborate magic trick. The coach, with its fifty-five passengers, must have weighed tonnes but it was levitating, in front of his eyes. He knew that the Super Stallion would have no trouble with the weight, but the magnetic hoist...? It would have to be incredibly strong to maintain its grip. But this wasn't the time to worry about the science of what was happening. The coach was being snatched away in front of their eyes. They had to stop it.

Ben Daniels hit the accelerator one more time and the Vauxhall Astra leapt forward, the engine howling, the floor vibrating, on the edge of total breakdown. Alex craned his neck, looking through the sunroof. They were now nearly underneath the coach, which was already six or seven metres above them and rising all the time.

"What can you do?" he shouted. "What else did Smithers put in this car?"

"Nothing!" Ben shook his head.

"Does it have an ejector seat?"

"Yes!"

Instantly, Alex saw what had to be done. "Hit it!"

"I can't, Alex!"

"Just do it!"

Ben hesitated. The coach was moving ever further into the sky. Alex ripped off his seat belt. "We haven't got time to argue."

"You won't survive it! And then Mrs Jones will kill me!"

"Just do it!"

Ben let out a cry of exasperation and punched forward with his left hand, finding a button on the control panel. The sunroof flew off and at the same time Alex yelled as his entire seat was pro-pelled upwards, bright red flames blasting out beneath his feet. He felt the rush of the wind. For a hideous moment, he thought the helicopter had dropped the coach and that he was going to be crushed. It seemed to be plunging towards him, filling his vision. But it was actually the other way round. *He* was the one who was rocketing towards *it*. Everything else had disappeared: the motorway, the Vauxhall, the other cars, the sky. This was the moment of truth. He was hurtling towards a black metal wall ... the underbelly of the coach. If he was travelling too fast, he would be splatted against it like an insect on a windscreen: too slowly and he would fall back to certain death below. He stretched out, his hands scrabbling for anything that he could cling on to. He had been fired like a bullet. Was he going to reach it? The next moment he did! He saw a metal bar running across the chassis, just in front of the back wheels. The bar was filthy, thick with oil. With a yell, he hooked his hands over it. The seat fell away from beneath him, plunging back down to the road. Somehow, he managed to hold on. Already he could feel the weight of his body, putting the strain on his arms.

He was dangling. He looked down at his feet and beyond them, far, far away, the motorway. The cars were already the size of toys.

The Super Stallion rose ever higher, arcing through the air, heading west, carrying three adults, fifty-two children and one uninvited passenger into the unknown.

INTO THE DARK

Sitting behind the controls of the Sikorsky CH-53E, Slavko Novak reflected on his good fortune. The telephone call had come out of the blue, from his cousin, Dragana. The two of them had never really got on but now it seemed she was offering him a job. Was he available to leave straight away for England? He would only be required for one day. He would be paid fifty thousand pounds. Slavko didn't need to think twice. He was a test pilot at a Serbian aircraft factory, a highly qualified job, but he hadn't had a payrise in twelve years. His wife nagged him. He had four children – Miljan, Mudras, Milun and Milinka – who were rude to him. He needed an adventure. And who could say what he might do with the money? He certainly wasn't going to tell his family.

Eight hours later, he had found himself in a hotel in London, being briefed by his new employers. It was rather odd that they were identical twins. They showed him the route that he would take and they explained the revolutionary magnetic hoist he would be carrying. It had been developed by the National High Magnetic Field Laboratory at Florida State University and it used nanoparticle wire, a blend of copper and silver, at the core of nine separate coils. It would produce a magnetic field of five teslas ... about five thousand times the strength of a fridge magnet. He would have to position it very carefully, right at the centre of the coach. It was all a question of balance.

Slavko was a shy, unsmiling man with grey hair, grey skin and a nose that looked broken although it had naturally grown that way. He had never been particularly imaginative. He had no idea why the twins wanted to steal a moving vehicle off an English motorway. Nor did he want to know who would be travelling in the coach. It was the second part of the operation that occupied his mind. Lifting the coach would be hard enough but locating the target and releasing it would require total concentration and perfect timing. At the very last moment, before he left the hotel, he had questioned the amount he was being paid. Fifty thousand pounds really wasn't enough for an operation of this size and complexity. He wanted twice as much.

The two brothers briefly discussed his demand between themselves. Slavko had thought they might turn nasty and was surprised when they had agreed. In fact there seemed to be no hard feelings whatsoever ... quite the opposite. They gave him a cheque there and then, drawn from a bank in Panama City. Slavko had rarely seen so many noughts at the end of a number. He had twenty thousand Serbian dinar in his personal bank account but he was painfully aware that was the equivalent of about a hundred and forty pounds. The cheque was folded in half and lodged in his top pocket like a good-luck mascot. He would cash it in once this was over.

Now Slavko noted his position and pressed down with his right foot, adjusting the tail rotor. The helicopter responded immediately. Despite its huge size, the Sikorsky really was quite a delicate machine. He had just nine minutes left to reach his destination. He had been told that he would be tracked and guessed that the RAF would already be scrambling its fighter aircraft at its bases in Northolt, Brize Norton, High Wycombe and everywhere else.

Nine minutes. Then he had to disappear.

About ten metres underneath him, Alex Rider was, quite simply, clinging on for dear life.

As they rose away from the ground, the air became colder and the currents much stronger and if he had tried to hang on to the coach with his hands alone, he would have been quickly ripped away and sent spinning to his death. But the underbelly of the Mercedes-Benz Tourismo was a strange labyrinth of twisting pipes and brackets with thick cylinders, shelves and ridges. He identified an area that provided a sort of crawl space above the main axle and, using all his strength, he managed to bring his legs up and fold them into it so that he was tucked inside a metal box, protected from the rush of the wind. He still had to hold on. If he relaxed for a moment, he would fall away. The compartment was filthy, covered with the oil and dirt that had built up over years. Alex could feel the massive weight of the coach, which seemed to be crushing him even though right now it was effectively weightless.

He risked a look over his shoulder and wished at once that he hadn't. They were thousands of feet above the ground. The roads were little more than scribbles, the cars moving dots. The fields had turned into a multicoloured patchwork and they were a very, very long way away. He had no idea where he was heading but he saw a city, surrounded by fields, a railway line twisting through it, neat houses in rows, a cathedral. Was it Bath? Gloucester? He closed his eyes and focused instead on the bottom of the coach, keeping his grip, not moving, his whole body locked into place. The noise of the helicopter was deafening. He could feel the vibrations from the blades. He wondered about the children inside the coach. They would be terrified. How long was this journey going to last? Were they leaving the country? No. Surely that was impossible. The RAF would intercept them. Their fighter planes must already be on the way.

They were dipping down. Alex hadn't dared look for the last few minutes but he felt the change of pressure in his ears and opened his eyes to see that they had descended several thousand feet. They were flying over countryside – fields and mountains with a few scattered houses and farms. For some reason he thought they might be in Wales. He didn't have much of a view. His head was crushed against the underside of the coach, thick oil clogging his hair, and he had to twist round to look over his own shoulder. The wind battered his eyes, making it painful to keep them open. His arms were getting very tired. How long had he been hanging here? And where exactly were they going to land?

Adjusting his grip, Alex took another look and saw that they were following a single-track railway line. It was running directly beneath them, cutting through fields that were green and ancient with low flint walls and grazing sheep. There was a train a couple of miles ahead of them and he realized they were chasing it. Alex lowered himself a little, hanging down so that he could see more. It was a steam locomotive. From this height it looked exactly like a toy – something from long ago. In fact, it could have come straight out of a museum. He could see the driver leaning out of the side and the clouds of smoke puffing out of its chimney.

Behind the main locomotive there was a tender, piled high with coal. And behind that, a single wagon had been attached. It was a low-loader – nothing more than a long, wooden platform with open sides. As they closed in on it, Alex's heart began to race. He understood exactly what was going to happen.

They caught up with the locomotive. The helicopter was only five hundred feet above the ground and the coach, at the end of the magnetic hoist, was much nearer. For Alex, the situation had suddenly become far worse as the wind whipped the smoke up and into the underbelly of the coach, burning his eyes and making it difficult to breathe. He was blinded, drowning upside down in a thick fog that stank of soot. He was coughing uncontrollably and what little strength he had left was rapidly draining out of his arms. Vaguely, he was aware of the sleepers rushing past, each one blurring into the next. The helicopter edged forward and began to drop and at last the smoke cleared. Now Alex saw the wooden platform, right underneath him. That was where the helicopter was going to position the coach! It was a brilliant scheme. The locomotive train would carry the coach on the next leg of its journey while everyone kept following the helicopter. But by the time they caught up with it – if they ever did – they would be too late. The coach would be miles away, carried in a completely different direction.

They dropped lower and Alex was seized by a new terror. There couldn't possibly be enough room between the bottom of the coach where he was clinging and the platform that was travelling beneath him. From the very start he had felt as if he was being crushed, but now it was actually going to happen. He wondered if he could drop down and somehow roll out of the way, but he knew that would be just another way to commit suicide. All he could do was stay where he was and hope for the best. But the weight above him was almost beyond comprehension ... tonnes and tonnes of it. The platform was solid, unforgiving. He felt like an insect trapped between the pages of a slowly closing book. Part of him wondered how he had got into all this. All he had ever wanted was to find Jack!

It was very dark. The low-loader, the tyres, the huge bulk of the coach – between them they had blotted out the light. Now he was so close to the platform, he could see the knots in the wood. Even with the roar of the helicopter, he could hear the train's wheels clanking as they rolled over the sleepers. The coach touched down. Alex cried out as the wooden surface touched his shoulders. This was where it ended. This was death. The huge rubber tyres bulged, taking the weight. There was just enough space for him after all! Then the coach rose slightly and Alex knew that it had been released from the magnetic hoist. Almost at once, the sound of the helicopter grew fainter and the chuffing of the steam locomotive took over. He had passed from one technology to another – two centuries apart.

He was still trapped. Alex had briefly hoped that once the coach had been set down, he would simply wait for the right moment and then steal out of his hiding place. For now, that was impossible. He was still being carried forward and he could only stay where he was until they arrived wherever they were going. At least he didn't have to cling on any more. He let go of the metal bar and sank gratefully onto the platform below. Looking through the sides, he could see grass and gravel rushing past. They had to be somewhere rural and isolated. The fact that the railway could accommodate a steam train spoke for itself. This couldn't be a main line. It belonged to the Victorian age. If this was Wales, perhaps it might lead to an old mine?

The sound of the train amplified and in a split second everything went dark. Once again Alex found himself choking on thick, black smoke and for a moment he was confused. What had happened? How had day turned into night? Then he understood. They had entered a tunnel, a long one. The train was slowing down. Now it stopped. As Alex lay there, fighting the sense of being buried alive, he wondered what he was going to find when they finally came out on the other side.

* * *

It had all gone perfectly.

Slavko Novak wanted to laugh out loud. He had plucked a moving coach off a motorway, carried it a hundred and twenty miles across the country and deposited it on a moving train. It had taken an extraordinary amount of skill and almost nobody in the world would have been able to pull it off. That made him think of his cousin, Dragana. He briefly wondered what had happened to her, then put her out of his mind. Her loss was his gain. And now he knew what he was going to do with the money. There was a barmaid he knew at a little place in Pazinska Street in Belgrade. He had always liked her. Perhaps he would invite her to come away with him for the weekend. Of course, he wouldn't tell his wife.

It wasn't quite over yet. He had been instructed to fly north towards Shropshire, keeping low to avoid the radar. There was a red button mounted on the control panel in front of him. The Grimaldis had instructed him to press it as soon as he was within five miles of his destination – transmitting a signal to the car that would be waiting for him just outside the town of Montgomery. That was where he was to land the helicopter. By the evening, he would be back on his way home.

He checked his bearings. Seven miles ... six miles ... five... He was finally within range. He leaned forward and pressed the button although, even as he did so, it occurred to him that it was rather odd. Why did it need this extra device? Surely the car would be able to see him anyway?

They were the last thoughts he ever had.

Two Tornado jet fighters from RAF Brize Norton had caught up with him and were swooping down from fifty thousand feet. But neither of them was close when the bomb, activated by the red button, exploded. The pilots saw the missing Super Stallion tear itself apart in a gigantic ball of flame. A few moments later, scattered pieces began to fall out of the sky onto the fields below.

But as the pilots radioed in what had happened, they were also able to confirm a negative sighting – repeat, a negative sighting – of the coach. It seemed impossible but the Mercedes-Benz Tourismo and fifty-two children from Linton Hall had simply disappeared mid-flight.

"How is it possible?" Mrs Jones demanded.

She was back in her office. Just two men were with her: John Crawley and Ben Daniels. It was hard to tell which of the two of them was looking more uncomfortable.

"The Super Stallion was last seen over Gloucester and then over Monmouth," Crawley replied. "It seems to have been heading into the Brecon Beacons. Unfortunately, it dipped down after Abergavenny and that's when we lost it. It was actually flying under the radar. The area around there is very hilly and that would have helped."

"And then?"

"It reappeared briefly. We have reports from two pilots that the coach had been detached. The magnetic hoist was still in view but it was empty. And a moment later, the helicopter blew up. It's very lucky there was no one underneath. Only the pilot was killed."

"Do we know who the pilot was?"

"Not yet."

"But the helicopter must have landed somewhere. It was heading towards the Welsh borders with a bright blue Mercedes-Benz Tourismo dangling underneath it! So how come nobody has seen it?"

Crawley sighed. "We're still trying to work it out, Mrs Jones. You're right. A coach like that would stand out like a sore thumb in the Welsh countryside and we've had half a dozen aircraft searching the entire area. But there's nothing. They must have gone to ground."

"Well, I hope you're pleased with yourself, Crawley. We had over seventy personnel watching the Ashmolean Museum and the whole city of Oxford on lockdown. We made complete fools of ourselves." She turned to Daniels. "And what do you have to say for yourself?"

"Alex worked it out but we got to the motorway too late," he said.

"That's not what I'm talking about. I told you to look after him. And by that I didn't mean that you should fire him into the air over a crowded motorway and allow him to get snatched by the opposition!"

Ben Daniels met her eye. "Do you want me to resign, Mrs Jones?" he asked.

"No." Her voice softened. "I don't want either of you to resign. This is my fault as much as yours. This is the first major situation we've had to face since Alan Blunt left and so far I've made a complete hash of it."

"What next?" Crawley asked.

"We look for the coach. It's not easy because, as far as I can see, it could be anywhere. We're recovering the black box from the wreckage of the helicopter and that may give us a clue – but that's going to take time and I have a feeling that time is something we don't really have."

As if on cue, the telephone rang. Mrs Jones snatched it up and listened for about a minute, then slowly lowered it. Her face showed no emotion at all. "We've heard from the Grimaldis," she said.

"What do they want?" Ben asked.

"They didn't identify themselves, of course. Half an hour ago, the school received a video file. It was sent over the Internet and Special Branch are examining it but it's going to be nearly impossible to trace."

John Crawley had a laptop with him. He passed it to Mrs Jones who tapped in the access code she had just been given. At once, a film began to play. The image showed the Mercedes-Benz Tourismo as it dangled underneath the Super Stallion, flying over the English landscape.

"This is a message to the parents of fifty-two children from the Linton Hall Preparatory School," a voice announced. It was flat, emotionless and had been electronically distorted to disguise whoever was speaking. "The children are being held in a secure environment," the voice continued. "They have not been harmed. They are being well looked after.

"However, we will kill every one of these children in forty-eight hours if the ransom we demand has not been paid. We are asking for the sum of two hundred and sixty million pounds. This is the equivalent of five million pounds per child. The money is to be paid into a bank in Panama. The details of the bank will appear at the end of this short video.

"Please be aware that we are treating the children as a single unit and we are demanding one single payment. If any of the parents refuse, or are unable, to pay, then it is for the other parents to make up the shortfall. And if the exact amount of money is not received by the time stated, all the children will die. There will be no exceptions.

"Do not attempt to find the children. We are extremely well armed and will fight back if we find ourselves under attack. You can be certain that, in this eventuality, none of the children will survive."

On the screen, the helicopter and the coach had disappeared into the distance.

"Do not attempt to negotiate with us," the voice concluded. "Do not ask for more time. I repeat. The sum of money is two hundred and sixty million pounds. You now have forty-seven hours and fifty-eight minutes. That is all."

The screen went black and a name came up. It was a bank: the Caja España in Panama City. Written beneath it were the details of the bank account into which the money had to be paid. Mrs Jones had no doubt that it would be untraceable.

For a long time, nobody spoke.

It was Ben who broke the silence. "Two hundred and sixty million!" he said. "Can they afford that?"

"From what I understand, there are parents at Linton Hall who could afford the full amount on their own," Mrs Jones replied. "Some of them will have insurance for exactly this sort of eventuality. There may be a few who find five million a stretch ... although anyone who can afford to educate their children at a cost of thirty-thousand pounds a year probably isn't going to be too hard up." She paused. "The Grimaldis have been very clever. By treating the children as a single package – all or nothing – they've made it absolutely certain that the parents will raise the money. They may argue among themselves but they have no choice."

"Forty-eight hours," Crawley muttered. "That's not a lot of time."

"No." Mrs Jones flicked open a box of pepper-mints and took one out. "But they've made one mistake."

"Alex Rider."

"Exactly. Wherever they are, he's with them – and they don't know it." She slipped the peppermint into her mouth. "It seems that once again he's our only hope."

SMOKE CITY

Alex had no idea how long he had been in the tunnel. He was wearing a watch but his face and eyes were so blackened by soot that he was barely able to open them to look at it. He was only breathing with difficulty. The steam engine might not be moving but it was still burning coal and the smoke had wrapped itself around him, smothering him. They were about a hundred metres from the entrance and a single draught of cool air was making its way down the length of the shaft towards him. Alex knew he owed his life to it. The entrance was also providing a small amount of daylight. Otherwise, he would have been completely blind.

He heard footsteps. Two men were walking along the side of the track between the train and the tunnel wall, talking to each other in low voices. Alex was crushed between the bottom of the coach and the low-loader, with barely enough room to turn. Looking over the crook of his arm, he could just make out the lower parts of their legs as they came to a halt. For a moment they were so close that he could have reached out and touched them. Then the coach door opened with a hydraulic hiss and they climbed out of sight.

"All right! Listen up, everyone!" It was difficult to make out the man's voice but Alex knew it wasn't one of the Grimaldi brothers. He was talking to the schoolchildren and, although Alex could only hear half of what he said, the general sense was clear. "You're going to have to wait here another twenty minutes ... no need to be scared. We're not going to hurt you if you behave yourselves ... need to cover the bus. It's going to get dark. Move soon. You'll be staying with us a couple of days ... return to your families ... dinner and bed when you arrive."

The men climbed down again and Alex saw them busy themselves with a long roll of tarpaulin which must have been lying beside the track, waiting for this very moment. When he had met the Grimaldis, he had been unimpressed. He had thought there was something almost childish about them, their schoolboy spite, the way they hung on each other's every word. But he had to admit that their operation – Steel Claw – had been worked out to the last detail. They had stolen an immensely powerful helicopter and used it to snatch a bus full of children in a way that had made a complete mockery of all the security around it. Now, he guessed, the coach was being disguised in some way so that when it finally emerged from the tunnel, it would be hidden from passing aircraft, from satellites, from anyone who happened to be watching.

And what then? Where exactly were they? Alex was surprised he had managed to survive so far but he suspected the worst was still to come. He had arrived in the lions' den – and he had no doubt that the lions were about to show their teeth.

He lay there for what seemed like an eternity. The men finished their work and walked away and suddenly the tunnel was full of fresh smoke as the train shunted forward, pulling the coach – now concealed underneath a giant sheet of tarpaulin – behind it. It took them a long time to reach the end of the tunnel and by then Alex was almost at the end of his endurance, sweating and choking. His nose and throat felt completely clogged up and the fresh air, when it came, washed over him deliciously, wiping away all the fears and doubts of the last hour. Perhaps things weren't as bad as he thought. The Grimaldis had no idea he was here. In fact, they believed he was dead. All he had to do was find out where he was and contact MI6 and this would all be over.

Looking out of the narrow slit that was all he had beneath the coach and its tarpaulin cover, Alex watched the countryside sliding past. The locomotive was moving quite slowly. The railway was level and straight. There were no buildings that Alex could see – just wild grass dotted with flowers. The puffing of the engine, the constantly shifting pistons and the grinding of the wheels would have blocked out any other sound, but Alex sensed that they had arrived at a part of the country that was as silent as it was remote. Finally, they began to slow down. The edge of a station platform blotted out Alex's view. The train drew to a halt, steam exploding out of it like exclamation marks. The tarpaulin cover was removed. They had arrived.

He had a choice. He could stay where he was underneath the coach. At least nobody could see him there and he knew he was safe. Or he could move out at once, find somewhere else to hide and see what happened next. He decided on the second option. Apart from anything else, he needed to escape from the narrow space in which he'd been trapped for so long and he knew it was important to keep track of the children from Linton Hall, to watch where they were taken. The locomotive was already settling down, the steam hissing and the various metal parts clicking as they began to cool. Alex slithered sideways, edging across the wooden floor of the low-loader, away from the station platform. He stopped behind one of the coach's tyres and checked around him. There didn't seem to be anyone near by. He wriggled out, then dropped to the ground, squatting beside the railway track with the low-loader above him. Nobody had seen him. His lungs gratefully sucked in the clean afternoon air.

But where the hell was he? What sort of place was this? Alex stared around him, trying to take it all in.

It was an industrial complex – although one that had long ago been abandoned. He could tell that instantly from the silence, from the rusting pipes, from the tufts of wild grass sprouting out of the broken concrete and the puddles of stagnant water. There was a massive square tower in the middle of it all, grey and windowless, made out of concrete. It rose about fifty metres into the air. A conveyor belt surrounded by corrugated-iron walls sloped down from the top, reaching all the way to the end of the platform. It must have been used to carry some sort of product – either into the tower or away from it. But what? The answer was right in front of him. The lower end of the conveyor belt stopped a few metres short of what looked like a black pyramid. It was coal. Alex's first thought had been that this was an old Welsh mine. But it might well be that coal hadn't actually been dug up here. It could have been brought from somewhere else, offloaded and then used in some sort of industrial process.

He examined the rest of the complex, trying to get his bearings. A brick chimney, the same height as the tower, stood to one side with half a dozen smaller, steel chimneys glinting in the sun. All around there were giant fuel tanks, oil drums, rusting tractors and wagons. Everything was connected by a network of twisting pipes and girders, cables, bridges and walkways, as if the whole place were some extraordinary machine and it might all be turned back on with a single switch.

Curiously, one or two of the buildings looked new, as if they had recently been restored. At the far end, Alex saw two blocks, one-storey high, with a corridor joining them together so they formed a letter H. They immediately reminded him of the prison quarters where he had been held at Siwa. Even at this distance he could see the windows were barred. The fence that surrounded the complex and the searchlights on aluminium poles were all brand new. The Grimaldi brothers must have taken over the place and added their own security. Guards with machine guns were patrolling the perimeter. As far as he could see, there was no road leading out. Certainly, there were no cars in sight. He looked behind him and saw that the locomotive had crossed a turntable before it had arrived at the platform. Presumably it would back onto it and then – assuming that it actually worked – the whole thing would rotate so that it could leave the same way it had come.

"OK, kids. Let's have you out of the coach! Quickly now!"

Alex twisted round. He recognized the voice. It wasn't one he would ever forget easily. Frankie Stallone, the gangster who had tried to kill him, had followed him here from the South of France.

It seemed that he was in charge of this part of the operation.

Alex hadn't heard the doors open but now he watched the children climbing down – or at least their feet and the bottoms of their legs, which was all he could see beneath the coach. They were being assembled on the platform on the other side of the train. One or two of the younger ones were crying. Finally they were all out. Alex guessed that it must have been Stallone who had addressed them in the tunnel. Now he spoke to them again.

"I want you to line up in pairs," Stallone ordered. "You're going to be taken to the accommodation block, which is just over there. We have bedrooms for you to stay in, just like at school. There's a TV room and a dining room – you'll all get something to eat very soon. Like I told you, you're going to be with us for forty-eight hours and if you all behave yourselves, nobody needs to get hurt. We have someone to look after you and if you need anything – medicine or stuff like that – you can ask. Are there any questions?"

"I have several questions." It was another man speaking. Alex wished he could move round to the other side of the train so that he could actually see what was happening, but it was too dangerous. "What have you done to Mr Philby?"

"Who are you talking about?"

"Our security man. He's unconscious."

"Don't worry about him. He's been knocked out.

He'll be fine in an hour or two."

The man hadn't finished yet. "Who are you, and what do you want?" he demanded. His voice was high-pitched, trembling. "This is an outrage!"

"Who are you?"

"I'm Jason Green. I'm their drama teacher."

"And you're going to be their dead drama teacher if you don't shut your mouth. It doesn't matter who I am. All that matters is that you do as you're told."

"You've kidnapped us!"

"That's right, Jason!" Alex could hear the mockery in Stallone's voice. "How very smart of you to notice. Now shut up and get in line. Let's move out of here."

There was the shuffling of feet as the children formed a line and Alex watched them set off. They walked past the steam locomotive, which was sitting there, puffing quietly after its labours, like a great, metallic beast. He saw them disappear into the distance, heading for the prison block he had already identified. It was time to move himself. There were two wagons parked near by, no longer on the track ... fuel tanks on wheels. They were rusty and the paint was faded but Alex could make out a word, painted in red letters on the side: BENZENE. Somewhere, in the back of his mind, he was sure he knew what it meant. He had heard it mentioned in chemistry class. Some sort of fuel? Not for the first time, he wished he had spent more time in school.

Keeping low, he ran a short distance across the ground, away from the locomotive and over to the wagons. He skidded underneath one of them and lay there panting, once again out of sight.

Already he was running through his options. All he had to do was contact MI6, but how was he going to do that when he no longer had a mobile phone? He had lost his in the South of France, along with everything else, and he hadn't had a chance to replace it. He might be able to break into an office but he couldn't see any telephone lines running in or out of the compound, which suggested there might not be any phones and anyway, they probably wouldn't be connected. That left the guards. He could knock one of them out and steal a mobile but he wondered if he'd even get a signal. Worse than that, once they knew he was here, he would lose the one advantage he had. They would quickly hunt him down.

He was on his own. He was unarmed. There were at least a dozen guards with machine guns. He had no idea where he was ... he only knew that it was the middle of nowhere. He was fenced in, surrounded by steep hills and, unless there was a road somewhere that he couldn't see, it looked as if a long tunnel was the only way back into the real world.

Not good.

So what next? Even as he asked himself the question, Alex knew that the answer lay in the accommodation block. Maybe the drama teacher or one of the children had managed to hang on to a mobile. There were fifty-three of them. Was it too much to hope that between them they might have some weapon he could use, even if it was only a penknife? And then there was the security man, Philby, that the teacher had mentioned. Surely he'd be able to help, once he'd come round. The more Alex thought about it, the more he saw what he had to do. There was safety in numbers. Out here, he was on his own.

He couldn't make his move yet. There were too many guards around and too much chance of being seen. Alex reached up and touched the surface of the metal fuel tank. Benzene. He suddenly remembered. It was a by-product that came from coal. It was used in motor cars, blended with petrol. It was highly flammable. If the tank was full, that might be useful.

He looked at his watch, then wiped the surface with his thumb to remove the coating of soot. It was four o'clock. The sun wouldn't set for another few hours.

Alex settled down to wait.

The compound was called Dinas Mwg – a Welsh name which translates roughly as Smoke City.

A thousand men and women had once worked here, turning coal into an industrial fuel known as coke; it was a strange thing that it should share its name with a soft drink. The process was long and dirty and began in the cement tower that Alex had noticed. It was known as the retort house. The coal would have travelled up the conveyor belt before being heated in enormous steel tubes. The resulting product, coke, was very pure and smoke-less, used in the steel manufacturing industry. It also had remarkable heat-shielding properties. NASA had used it on many of their space vehicles. In addition, there would have been a number of by-products including gas, tar, ammonia, sulphuric acid and benzene. All of these had been separated, stored and finally sold.

Unfortunately, the collapse of the steel industry had spelled the end for Dinas Mwg. The place had closed down eleven years before and effectively it had been left to rot. The countryside was dotted with old mines and factories that had been aban-doned as the twenty-first century had taken its toll. One more wouldn't make any difference. And so it might have remained – but then the Grimaldis had come along. They had bought the compound from the Welsh authorities for next to nothing, claiming that they were going to turn it into a museum and a heritage centre. Of course, that had been a lie. From the very start, they had seen it as a perfect location to hide fifty-two extremely wealthy children while the police and the security services scoured the country for them.

Dirty, lost and forgotten, Smoke City lay

concealed in a valley, surrounded by mountains. A narrow road had once led there but a landslide five years before had closed it and now the only way in and out was a single, old-fashioned railway line. The Blaina Tunnel, where Alex had waited in the dark, was half a mile long and connected directly with the main line. The Grimaldis had been forced to purchase the train that had brought them here. It was called *The Midnight Flyer* and it was a Standard Class 5 steam locomotive, built in Doncaster in 1950. It was a beautiful piece of machinery, bringing back memories of the age when it had been constructed. As well as being restored to working condition, it had been repainted and polished so that it looked as good as new, gleaming black with its name picked out in gold letters and a single bright red pilot bar just above the ground at the front. Rebuilding the engine had been the most expensive part of the operation. In fact, the Grimaldis had spent just over five million pounds setting up Operation Steel Claw. That left them with an expected profit of around two hundred and fifty-five million pounds, which they both considered perfectly acceptable.

It had been necessary to make certain modifications to the compound itself. What had once been an administration centre with a number of offices had been turned into the prison building that Alex had seen. They had put bars on the windows and brought in fifty-two beds. The Grimaldis had also built an accommodation block for themselves. It was basic but comfortable, with two bed-rooms, both of them identical with a connecting door. They had one large living room and a small kitchen – but no bathrooms. The water supply had been cut off when the compound was closed down. It didn't matter. They could easily go without a bath for a couple of days and there were chemical toilets and bottles of drinking water.

Two hours after the children had left the train and as Alex waited for darkness to fall, the two brothers were sitting in the living room on the first floor, having tea. They were not alone. Jane Vosper was sitting opposite them, her legs crossed, balancing a cup and saucer on her knees. Giovanni and Eduardo were dressed very much like the gang-sters that they were: in dark suits with white shirts and narrow ties. Their shoes were highly polished, their black hair slicked back with gel. Giovanni had a gold ring on the fourth finger of his right hand, Eduardo on the same finger of his left.

The tea was very good. There were sandwiches cut into triangles, a sponge cake, a variety of choc-olate biscuits. They had poured Earl Grey tea for their guest. They were drinking coffee themselves.

Even so, Jane Vosper was in a bad mood. "How long am I going to have to stay here?" she demanded.

"I think we agreed that you would stay here until the operation was concluded," Giovanni replied.

"Two days," Eduardo added.

The woman sniffed. "So what am I supposed to do for two days?"

The brothers exchanged a sly glance, as if there was something they weren't telling her. "I'm sure you'll think of something," Giovanni said.

Mrs Vosper turned and stared out of the window at the silver chimneys, rising up in the afternoon sun, the long stretches of pipes criss-crossing each other, weaving in and out of the walkways. In the distance, the locomotive with its tender had backed onto the turntable. It was about to be rotated one hundred and eighty degrees, ready for the return journey. Smoke was still belching out of the chimney. Meanwhile, the coach had been driven off the low-loader and concealed underneath a wooden canopy. It was standing on a patch of concrete, surrounded by wild grass and rubble. "When do I get my money?" she asked.

"As soon as we have the ransom, you'll be paid."

Mrs Vosper finished her tea, noticing for the first time how bitter it tasted. She turned away from the window. "Why have you taken my mobile?" she asked. "I want to telephone my husband."

"I'm afraid you can't," Giovanni told her. "We have to think about security. It's always possible that your calls are being monitored."

"You have to be very careful," Eduardo agreed. "I'm afraid it's quite likely that the police are going to suspect you were involved."

"I'll tell them I was taken prisoner with the rest of the children," Mrs Vosper retorted. "There's nothing to make them think otherwise."

"Of course, dear lady. That's how we planned it. So obviously you can't make phone calls. That would give the game away!"

"I suppose that's true." Mrs Vosper put down her cup and saucer. She was certain that the air at Smoke City was making her ill. She was a little breathless and there was a burning sensation in her throat. She sat down in her chair.

"Are you all right?" Giovanni asked. "You're looking a little pale."

"Perhaps you'd like to lie down?" Eduardo suggested.

The two brothers stared at her with concern. Mrs Vosper said nothing. She had suddenly become very still. In fact, she was staring at the ceiling with empty eyes. Her tongue was sticking out of the corner of her mouth. Her face had gone mauve.

The brothers gazed at her curiously.

"How much cyanide did you put in her tea?" Eduardo asked.

"Half the bottle."

"It took its time."

"Yes. But it's over now." Giovanni helped himself to another sandwich. "That will save us a bit of cash!"

Eduardo picked out a chocolate finger. "We'll

have to kill her husband too, of course."

"Yes. I'll give the order as soon as we're out of here."

There was a brief silence as they finished what they were eating.

"Are you sure the parents will pay?" Eduardo asked.

"They'll pay, Eddie. But I'm afraid I've got some bad news. They've sent us an email via the bank in Panama. I picked it up just before we sat down."

"And?"

"They've asked us to reduce the ransom. They've offered to pay one hundred million pounds instead of the two hundred and sixty that we're asking. Less than half!" Giovanni shrugged. "I can't say I'm surprised. They'll try to get the best deal for anything ... even the lives of their children."

"They're business people, Gio. That's how they behave."

"Exactly, Eddie."

"So...?"

"So tomorrow morning we'll have to kill one of the kids. It's a little cruel but we always knew it was a possibility. We'll get Mr Stallone to film it. The important thing is to make sure it's one of the poorer children. We don't want to upset any of the billionaires. We'll send the school a copy of the file and after that I'm sure there won't be any more arguments. And then we'll raise the ransom amount to three hundred million pounds."

Eduardo Grimaldi walked over to the window. The locomotive engine was now facing back down the line, in the direction of the tunnel. His brother joined him. Jane Vosper sat, lifeless, behind them. They had already forgotten she was there.

At last the sun had set over Smoke City.

Alex's eyes flickered open. Somehow, without meaning to, he had managed to fall asleep. Well, that was good. He needed all the energy he could muster. His stomach felt empty. He hadn't eaten since breakfast and he'd had little enough of that. His hands were black. He wondered what he must look like ... a Victorian chimney sweep, probably!

He watched as, one by one, the searchlights crashed on. The Grimaldis were taking no chances. Nobody knew they were here but they still had their guards out, marching back and forth, following the line of the fence. Even so, it was impossible to illuminate the entire compound. It was exactly what Alex had hoped. There were so many different shapes – buildings, pipes, old bits of machinery – that the beams of light created a fantastic network of shadows which themselves provided places for him to hide.

He took a quick look around him, noting that the steam train had been turned and that the coach had been driven off the low-loader. The coach was of particular interest to him. He couldn't drive but the security man, Philby, certainly could. He was beginning to see that this was his best option. Find the schoolchildren, put them on the bus, drive out of here. It sounded desperate but at least it was a plan.

It was time to go. Alex stretched his cramped muscles, then slid out from underneath the benzene wagon. A single drop of evil-smelling fuel dripped onto his neck and he saw that the metal casing was badly rusted – that it might wear through at any time. Could he help it on its way? It was a thought which he filed away in some corner of his mind. If he could start a fire, that might provide a distraction. It might even be spotted by someone flying overhead...

The prison block was straight ahead of him, half concealed by the concrete tower. The conveyor belt slanted down high over his head, reaching back to the pile of coal on the station platform. For the moment there were no guards in sight and Alex hurried forward, keeping in the shadows, avoiding the light. He came to a brick-built shed, some sort of storage facility. Once it had been securely fastened with a steel door but someone had forced their way in and the door was hanging off its hinges. Alex ducked inside, still hoping he might find something he could use as a weapon.

There was nothing. The light, streaming in through a small, dusty window, revealed shelves lined with laboratory equipment that hadn't been used for years. Alex saw a couple of glass jars marked H_2SO_4. At least that was one thing he remembered from school: the chemical formula for sulphuric acid. He turned to leave and stepped on something lying on the floor. It was an old chisel. He picked it up and tucked it into his belt. It wasn't much but it was better than nothing.

He reached the doorway and was about to pass through when the sound of approaching footsteps made him stop and retreat quickly into the darkness. A guard walked past, dressed in dark combat trousers and an anorak with a machine gun hanging diagonally across his chest. He was speaking on a walkie-talkie.

"Sector Seven ... all clear. Over."

Alex heard the buzz of static as the message was relayed to wherever the control centre happened to be. He waited until the man had gone, then crept forward, not wanting to waste any more time. There were lights on inside the building ahead of him and Alex briefly wondered where the electricity was coming from. If there was a generator somewhere, he might be able to sabotage it, although so much power was being used in the compound that he was fairly sure it must still be connected to the mains.

The entrance to the accommodation area – the only way in as far as he could see – was in the middle of the passageway that connected the two blocks. It was open but it was also guarded. Alex could see a chair and a table on the other side and a man sitting with his feet up, reading a magazine. With his attention distracted, it would be easy enough to sneak in and take him out, using one of any number of karate moves. But that wouldn't work. As soon as someone noticed that the man had gone missing, the alarm would be raised. Somehow Alex had to get past without being seen.

For once, luck was on his side. The man's walkie-talkie crackled and he held it to his ear. He must have received some sort of instruction because a moment later, he got up and walked off down the passageway. Alex seized the opportunity to slip inside, heading the opposite way. The passageway was wide and, with its tiled floor and old-fashioned radiators, reminded him of an abandoned hospital. It had recently been given a coat of white paint and new light fittings but there was still a sense of emptiness and desolation. It led to a second corridor, this one running left and right with softly glowing light bulbs hanging down on wires and a long line of identical doors. Alex crept forward carefully. If anyone came out, he would have nowhere to hide.

He heard a sound coming from behind one of the doors. It was unmistakable: a child crying. Knowing that he shouldn't do it but unable to stop himself, Alex reached for the door handle and turned it. The door wasn't locked. It opened into a small room, barred, with two bunk beds, a table with a lamp, two chairs. It would have looked like a prison cell, except that the duvets on the beds were decorated with characters from *Star Wars* and the occupants were both about ten years old, boys wearing striped pyjamas. The boy in the lower bunk was in tears and the other boy, a little older, had climbed down to comfort him. The two of them stopped and stared, seeing Alex standing in the doorway. Alex quickly brought a finger to his lips, warning them not to call out.

"Who are you?" the older boy whispered.

"I'm a friend," Alex said. "I've come to get you out of here."

"They kidnapped us from school..."

"I know. I saw it happen. Is there anyone in charge?"

The older boy nodded. "They've got a nurse looking after us. Mr Green was here to begin with but now he's gone. He teaches us drama."

"What about your security guard? Do you know where he's being kept?"

"No." It was the younger boy who had answered. "They knocked him out when he was in the bus. We haven't seen him."

"Thanks." Alex took a step back. "You mustn't tell anyone you've seen me. You must both try and get a bit of sleep. With a bit of luck, we'll all be leaving here very soon."

"What's your name?" The younger boy looked at him anxiously.

Alex smiled. "Alex Rider. I'll be back as soon as I can."

He left the room, closing the door behind him. The most important thing was to find out where the security man – Philby – was being kept. He started down the corridor but he hadn't gone halfway when he heard a pair of doors swing open at the far end and a shadow stretched out, climbing the opposite wall. Someone was coming!

He was standing next to a store cupboard, between two of the cells. The door was half open and he quickly went inside, pulling the door shut apart from a small crack to allow in the light. He saw that he was in a laundry room. There were spare sheets and duvets, brand-new pyjamas and T-shirts, still in their wrapping. Outside, the footsteps were getting closer. Alex reached for the chisel in his belt and drew it free. The footsteps had stopped. The guard – or whoever it was – had stopped right outside. Alex tensed. He had nowhere to hide. If he was discovered, he would simply have to strike first.

The door opened. A figure stood in front of him, silhouetted against the lights in the corridor.

Alex lashed out, driving the wooden handle of the chisel upwards, a knockout blow to the side of the head. It was only some instinct that made him stop and pull back at the last microsecond. His fist froze, a few millimetres from its target.

He was looking at a woman dressed in the uniform of a nurse.

The woman was Jack Starbright.

NEVER SAY DIE

"Jack?" Alex dropped the chisel. It clattered against the floor.

"Alex?" Jack gazed at him in disbelief.

The two of them stood there for what felt like an eternity, then fell into each other's arms.

"I don't believe it!" Jack's eyes had filled with tears.

"I got your message, Jack. I've been looking for you all over the world."

"And you found me! You're in a laundry cupboard! How did you get here?" She pulled away. "You look awful, Alex! When was the last time you had a bath?"

"Jack!"

She stared at him, then grabbed hold of him again and Alex felt an extraordinary sense of lightness as all the fears and doubts of the past couple of months were wiped away to be replaced by the knowledge that he had been right all along, that Jack hadn't been killed and that he had found her. Apart from the strange uniform, which didn't suit her at all, she looked just the same as always with her tangled red hair and her wide smile. She was a little thinner perhaps and, with a jolt of unease, Alex noticed an old bruise, fading beside one of her eyes. But it was her. She was alive. That was all that mattered.

"I've missed you so much, Jack." The words came tumbling out. "After what happened, I thought you were—" He had to stop himself. He couldn't go on.

"I know. But never say die. We're together now!" She paused. "And we're still in trouble!"

It was true. They couldn't stay where they were. They both realized it at the same moment. It was time to move.

"We have to go somewhere safer," Jack said. "They patrol the corridors all the time. We can go to my room."

"What are you doing here, Jack?"

"God knows, Alex. The whole thing is a nightmare – or it was until you showed up." She poked her head out of the door and checked that the corridor was clear. "Follow me! I'm just up here."

Signalling, she hurried back the way she had come. Alex followed her, his head spinning. Why was she here? Why was she dressed like a nurse? How had she even got here from the South of France? There were a hundred questions he wanted to ask her but he knew he would have to wait until they were out of sight. Together, they crept past a series of doors – old offices that had been turned into sleeping quarters for all fifty-two children. Alex saw a dining hall at the far end with trestle tables and simple wooden seats. It reminded him how hungry he was. But before they reached it, Jack opened a door and ushered him into a bedroom, a little larger than the one he had visited. There was an adult-sized bed, a wardrobe, a dressing table with a mirror. This was where she was staying.

She closed the door then embraced him for a third time, holding him close and saying nothing. When they finally separated, he noticed that he had left black smudge marks on her uniform and glanced at himself in the mirror. She was right. He did look terrible: ragged and scrawny, with his hair, his face, his clothes all covered in soot from the tunnel.

"Are you all right, Alex?" she exclaimed. "I've been so worried about you. Ever since Siwa..."

"What happened in Siwa?" Alex asked. "I thought you were killed..."

"I know." She was about to explain, then stopped herself. "Do you need something to eat or drink?" she asked. "You're very thin. Who's been looking after you?"

"I've been with Sabina and her parents," Alex said. "And yes. I'm starving. Can you get me a sandwich or something?"

"Wait here." Jack went to the door. "I want to make sure the children are asleep. Some of them are terrified, poor things. Then I'll get you something from the kitchen. It'll just take me a couple of minutes." She pointed at a second door leading out of the room. "There's a bathroom in there. There's no plumbing but I've got bottles of water..." She ran over to Alex, hugged him one last time, and left.

Alex went into the bathroom. There was a sink and a supply of water in five-litre bottles. He had no change of clothes but at least he was able to wash the soot out of his hair and clear his eyes. He drank half a litre of water too, then went back into the bedroom and sat on the bed. He wasn't tired. Finding Jack had energized him in a way he wouldn't have thought possible. Right now, the fact that he was a prisoner in a compound surrounded by armed guards didn't mean anything. He would fly out of here if he had to. Nothing was going to stop him.

He was still sitting there, a smile on his face, when Jack returned clutching sandwiches, fruit juice and chocolate biscuits. "This is all we have," she explained. "There's no proper kitchen."

"It's perfect, thanks." Alex grabbed a sandwich, noticing that it was egg mayonnaise. She had even chosen his favourite. He wolfed it down. "How much time do we have, Jack? There was a guard at the door when I came in. Are there any others?"

Jack shook her head. "There's only one way in and out of this building. They've had a guard sitting there the whole time. The Grimaldis brought me here to look after the children. They didn't want to have a riot on their hands. But they don't trust me. As soon as this job's over, I don't think I'm getting out of here alive."

"I'm here now."

"I know. I know. I still can't believe it. Tell me you're not on your own. Tell me you've got Mrs Jones and the whole of MI6 waiting outside."

"I am on my own and they don't even know where I am."

"Alex!"

"I'll work something out, Jack. I promise you. But first of all, I've got to know how you got here. What happened in Siwa? I know they tricked me with the film of you being killed but that still doesn't explain how you ended up dressed as a nurse in the middle of Wales."

"And I want to know how you found me, Alex. I can't believe you managed to work out my email. I wanted to tell you where I was but I didn't get the chance—"

Alex held up a hand – and a half-eaten sandwich. "We don't have a lot of time, Jack," he said. "You start at the beginning. Then I'll tell you my side of it. And then we'll work out what we're going to do."

"OK." There were two chairs in the room. Jack

rested one against the door to stop anyone entering. "Just in case..." she said. "Nobody has come in here yet. But if they do, you can hide in the bathroom."

She sat down on the other chair. Alex was sitting on the bed, drinking orange juice through a straw. At last she began.

"It still makes me ill thinking about Siwa," she said. "I felt awful because I thought it was my fault that you got captured ... I mean, you only went there to rescue me and I blamed myself for getting you into trouble. And I couldn't believe those two creeps ... how horrible they were. Razim and Julius Grief."

"They're both dead," Alex said.

"I heard. All I can say is, it's an improvement." She drew a breath. Just as Alex had discovered when he was in San Francisco, it was still painful remembering what had happened. "I tried to escape," she went on. "I thought I was being so clever. I managed to get out of a window and I stole a Land Rover and I was driving into the desert to get help when it just stopped. There must have been something in the engine. They flicked a switch and stopped it by remote control.

"So I was sitting there like an idiot, trying to get it started again, when these men appeared and dragged me out. I tried to fight but they were too strong for me and there was nothing I could do. About five seconds later, the whole car blew up. It

made me sick, realizing I had just been inside it.
I mean, I'd been sitting on a bomb for goodness'
sake! After that, they dragged me back to my cell
but this time there was a man standing outside the
window so I couldn't climb out again.

"I don't know how much time went by. I didn't
have my watch and I was half out of my mind,
worrying about you. But after a while the door
opened and two men came in. Actually, it could
have been one man carrying a mirror. Talk about
peas in a pod! They were twins, obviously. But
they were also identically dressed in old-fashioned
safari suits. They would have looked ridiculous,
except for the fact that they were clearly so dangerous. I saw that at once.

"'Miss Starbright...?' one of them said. He could
have been introducing himself to me at a cocktail
party.

"'We are the Grimaldis.' It was the other one
who finished the sentence. That's how they talk."

"I know," Alex said. "We've met."

"Anyway, they said they had a job for me. They
didn't ask me if I was interested or anything like
that. They just looked me over, nodded at each
other and walked out. I was shouting after them,
asking about you, but the door slammed shut and I
was left on my own.

"There was only one thing I could do. I had
to leave you a message in case you came looking
for me and I'd already managed to get one of the

screws out of my bed. I used the point to scratch their name into the wall."

"I saw it!" Alex said. "I went to your cell. I found it under the bed."

"I would have written more but I didn't have time. The door opened again and two of the guards came in. They handcuffed me and dragged me outside. There was an SUV parked in the courtyard. They bundled me in and off we went.

"So that was how I met the Brothers Grimm. Eduardo was driving and Giovanni was in the front seat – or maybe it was the other way round. I don't know. The two of them drove off and as it turned out, we were going to be together for the next seven hours which, I can tell you, felt like a very long time indeed. We drove all the way to Alexandria ... through the desert to a place called Mersa Matruh and then along the coast. In a way, they were as horrible as Razim and Julius. If you ask me, they're completely mad. They're like one complete nutcase in two bodies.

"At least they didn't hurt me. In fact they were quite polite. They told me they had been sent by Scorpia to check up on Razim and to see how things were going. They didn't much like him, by the way. They thought they should have been put in charge. But at the same time, they were planning an operation of their own, something they called..."

"Steel Claw," Alex said.

"Right. They didn't tell me what it was while we were in the car but they did say that Razim had been planning to kill me – simply to hurt you – and he would have gone ahead with it if the two of them hadn't turned up at just the right time. You see, they needed someone to keep control of a bunch of children ... a nurse or a matron, I suppose. Somehow they found out that I'd been a nanny once and that was enough for them. They told Razim they wanted to take me away and I don't think he was too happy about it. But they must have persuaded him because off I went and here I am."

She smiled. "I can't tell you how happy I am to see you again, Alex."

"Me too." Alex tore open a packet of biscuits. He had eaten four of the sandwiches. "Go on!"

"They took me to a boat which they had moored at Alexandria. It was called *Quicksilver*. I have to admit that actually it was quite beautiful ... well, not the part of it where I was locked up. That was in the hold. There were two men who looked after me. One of them was Mr Stallone and the other was called Skunk. They weren't very nice."

"I've met them too," Alex said.

"Where are they?

"One of them is here. I saw him at the train. I don't know about the other."

"They were both pretty mean." Jack sighed. "I'm amazed how many really evil people there are in the world. How did they get to be that way?"

"I've often wondered about that," Alex said.

"They kept me in a tiny cabin and for the next few days we didn't move at all. We just stayed there in Alexandria. Then the twins came to see me again. They told me that Razim had been killed and that you had escaped from Egypt. In a way, they were quite amused about it. I told you – they didn't like him. I begged them to send a message to you, to tell you that I was still alive, but they weren't interested. The next day we left and as we slipped out to sea I had this awful feeling that I'd never see you again. I thought I was leaving my whole life behind.

"I had no idea where we were going but after a while I could tell we were heading north because it was getting cooler. Finally, we arrived off the coast of France, near Marseille, and we stayed there for ages. Giovanni and Eduardo went ashore and that was the last I saw of them until I arrived here – but I was still kept prisoner on the boat. They told me they were taking me to England and they also told me about Steel Claw. They were so proud of themselves. They were going to make millions ... even if it meant terrorizing a bunch of ten-year-olds.

"About a week later, we moved up the coast to Saint-Tropez and moored in the harbour. A woman came on board. I think she was Russian or Serbian, but I never saw her because she was in the luxury cabin while I was down below. I was still tearing my hair out, locked up on my own.

But one evening the younger one, Skunk, made a mistake. I wasn't let out on the deck in case I shouted for help. But they allowed me to have a shower twice a week and he had to take me there. Anyway, he got distracted and somehow he managed to forget about me for a couple of minutes. I couldn't believe it when I came out of the shower room and saw that there was nobody waiting for me. My first thought was to get off the ship but that wasn't going to be as easy as it sounds. All the main doors were kept locked and there was always someone out on the deck.

"I sneaked down the corridor and the first thing I saw was an open door and a cabin with a laptop on a table. That was all I needed. If I got a message to you, you could contact Mrs Jones or someone and that would be the end of this whole horrible business. So I slipped inside and sat down at the laptop. It was connected to a local wireless network. I began to type.

"I'd only written three words when the door crashed open and suddenly Skunk was there. He slammed down the lid of the laptop. He almost smashed my fingers. He was furious. Then he hit me." She pointed to the bruise on her face. "It was a scary moment. I really thought he was going to kill me, and he might have done if the brothers hadn't needed me. As it was, I don't think he ever told them what had happened. He was too afraid of them. I was taken back to my cabin and I've been wondering ever since if you'd got the message and what you made of it."

"I knew it was from you," Alex said. "It led me to you." He shrugged. "It just took me a little longer than I thought..."

"I was so cross with myself. If I could have told you the name of the boat, it would have made everything so much easier. But I never got the chance. I was locked up all the time after that and then one day – actually, it was the middle of the night – they dragged me off *Quicksilver* and transferred me to a huge truck carrying olive oil into England. That's how they smuggled me into the country ... tied up and gagged in the back. They must have driven me up to one of the Channel ports and brought me over in a ferry.

"And that's about it, really." Jack had been talking for a while. She looked tired but she was still smiling. "You wanted to know what I was doing here. The children from Linton Hall arrived this afternoon. I had to get all their names and addresses plus their parents' names and phone numbers. I had to give them rooms. Then I got them something to eat. A lot of the younger ones are very upset and I've tried to look after them. That's what the Grimaldis wanted me for."

She stopped.

"And now it's your turn. What about you? I want to know where you've been and how you got here and why you're on your own..."

Alex was about to reply when he heard footsteps walking down the corridor, approaching the room. They stopped outside. Alex and Jack exchanged a quick look, then moved at the same time. Alex slipped into the bathroom while Jack snatched the chair away from the door. As an afterthought, she gathered up Alex's sandwich and biscuit wrappers too. She had just thrown them under the bed when the door opened and Frankie Stallone walked in. She hadn't seen him since he had kept her prisoner on board *Quicksilver* and she winced at the sight of his face with its multiple burns.

"Miss Starbright," he muttered.

"What do you want?" Jack stood in front of him, purposefully barring his way.

Stallone looked past her suspiciously. "Did I hear you talking just now?" he demanded.

"I was saying my prayers before bed."

The room seemed empty. Stallone nodded. "We need you to get one of the kids up at seven o'clock tomorrow morning," he said. He handed her a slip of paper. "This one."

Jack took the piece of paper. "Why?"

"It seems that some of the parents are having second thoughts about paying for their little darlings. So we're going to shoot one of them to make an example. And we're going to film it. That should encourage them all to think again."

"You're sick!"

"You should be careful how you talk to me, Miss

Starbright." Stallone glared at her. The red smears where his eyebrows had been twitched slightly. "All we want is the money. If they're going to argue about it, that's their look-out. Get the kid out of bed. Get him dressed. Bring him outside. And if you're very good, we won't make you watch."

He left, closing the door behind him.

Jack waited until his footsteps had disappeared down the corridor. When she turned round, Alex was back in the room. "Did you hear?" she asked.

"Every word."

"Seven o'clock." She looked at her watch. "That's twelve hours from now."

Alex nodded, his mind already racing ahead. "I don't suppose there are any phones anywhere?" he said.

"All the kids were searched. They had their phones taken off them. Anyway, there's no mobile signal here. They have Internet, I think, but I don't have the access code."

"There was a security man travelling with them on the coach. Do you know where he is?"

"Yes. There's another accommodation block over on the other side. I can show you. It's where the Grimaldis hang out. The security guy is called Ted Philby and he's locked in a sort of outhouse just behind. Sector Five – that's what they call it. There's a teacher with him – and also the coach driver. But you need to watch out for her, Alex. She's part of it."

"I know," Alex said. "I met her husband." He thought for a moment but he already knew what he had to do. "We have to get the children out of here. Maybe we can get out by train. If not, there's the coach."

"There's no road."

"Then we'll drive along the tracks."

"In the dark?"

Alex remembered what he had just heard. Sitting here with Jack, he had thought he had time to work out a plan, but in an instant everything had changed. "We have no choice, Jack," he said. "We're leaving here tonight."

BREAK-OUT

Almost at once they had a problem.

The guard had walked away when Alex first arrived at the accommodation block and he had been able to slip in easily. But now as he crept back to the corner and peered round to the main door, Alex saw that his luck had run out. Frankie Stallone had taken his place. He was sitting there reading the magazine that the other man had left behind. His hand was curled loosely round the cover and Alex could clearly see the flame tattoo stretching out over the back. He had a gun, lying inches away.

He was smoking a cigarette, holding it in his left hand. There was a walkie-talkie strapped to his chest. There was no question that he was fully alert. Even seeing him made Alex's skin crawl, reminding him of what had happened at Needle Point. There was a fresh bandage on his neck where Alex had stabbed him with the nail. Hearing his voice in Jack's room was one thing. But seeing him in the flesh was quite another. How could Alex get past?

There seemed to be no way that he could approach the front door. The passageway was wide and well lit and it would be impossible to cover the area that separated them without being seen. The moment Alex turned the corner, he would be in full sight and the man would gun him down before he had taken two paces. Somehow, he and Jack would have to distract him so that they could get close enough to take action. They still had the chisel with its heavy wooden handle. But they were up against a professional gangster, a man who wouldn't hesitate to kill.

Alex signalled, and he and Jack made their way back until they were out of earshot. Even so, they still whispered to each other. Alex was aware of the line of closed doors that ran along the corridor behind them and the children tucked away in their cells. He wondered which one of them had been chosen by the Grimaldis for execution. It wasn't a question he wanted to consider. He was going to save them – all of them. There was going to be no compromise.

"Are you sure there's no other way out of the building?" he asked.

Jack shook her head. "I've already looked. All the windows have got bars on and there are no other doors. This is the only way." She thought for a moment. "Give me the chisel!"

"Why?"

"I can take him out. I'll whack him with it." She thought for a moment. "Or stab him."

"No." Alex shook his head. Jack might be fast but he remembered what had happened at Needle Point and knew that Stallone would be faster – and he wasn't going to put her in danger, not having found her at last. "I'll do it," he said.

"You can't, Alex. The passageway's too long. If he sees you, you won't have a chance and this time he'll kill you for real. But I can take him a cup of tea. That will allow me to get close. And I can hide the chisel under the tray..."

Kill you for real. Of course, Stallone thought Alex was dead. He had actually seen him drown. Suddenly Alex had an idea. All he had to do was neutralize Stallone for two or three seconds and that would allow Jack the time to strike out. He remembered the bathroom with the five-litre bottles of water. He looked at the corridor with its freshly whitewashed walls. He smiled to himself. Would it work? Yes. He was sure of it.

Ten minutes later, Frankie Stallone looked up as the woman, Miss Starbright, approached, holding a tray with a cup of tea and a few biscuits. She was smiling but he was suspicious at once. In fact, he was always suspicious. It went with his line of work and over the years it had helped keep him alive. The woman was a prisoner. His bosses had already told him that he was to kill her the moment the ransom had been paid. The two of them had barely spoken up until now, so why was she being nice to him?

She stopped next to the table, the tray still in her hands. "I brought you some tea."

"I don't want tea," Stallone said. His hand with the tattoo was stretched out on the table in a way that looked completely casual but he knew that he could snatch up the gun, aim and fire in less than a second. "I thought you said you were going to bed."

"There's something I want to ask you first," Jack said.

"What's that?"

"I have a lot of money in my bank account. Over two thousand pounds. If I paid you, would you help me? I just want to leave. If you let me go, I'll give you everything I have."

So that was what it was all about! She was scared. He could see that now. And she wanted to bribe him to let her go. Stallone sneered at her. Who did she think he was? She said she had a lot of money but two thousand pounds was nothing to him! It was pathetic...

He was about to tell her to get lost when he saw it. A movement in the shadows. He looked past her and for a moment he forgot everything. Even the gun went out of his mind. It was impossible. And yet it was there, standing at the end of the corridor. He had to believe it. It was in front of his eyes.

It was the ghost of the boy he had killed.

Frankie Stallone didn't believe in ghosts. It was

true that he sometimes saw the faces of the people he had killed: in moments of idleness, in his sleep. There were plenty of them. Some of them had died pleading with him. Some of them had looked shocked. But he was able to get rid of them easily enough. He just had to remind himself that they were figments of his imagination and they would disappear.

This was different. The boy was standing quite still, half naked and with no shoes, at the end of the corridor. Frankie knew he was dead. He had seen him plunge into the Mediterranean, dragged down by the weight attached to his foot. There was no possible way he could have survived. But now the boy was staring at him with empty eyes. He was completely white – the colour of the drowned. And there was water dripping from his hair, down his face, off his shoulders and arms. Frankie was gripped by something he had never felt before. It was sheer terror. It paralysed him.

It might have taken him three seconds to work out how he had been tricked. First of all, Alex had stripped off his shirt, shoes and socks. Then he had rubbed his body against the newly whitewashed walls, transferring the paint onto his own skin. Finally, as Jack had turned the corner, carrying the tray, he had poured water over his head. He had waited until she had started speaking and then he had stepped forward, making no sound. It felt odd. He was the target. He could be shot dead in an instant. But his best protection was not to move.

It had worked. Three seconds was all Jack needed. The bald man was sitting in front of her, his eyes wide. She saw that he had forgotten her and, dropping the tray, she swung her fist with all her strength. Her fingers were curled round the chisel and she lashed out. After what he had done to Alex, she had been very tempted to use the metal blade. She was quite sure the world would be a much better place without him. But it was the wooden handle that slammed into his skull, and with a grunt he fell to one side. Jack lifted the chisel, still prepared to stab him if she had to. There was no need. He was out cold.

Alex had run forward, ready to help Jack if necessary. He saw from her smile that it had worked as he had hoped. The side of the gangster's head was starting to swell – another injury to go with the others. Jack reached into her pockets and took out several strips of torn sheet. Quickly, the two of them tied up his hands and feet, also forcing a gag into his mouth. Alex knew it would be a while before he woke up. He briefly remembered Needle Point, the camera turning. He didn't really care if Stallone never woke up at all.

They were about to drag the body away when Alex noticed the gun on the table. He swept it up and slipped it into the waistband of his trousers.

"Are you sure you want that?" Jack whispered.

"Why not?"

"I don't think you should have a gun, Alex. It doesn't feel right."

"I promise I won't use it, Jack," Alex said, adding under his breath, "until I have to."

They dragged Stallone over to the storage cupboard where the two of them had met. They both knew what they had to do. Jack was going to wake the children and prepare them for what lay ahead. Alex had the more dangerous task. He had to free the security man and the drama teacher. He would need their help if he was to have any hope of starting the coach. Jack and Alex gave each other a quick high five.

"Good luck."

"You too."

Alex had put his clothes back on. He took the gun and the walkie-talkie, then snatched up the chisel. Finally he slipped out into the night.

Once again the compound was criss-crossed by powerful beams of light, but Alex easily slipped through them. He was full of confidence since finding Jack. He also knew that there was no going back now. Quite soon, someone would discover that Frankie Stallone had disappeared and at that moment, the element of surprise would be gone. It was a warm evening with a strange stillness in the air, as if there was about to be a storm. But there were no clouds. Looking up, Alex saw a mass of stars in an ink-black sky. The moon was reflected in the steel lines of the railway, which stretched into the distance like some sort of magical pathway. The tunnel was several miles away and out of sight, although Alex could make out the shape of the hills that rose up, surrounding them. Safety lay on the other side.

He crouched down behind an oil drum as two guards walked past, heading for the steam train which was sitting beside the platform with its tender full of coal, quietly puffing. That was one good thing about the abandoned coke works: there was no shortage of hiding places. Alex's thoughts were already racing ahead. He needed to give the Grimaldis something to think about while he and Jack led the children out of here. He had a gun now ... and – he had checked – six bullets. How could he use them? Briefly, Alex considered sneaking into the building that the two brothers occupied. Two shots and it would all be over. But, like Jack, he knew he couldn't do it. Despite all the things that had happened to him, he was no assassin, and anyway, there were all the other guards to consider. It might be the start of a bloodbath.

He had another idea. Briefly he weighed it in his mind, balancing it against any other options – then smiled to himself. Yes. It might work. He waited until the two guards were out of sight, then crept over to the shed where he had found the chisel. He knew that time was against him but this would just take a few minutes. Sulphuric acid.

BREAK-OUT

The question was – how long would it take to eat through rusting metal? Well, that was certainly something that had never come up in science class.

Ten minutes later, he was approaching the block where Giovanni and Eduardo were staying. It was easy enough to find: the only brand-new building in the entire compound. There were no lights on behind the windows. The twins must have gone to bed. Nor did there seem to be any guards around at the moment. At least, that was what Alex thought. He froze. There was somebody outside after all, lying face upward in a wheel-barrow, hands hanging limply towards the ground. Drunk? Asleep? It took him about half a second to realize the answer was neither.

With a dry mouth and an uneasy feeling in the pit of his stomach, Alex drew closer. In the beams of light, it was easy to make out the drab, brown hair – lifeless in every sense – and the heavy shoulders, the stout legs. It was a woman. Bizarrely, she had her handbag resting on her lap. Although he had never met her, Alex knew that he was looking at the coach driver, Jane Vosper, another victim of the brothers and their twisted plan.

He didn't want to go near but there was one thing he had to do. Alex went over to the wheelbarrow, doing his best not to look at her face. He was interested in her handbag. He clicked it open and looked inside. And there they were, exactly as he had hoped! He reached in and took out a bunch

325

of keys. One of them was an ignition key, clearly marked with the Mercedes-Benz logo. He slipped the whole bunch into his pocket. Now all he had to do was to find the security man and the teacher and they could drive the coach out of here.

The outhouse that Jack had described was a short distance from the new building, close to the perimeter fence. Alex wasn't surprised to see a man standing guard outside, a machine gun cradled in his arms. He backed away. He couldn't risk using the gun. If a single shot was fired, the entire compound would be alerted. But he had another idea.

He pressed the button on the walkie-talkie that he had taken from Stallone and held it close to his lips. He spoke in a low voice. "Sector Five – do you copy?"

In front of him, he saw the guard reach for his own walkie-talkie. "This is Sector Five, over."

"We have a disturbance in Sector One. Request backup."

"Heading there now. Over."

Alex had no idea where Sector One was but he hoped it was far away. He reckoned he would have a few minutes before the guard discovered that something was wrong and hopefully he wouldn't realize that he had been deliberately tricked. He watched as the man walked away, then Alex crept through the shadows until he reached the door. The outhouse was made of brick with a wooden door that was fastened with two sliding bolts but no lock. Alex had brought the chisel with him in case he needed it to break in, but this was going to be easier than he'd thought. He slid the bolts across, opened the door and entered.

The room was completely bare. There were two men slumped on the concrete floor, surrounded by water bottles and a scattering of sandwich wrappers. One was small and crumpled with thinning brown hair, dressed in a suit that was hanging off him. The other was younger and tougher, with the square shoulders and cropped hair of an ex-soldier. The drama teacher and the security man. It was easy to tell which was which. They both leapt up as Alex came into the room.

"Who the hell are you?" the security man demanded.

"I'm Alex Rider," Alex said. "Are you Ted Philby?"

"That's right. Deputy head of school security." Philby examined Alex suspiciously. "Where have you come from? You weren't on the coach."

"I can't explain right now. We don't have any time. I distracted the guard but he'll be back any moment."

"Whoa! Wait a minute!" Philby wasn't moving. "I'm not going anywhere until you've told me how you got here and shown me your ID."

Alex's heart sank. He'd met people like this before. Philby was taking charge. He was a fully paid-up member of the school security team – the deputy head no less – and if Alex reminded him that actually, the school hadn't been secure at all, it wouldn't help. "I haven't got ID," he said.

"Then how do I know that this isn't a trick? For all I know, you could be working for them!"

Philby didn't even know who "they" were. Alex was about to back out and slam the door when the drama teacher came to his rescue. "I really think we should go with Alex, Mr Wilby," he said.

"It's Philby."

"Whatever." The teacher nodded at Alex. "My name is Jason Green. Have you seen the children? Are they all right?"

"They're fine. They're getting ready to leave." Alex turned to Philby. He could feel the weight of the gun in his back pocket and hoped he wouldn't have to use it to threaten the man. "Are you coming or not?"

"You've got the kids?"

"Yes."

"Then I'm coming. They're my responsibility. And from now on, you do what I tell you. All right?"

"Sure."

There was no time to argue. The three of them went outside and Alex slid the bolts back across the door. With a bit of luck, the guard wouldn't notice that anything was wrong when he returned. He might even forget about the message he had received. Philby was looking around him, suddenly aware that he had no idea where the children actually were.

"They're over there." Alex nudged him and pointed.

"Good. Follow me."

Keeping close together, the three of them made their way back.

Meanwhile, Jack had been busy. She had got all fifty-two children out of bed and told them to make as little noise as possible as they got dressed. The children were scared and they had lots of questions but they were also used to doing what they were told. By the time Alex and the two men had returned, they were lined up in the corridor, quietly waiting for whatever was going to happen next.

Ted Philby had led Alex and the drama teacher through the main door and along the passageway, as if it was he who had managed to break them out of prison, getting rid of the guards at the same time. He took one look at Jack Starbright, still in her nurse's uniform, and decided to ignore her. He raised a hand to the waiting children. "Hi, kids," he said. "You don't have to worry. I'm in control of the situation and I'm going to get you out of here."

Jack glanced at Alex. Alex quietly shook his head.

"You just have to do everything I tell you. You know who I am. You've probably seen me in the Hub. I've been trained for this."

There was a long silence. The children were silent and pale in the soft light of the corridor, standing together in pairs. They did not look convinced.

Jack stepped forward. "So what exactly is your plan?" she asked.

"Who are you?"

"I'm with him." Jack pointed at Alex.

"Right." Philby stroked his chin, considering his options. "The first priority is to move these kids and find somewhere for them to hole up. My guess is that we're in Cornwall or Devon."

"We're in Wales," Jack told him.

"Well ... that doesn't matter. We have to bust out of here. We don't have any transport, so that means we're going to be on foot."

"We have the coach," Alex said.

"Yeah. But the coach needs keys."

"I have those too." Alex produced the keys he had taken from the dead woman. For a fleeting moment, he saw her, lying on her back, stretched out in the wheelbarrow.

"That's very good," the drama teacher muttered. He turned to the children. "We're going to be all right, boys and girls. We're in safe hands."

"Thank you." Philby assumed that the teacher had been referring to him. "The coach is out of the question," he went on. "First of all, we're never going to be able to reach it without being seen. Secondly, it's noisy. The moment we start the engine, these people are going to come running. No. We need to get out there into the hills. We need to put as many miles between ourselves and this place as we can."

"Wait a minute," Jack said. She went over to Philby and spoke in a quiet voice. "That's crazy. Some of the children are as young as nine. They're already terrified and most of them are exhausted. Even assuming we can cut our way through the fence, how far do you think they're going to get? We have no idea where we are. It's dark. You should listen to Alex—"

Philby cut in before she could continue. "Lady – I don't know who you are but I'm a professional. He's just a kid. OK?" He turned to the children. "We're leaving now!"

Nobody moved.

Then one of the children put up his hand. Alex recognized the boy he had spoken to when he first arrived. "I don't want to go with you," he said. "I want to go with Alex."

There was a murmur of agreement along the line.

Philby scowled. "You don't get any choice in the matter, son. I'm calling the shots."

And that was when the sirens went off, echoing across the compound, howling into the sky. Perhaps the guard had returned and discovered that that his prisoners had gone. Perhaps it was Frankie Stallone who had failed to report in. Either way, it was too late for any further discussion. The alarm had been raised.

Alex stepped forward.

"I want everyone to grab a pillow," he said. "Then follow me."

DOWNHILL ALL THE WAY

"Pillows?"

Ted Philby was standing in front of Alex. He was several inches taller than him and quite a lot heavier. He had fallen into a combat stance and Jack wondered if he was about to start a physical fight. Meanwhile, Alex stood his ground. Outside, the sirens were still blasting. The children had disappeared back to their rooms. "Pillows aren't going to protect the kids from gunfire."

"I'm not going to argue with you, Mr Philby," Alex said. "We're leaving now. I need you to drive the coach. I think it's the only way out of here. If you won't do that, Jack will."

"I can drive it," Jack said, although she wondered if she would be able to manage such a massive vehicle as a school coach. She noted that Alex hadn't handed the security man the keys.

"The coach is parked right next to the train," Philby said. "It's in plain sight ... in open ground. How are you proposing to get anywhere near? Are you going to hide behind the pillows? Is that your big idea?"

Alex didn't answer. The schoolchildren were reappearing, each one of them holding a pillow made of thick foam, which they had taken from their beds. Jack was pleased that they had all decided to rally round Alex. They were young and they were afraid but they believed in him.

Alex ignored the security man. "Let's go," he said.

He led the way to the main door. There was activity all over the coke works, with men running in different directions, shouting orders at one another as if they had forgotten the walkie-talkies they all carried. The lights had come on in the block which Eduardo and Giovanni Grimaldi occupied. Alex swept his eyes across the tangled pipework, the huge tower with its slanting conveyor belt, the steel chimneys, the locomotive and the coach. For the moment, it seemed that the guards were concentrating their efforts on Sector Five, the area where Philby and Jason Green had been kept prisoner. The guard must have returned to find them missing and that was why he had raised the alarm. So far, it hadn't occurred to the twins or to anyone else that the schoolchildren might be trying to escape. That would change soon enough. They had maybe two minutes to make their move before they were discovered.

Alex looked back at the children, crowded

together in the corridor, still in pairs. "I want you all to stay close together and look after each other," he instructed them. "There may be gunfire but don't be scared. Remember that these people need you alive. You've got a teacher with you. You've got Jack. And you've got the deputy head of security. So let's go."

He stepped outside and ran the short distance to a cylindrical gas tank which he had noticed earlier and which would provide cover for all of them before they set off on the next part of the journey. The worst of it was that they were fully exposed for the first twenty paces and Alex counted every one of them, worried that someone would hear the crunch of so many footsteps on gravel. In fact, the noise of the sirens drowned out any sound and it occurred to Alex that the Grimaldis had made another mistake. Their own security system was working against them. Even so, he hardly dared breathe until the last of the children – two girls in pigtails, both of them clutching their pillows – had arrived, with Jack bringing up the rear.

Meanwhile, Ted Philby took in his surroundings. The station platform with the locomotive train was directly in front of them. It was on the other side of the retort house, the concrete tower which rose fifty metres over their heads, blocking their way. The coach was parked right next to the locomotive, facing the same direction, as if the two technologies, one old and one new, were in competition with each other. If Alex really was determined to reach the coach – and Philby still thought it was suicide – he should go straight ahead. Instead, he veered over to the right, actually steering the children away from the relative safety of the platform.

Philby caught up with Alex and hissed, "You're going the wrong way! The coach is over there!"

"We can't go that way," Alex said. "Look!"

He pointed. There were two more guards, both armed with machine guns, positioned high up on a steel bridge that ran across the compound. They alone had remained where they were when the alarm broke out. They had a commanding view of the ground below them – and that included the open space beside the coach. If Alex tried to take the children that way, they would be mown down before they could get anywhere near.

"OK." Philby scowled. "That's exactly what I told you. We can't get anywhere near the coach. So let's do this my way. Out through the fence..."

But Alex was already moving. He had seen more guards moving through the latticework of light and shadow, approaching the accommodation block they had just left, finally coming to check up on their most valuable prisoners. It was time to get out of here.

He ran forward, not heading for the platform but the base of the retort tower and the door that led into it. Alex was gambling everything on the next few moments. If the door was locked, he would have to use the chisel – or worse still, the gun – to break it open and that would not just waste precious seconds, it might alert the guards as to where they were. He reached it ahead of the others and grabbed the handle. With a sense of relief, he felt it turn. The door was stiff but it opened. He went inside.

He found himself in a vast brick chamber, with light shafting in through windows that rose all the way to the ceiling, at least eight storeys above his head. It was impossible to say how this building had once operated. Everything was black. The floor and the walls were covered with soot that hadn't been touched for years. The very air stank of it. There were great lumps of machinery clinging to the brickwork, sitting on brackets. Pipes big enough for a man to crawl through ran past steel ovens suspended over what must have been a furnace. Alex guessed that this was where the whole process had taken place. The coal was brought in by steam trains. It was carried up the conveyor belt into the tower. It was heated and turned into coke with all the gases and other chemicals being separated before they were whisked away to other parts of the compound. He had arrived at what had once been the flaming heart of Smoke City. But the fires had gone out long ago and all that remained was blackened and dead.

There was only one thing he had been hoping to

see and there it was in front of him: a spiral staircase leading all the way to the loading platform at
the top. It was made of steel, with a low rail twisting round and round. It looked safe. It would need
to be, to take the weight of fifty-six people.

Alex waited until all the children were assembled and Jack had closed the door behind them.
The sirens were still wailing but they sounded more
distant. The walls were thick, almost soundproof,
and he could speak without fear of being overheard.

"Is anyone afraid of heights?" he asked.

Quite a few of the children looked doubtful but
nobody put up their hand.

"We have to get to the coach without being
seen," Alex explained. "This is the best option.
There's a slide that goes all the way to the platform next to the railway. That's what we'll use.
We're going to sit on the pillows and slide down ...
just like a ride in a funfair. If you're nervous, don't
look down. I'll go first to make sure it's all right."

Jack was listening to all this in amazement.
She had secretly wondered why Alex had brought
them all here and had very nearly challenged him.
Now she understood. The conveyor belt couldn't
be seen from outside: it was enclosed by two walls
and a ceiling made out of sheets of corrugated
iron. Alex could use it to smuggle the children
out and the guards wouldn't know what was happening. Once they had reached the platform, they
would be concealed behind the steam engine and

they could slip round to reach the coach. She looked up, craning her neck. The top of the conveyor belt was a very long way away, at least two hundred steps, but she was sure they could do it. Briefly, she met Alex's eyes and nodded at him. She had never seen him like this before. Perhaps it was because he was getting older but he seemed more confident than ever.

Ted Philby wasn't impressed. He had already reached the metal staircase and was staring up with a frown on his face. "I'll go first," he said, "if you really want to go through with this. But if you ask me, you're going to get the whole lot of us killed."

He began to climb. Alex went next, then half the children, then the drama teacher, the rest of the children and finally Jack, her white nurse's uniform already very much the worse for wear. The steel steps shuddered slightly as they took the weight of so many people and soot showered down. But the staircase was securely bolted to the wall. It held. It was still a lot further than Jack had thought. She had counted one hundred and ninety steps when she made the mistake of looking down. Her stomach lurched. It would be all too easy to slip and tumble over the handrail and, falling from this height, she would be smashed to pieces on the floor below.

The sirens had stopped. There was a rattle of machine-gun fire from outside the tower. The children froze on the spiral staircase, the ones at the front high above the ones who were behind. A few of them began to whimper.

"It's all right," Alex called down. "Either it's a false alarm or they're shooting at each other. They don't know we're here. And we're almost at the top."

It was true. They set off again and a minute later, Alex turned the last corner and reached a metal platform with a square hatch in front of it. Ted Philby was already there, looking down the long, black slide that led to the platform. Once, machinery would have kept the conveyor belt moving slowly upwards, carrying the coal up to the top, where men would be waiting to shovel it away. Now it was silent and still. And steep. It disappeared into blackness.

"Great work, Alex," Philby sneered. "Just take a look at that! You come out the other end too fast, you're going to break both your legs."

"I thought you said you'd go first," Alex muttered.

"No way. This is your crazy idea. You try it out."

Philby stood aside and Alex edged past. He sat down, then had a last thought. "I need something to sit on," he said.

The security man swore under his breath, then stripped off his jacket and handed it to Alex. "Use this."

"Thanks." Alex folded it underneath him.

"Don't thank me. You're still going to get your-self killed."

Alex stared into the darkness. "I'll give you a

signal if it's clear. Then send the rest down."

He pushed himself forward. At once he began to slide, picking up speed very quickly. The conveyor belt was made of leather, or some sort of thick canvas, and apart from a few scattered pieces of coal, the surface was completely smooth. The jacket protected him from friction burns. There had been some light at the top and he could make out a very faint square at the end, but the middle was completely dark and as he shot down, Alex got a sense that he was being swallowed up, the corrugated-iron walls rushing past on both sides and over his head. It was only when it was too late that he remembered what Ted Philby had said. If he didn't slow down, he might do himself serious damage. There were no soft cushions waiting for him at the end, nothing but hard cement. Alex was half lying on his back, the stale breeze whipping across his face. He stretched out with his hands and dug his heels in. It made no difference. He knew that he was out of control. He couldn't see. His face was once again covered in soot. It was working its way into his eyes.

And then he was spat out into the fresh air. For a horrible moment, he felt himself falling with nothing beneath him. Then the backs of his legs and his shoulders came into contact with some sort of ramp, which he recognized, seconds later, as the pyramid of broken coal he had seen before. He was sliding down it, the loose pieces slowing his progress. By the time he hit the platform beside the railway, he was barely moving at all. He got to his feet, dusting himself down. He had made it – and in one piece.

Half a dozen guards had arrived at the accommodation block where the children had been held. Alex could hear them quite distinctly. But he was hidden behind the coal pile at the far end of the platform. He climbed back up and waved his hands, hoping that Philby would see him at the top end of the conveyor belt. About thirty seconds later, the first of the Linton Hall children appeared, shooting out of the corrugated-iron tunnel and ending his journey on the coal slide. He was a plump ten-year-old, whose face and blond hair were now covered in black smuts. Alex went over to him to check that he was all right.

"That was fantastic!" the boy whispered. "Can I do it again?"

It took another ten minutes for all the children to arrive. Alex suspected that quite a few of them might have needed persuading before they had launched themselves into the darkness. Jack and the drama teacher came down one after another and finally Philby arrived, his white shirt filthy, his trousers torn. Alex handed him back his jacket. It was completely ruined.

"So what next?" the security man asked, putting it back on with a scowl. He didn't seem impressed that they had got this far without being seen.

Jack had already begun taking a headcount.

Unlike Philby, she loved seeing Alex in command. She couldn't believe that they were together again. "They're all here!" she announced.

"Right." Once again, Alex addressed the entire group. He was grateful that the sirens had finally been silenced. The only sound in the compound now was the soft puffing of the train. He kept his voice low. "Nobody can see us here. We're going underneath the locomotive train. Be careful you don't touch anything or you may burn yourself. The coach is parked on the other side. Mr Philby's going to drive us out of here." He glanced at Philby who nodded, briefly. "Once we start the engine, the guards will hear us. There may be some shooting. I want everyone to lie down on the floor, under the seats. Whatever happens, don't stand up."

"And where exactly do you want me to drive?" Philby demanded. "You may not have noticed, but there's no road out of here."

"We'll have to drive along the railway track. We're quite a long way from the tunnel but we'll be safe once we're on the other side."

"Why don't we take the train?" It was right in front of them, still steaming. Ready to go.

"Do you know how to drive it?" Alex asked.

Philby thought for a moment, then shook his head.

"Then it'll have to be the coach."

The children were huddled together, waiting in the shadows. None of the searchlights could reach

the top end of the platform and they were concealed behind the great bulk of the train which
sat there, white steam writhing between its wheels
and coupling rods. The tender was behind it, piled
high with coal, and Alex could imagine himself
standing in the cab, feeding the furnace and feeling the extraordinary power driving him through
the night. He really wished he could take it instead
of the coach.

Alex signalled and they began to move. There
was only one way to keep out of the light and,
more importantly, out of sight of the two guards
on the bridge. They had to stoop low underneath
the driver's cabin, wriggle across the tracks and
then over the short gap to the waiting coach. With
so many of them making the journey, it took far
longer than he would have liked and he had heard
renewed shouting from the accommodation block.
Frankie Stallone had been discovered. The children
had gone! They had to be somewhere in the compound. The search had already begun.

Alex helped all the children as they emerged
from under the train. The front door of the coach
was open and he counted the numbers as they
climbed up, disappearing from view. Fifty, fifty-
one, fifty-two ... after what seemed like an hour,
they were all inside. The drama teacher followed
them in and suddenly, Jack was next to him. Philby
hadn't yet appeared.

Alex took out the ignition keys and handed

them to Jack. "Where's Philby?"

"I don't know."

"If he's gone missing, you'll have to drive," he said.

Jack glanced at the keys. "You've done brilliantly," she said. "I can't believe we're getting out of here."

"We're not there yet," Alex said.

She smiled at him and climbed up into the coach. Alex was left standing in the narrow corridor between the coach and the train.

He heard a sound and turned round, expecting to see Philby. Instead, a guard stood facing him, just ten paces away. Alex recognized the dead eyes, the mouldy skin. It was Skunk, the man who had been sent to film his death. He had come from behind the coal pile and there could be no doubt about what he was going to do. Skunk was carrying a machine gun. He had seen Alex. Slowly, smiling, he took aim.

Alex stood there, frozen, as the black muzzle of the automatic weapon rose up towards him. He knew that it was too late, that he had no hope of escaping. Even so, he reached behind him for the gun that was still tucked into the waistband of his trousers. Everything was happening in slow motion. He was rooted to the ground. His muscles seemed to be locked together.

And then Ted Philby appeared from nowhere, lunging out from behind the steam train, throwing himself at Skunk. Somehow he got his hands on the machine gun, the two men dancing together on the edge of the railway track, steam hissing around them as they fought for control. Philby had his back to Alex but he managed to twist round and shout over his shoulder. One word. "Move!"

A second later, there was a burst of machine-gun fire, deafening at such close quarters. Alex saw splatters of blood appear across Philby's back, forming hideous red stains which spread through his shirt. Alex had disliked the security man. He had found him annoying and unhelpful. But in the end, Philby had sacrificed himself to save him and the thought of it broke the spell and propelled him towards the waiting coach. Jack had seen what had happened. At exactly that moment, she started the engine. The Mercedes-Benz Tourismo coughed into life. There was a hiss of hydraulics and the lights came on inside. The headlights cut through the darkness. Alex reached the open door just as Skunk fired a second time. Bullets flashed over his head and smashed the wing mirror, sending it spinning into the night.

"Go!" Alex shouted. "We've got to go!"

Behind the wheel, Jack rammed the gear into first and stamped down on the accelerator. The coach was like nothing she had ever driven before but at least the controls were more or less the same as an ordinary car: a steering wheel, a clutch, brakes, a gearstick. There was a terrible grinding sound and for a moment she thought she was going to stall. Then the coach jerked forward. Alex was at the door, crouching down as more bullets slammed into the side, shattering one of the windows.

"Where am I going?" Jack shouted.

"Just keep moving!" Alex shouted back.

Somewhere in the compound, a searchlight swung round to find them and suddenly the interior of the coach exploded in blinding white light. The children lay stretched out on the floor, some of them hiding their eyes, terrified. Sitting in the driver's seat, her hands tight on the wheel, Jack stared through the front window, dazzled, hardly able to see anything. Then Alex was next to her, squinting through the glass.

"There!" He pointed and she saw what looked like two wagons.

"That's the wrong way, Alex!"

"Trust me, Jack!"

He was steering her away from the railway, away from the only route out of the coke works. They were heading back into danger, towards the guards, towards the other machine guns.

"Go round the wagons!" Alex shouted. "Make a circle!"

"This is crazy!" Jack shouted the words in exasperation but she did exactly what he wanted. He had crossed the world to find her. He had managed to get them at least some of the way out of here. She didn't doubt him for a second. Wrenching the wheel, she sent the coach in a twisting circle around the two wagons, the wheels spitting up gravel and dust. The movement caught the guards by surprise. For a moment, nobody fired at them. She noticed that Alex had taken out his gun. He was aiming out of the open door.

"OK! Now we need to get onto the railway!" he shouted.

"I'm heading there!"

Jack knew exactly what to do. Ahead of her, there was the turntable that had been used to rotate the train and beyond it, a crossing point, a ramp that had once allowed vehicles to drive over the rails. She steered towards it, feeling the huge weight of the coach behind her as it careered across the gravel. At the same time, Alex fired out of the door. He didn't seem to be aiming at anything in particular, but as the coach leapt forward, Jack saw the impossible happen. A massive fireball exploded behind them, spreading out and becoming a wall of flame that rose up to the sky, separating them from the rest of the compound. She could even feel the heat on the back of her neck. Alex had somehow created a furnace to protect them.

Standing in the doorway, Alex smiled to himself, pleased with his work. The idea had come to him on his way to the outhouse where the two men were being held. He had seen sulphuric acid in containers. He also remembered the two wagons that he had noticed when he first arrived. They were nothing more than oversized fuel tanks on wheels and they were filled with a highly flammable liquid ... benzene. Before he had released Ted Philby and the drama teacher, he had returned to the storage hut and used the chisel to break a hole in one of the flasks. Then, with great care – he would be badly burned if any of the liquid splashed onto his hands – he had carried the flask over to the wagons and poured the acid onto them. From that moment onwards, it had been eating its way through the metal, hopefully releasing the benzene onto the floor below.

And just now, as the coach swung past, he had fired all six bullets at the wagons. At least one of the bullets had hit and caused a spark. The result was more impressive than he could possibly have hoped. Several of the guards had been caught in the blaze. He had heard them screaming. The rest of them were on the other side of a barricade of fire. For the moment, the children were safe.

Alex was almost thrown off his feet as the front wheels of the coach hit the ramp that Jack had seen. He reached out and managed to grab hold of a silver railing as she swung round to the right. The coach tilted, threatening to crash onto its side. But a second later, she righted it so that now it was lined up on the track, two wheels on either side of the rails. The Blaina Tunnel was still a long way away, but if she continued in a straight line, eventually she would reach it.

She was driving over the wooden sleepers. Alex felt the vibrations punching through his legs and into his stomach as the wheels navigated the uneven surface. There was a fence ahead of them, a metal gate.

"Don't stop!" Alex muttered.

"I wasn't going to!" Jack replied.

It was too late anyway. The fence loomed up in the windscreen as the coach thundered into it, smashing it off its hinges and sending the pieces hurtling away into the night. There were more guards here, positioned on both sides. They no longer cared who they killed, lifting their weapons and strafing the coach with hundreds of bullets. The children screamed as the rest of the windows disintegrated, white glass fragments cascading down. Some of the bullets penetrated the coach-work, a jagged line of holes suddenly appearing in the metal panels. Light and dust poured in. It was incredible that the wheels hadn't been hit. Or maybe the rubber was thick enough to absorb the bullets. The coach seemed to be going through its death throes as it clattered out of the compound.

A few seconds later they had plunged into the safety of darkness. The air stank of gunsmoke. The windscreen was cracked and all but one of the windows had gone. The luxury seats were covered in dust. The engine was howling and the entire vehicle was rattling as it accelerated along the sleepers. All they had to do was keep going straight and they would reach the tunnel. It occurred to Alex that they had no choice anyway. They were trapped, straddling the railway line. They couldn't turn left or right.

But they were away. That was the main thing. Alex clambered back into the main body of the coach and quickly checked that none of the schoolchildren had been hurt. It was difficult to be sure, with so many bodies lying on the floor and smashed glass everywhere, but there didn't seem to be any blood. The drama teacher had taken charge and signalled that everything was all right so Alex turned and made his way back to the front, using any handhold he could find. They had slowed down but the floor was still shaking violently under his feet as they bumped over each and every one of the sleepers.

He reached Jack. She was hunched over the wheel, staring into the darkness. But even now there was a smile on her face. "You're doing brilliantly," he said.

"I can't believe we've made it," Jack said.

"We haven't yet." Alex looked out through the cracked front window. There was no sign of the tunnel but it was too dark to see anything. He guessed it was still a couple of miles away. "Can't we go any faster?" he asked.

"I don't dare, Alex. I'm going to rip out the tyres."

"OK."

Alex looked back the way they had come. The coke works were ablaze, the crimson glow stretching across the horizon and shimmering in the night sky. There must have been gallons of the benzene and it had spread everywhere, pooling around the other buildings which had themselves caught fire. The conveyor belt that had provided their escape was burning, the flames streaking diagonally up to the top of the bunker. There were other chemicals stored in the compound and these too ignited. Even as Alex watched, one of the out-houses blew itself apart with a blinding flash of yellow and red. Clouds of black smoke, like living things, were rolling over the ground. If the guards hadn't already fled, there was no way they would survive.

"Alex..." Jack began. Her voice was little more than a whisper.

She had seen it in the mirror. He had seen it too. He should have expected it, prepared for it. Perhaps it explained what Ted Philby had been trying to do before he was killed. He had known it could be used against them.

The Midnight Flyer burst out of the smoke and the fire, sweeping them aside like a curtain, steaming towards them, already picking up speed. Alex saw the headlights blazing, the wheels turning, the chimney blasting out yet more smoke. When he had seen it at the platform, it had reminded him of a sleeping beast, but now it was very much awake and it was coming after them in a fury. They had to move faster. Otherwise it would devour them.

Jack called to him a second time and Alex had never heard such despair in her voice. She was still steering the coach over the sleepers, fighting to keep it under control. Now, with one hand, she pointed to the dashboard. "We're running out of petrol!" she shouted.

Alex stared. How was that possible? He saw the fuel gauge, the needle hovering over the red. The engine coughed and the whole coach shuddered.

And still *The Midnight Flyer* came, drawing closer and closer, cutting down the distance between them, leaving the burning hell of the coke works far behind.

THE MIDNIGHT FLYER

Giovanni and Eduardo Grimaldi stood in the cab of the steam engine as it thundered through the night, drawing ever closer to the Mercedes-Benz Tourismo, no more than two miles ahead of them. Frankie "The Flame" Stallone stood sweating at the controls while Skunk shovelled coal into the firebox which bathed the whole interior in an intense, orange light. The twins had dressed hastily but had still managed to pull on identical clothes: jeans, cowboy boots and red-checked shirts. They were both holding mini-Uzi sub-machine guns, capable of firing 950 rounds a minute with a range of one hundred and fifty metres. They weren't close enough yet. They would be soon.

The brothers knew that Alex Rider was alive. When they had first been woken up by the alarms, they had assumed that the police or security services had somehow tracked them down to Smoke City and their first thought had been to evacuate. It was only when Frankie Stallone had broken out of the accommodation block that they had begun to piece together the truth. Alex Rider was here. Quite possibly he was alone. He and his friend, Jack Starbright, had released the children and were trying to escape with them. They had taken the coach.

"How could it happen?" Giovanni yelled to his brother as they stood together in the cabin. "How did he find us?"

"It doesn't matter!" Eduardo shouted back. "We'll catch up with him. We'll kill him. We'll kill all of them!"

"But the ransom!"

"It doesn't make any difference, Gio. They'll pay the money anyway. The parents won't know the kids are dead. By the time they find out the truth, we'll be on the other side of the world."

The twins had never argued with each other, not once in their lives, and they weren't going to start blaming each other now. If mistakes had been made, they were equally responsible. It was fortunate that *The Midnight Flyer* was kept permanently primed, ready to move at a moment's notice. The two of them had grabbed their weapons and leapt onto the locomotive. Stallone was the driver, Skunk the fireman. They had been shunting away from the platform even as the coke works exploded all around them.

Standing at the controls, Frankie Stallone knew what he had to do. He had to reach the coach before it entered the tunnel. That was the crucial thing. The Blaina Tunnel connected Dinas Mwg with the real world. On this side of it, there was no law. They could do anything. On the other side, the railway joined the mainline and there would be other trains, buildings, roads ... witnesses. The twins would use their machine guns to rip the coach apart as soon as they were near enough. The massive buffers and the pilot bar at the front of the locomotive would hammer into it, shunting it off the track. That was the plan, even if nobody survived.

The coach was directly in front of them. They could see its glowing tail lights. It was a miracle that it was moving at all. Half the windows had been shot out. The fuel tank had been ruptured and petrol was jetting out. It seemed to be stumbling over the railway sleepers. But *The Midnight Flyer* was in total command; a hundred tonnes of solid iron, powering forward with its pistons grinding, clouds of white smoke billowing out and brilliant sparks spinning into the night. Skunk fed it. Stallone coaxed it forward. And the twins watched with dark, glittering eyes as it carried them ever closer to their prey.

With a sinking heart, Alex stared at the gauges, trying to work out what had happened. The fuel tank must have been full when it set out for Stratford-upon-Avon – that felt an age ago now –

but it was almost empty. How could that be possible? He remembered the machine-gun fire. Obviously, they had been hit. Reaching out with his hands to help keep his balance, he pushed himself past Jack and leaned out of the broken window behind her. The wind slammed into the side of his head as he looked out.

The light from the coach showed him exactly what he had expected to see. A twisting line of bullet holes stretched along the entire side panel of the Mercedes-Benz Tourismo. It was a miracle that none of the children had been hit – but the fuel tank had been punctured. Liquid, silver in the reflected light, was spilling out, carried away by their own forward motion. If the coach continued much longer, they would simply grind to a halt. He looked back and saw a series of brilliant, white flashes on one side of the locomotive, as if someone was trying to take his photograph. It only occurred to him a few seconds later that it was a machine gun, firing at him. If it had been closer, he would have been hit, but fortunately it was still well out of range.

He ducked back inside. Some of the children were staring up at him, eyes wide open, waiting to see what he would come up with next. But he didn't have anything to tell them. The luxury coach was a complete wreck. Everything was shaking and shuddering. The luggage compartments had burst open and halfway down, the door of the lavatory was banging open and shut. Alex looked back and saw that the train had once again halved the distance between them. He could actually hear it now, huffing and puffing as it drew closer.

I'll huff and I'll puff and I'll blow your house down.

Strange that he should suddenly think of Jack reading nursery rhymes to him when he was seven years old. He had found her. The two of them had broken out of the compound, bringing all the Linton Hall children with them. Had it really all been for nothing? He refused to accept it.

They were rattling through the darkness but couldn't go any faster. The tunnel was still a mile or more away. The fuel was running out. *The Midnight Flyer* was almost on top of them. There was nothing he could do.

Alex forced himself to think.

Drop something on the track. Derail the train. But what was there inside the coach that he could possibly use? He had a gun with no bullets. Could he tear out one of the seats? No. It would take too long. He looked around him despairingly. There was a fire extinguisher beside the door. It was tiny. He might be able to drop it onto the tracks but *The Midnight Flyer* would probably bat it out of the way, and even if the train rode straight over it, the huge wheels would simply crush it. He noticed an oversized Thermos flask next to the front seat. Jane Vosper, the coach driver, must have tucked it in beside her. Fighting to keep his balance, Alex reached out and grabbed it. He unscrewed the lid and upended it. Tea poured out onto the floor. It was still warm, even though it must have been there for twelve hours or more.

Jack saw him. "Alex!" she shouted, fighting with the wheel. "This is no time for a cup of tea!"

But that wasn't what Alex was thinking.

The Thermos.

The fuel.

The Midnight Flyer.

He realized he had the answer in his hands. All he had to do was persuade Jack. He went over to her, leaning down so that he could speak directly into her ear. "How much further do you think we can go?" he shouted.

"I don't know. Maybe a few more minutes."

"I've got an idea."

Quickly he told her what was in his mind. He had known she wouldn't like it and he was right. She looked horrified. "Alex, that's madness. It will never work."

"It might work, Jack – and I can't think of anything else. You just have to let them catch up with us. Give me a minute and then start slowing down. Not too much. And be careful they don't ram us."

"Alex – they'll shoot you the moment they see you."

"With a bit of luck, they won't see me." There was no time for further discussion. He patted her on the shoulder, then reeled away from the front of the coach, stepping over the children in the aisle. He was still holding the Thermos flask and the lid.

"I need four people to help me," he shouted. "We've got to be quick!"

At once, several of the children got to their feet. Alex chose four of the biggest and strongest. "I'm going to lean out of the window. I need you to hold my legs and make sure I don't fall. And when you feel me kick out with my feet, you've got to drag me back in. Can you do that?"

The children nodded.

"This way!"

He had already seen which window he needed to use. It was about two-thirds of the way down, just past the central door. The glass had been smashed by machine-gun fire but he used the Thermos to knock out the final pieces. He climbed onto the seat. "Now!" he shouted. The four children grabbed hold of his legs. He lowered himself outside.

The wind almost tore him away. Holding the heavy Thermos flask, he couldn't use his hands to steady himself and he felt the strain on his neck, his ribs, his pelvis. It was as if he was being snapped into pieces. The blood was already rushing to his head as he hung upside down, and it was only with difficulty that he managed to snatch some air into his mouth and breathe. He risked a quick look back and saw that the train was much closer than he had thought. He was almost certainly in range of the guns. If he was seen, he was dead.

Something spat into his face, stinging his eyes and making him gag. He knew at once what it was from the smell – and the taste. Diesel fuel, thick and oily, was spluttering out in glittering jets. It was what he had come for. There were several bullet holes close to his head and they were acting as open taps, draining the tank. Gripping the Thermos with all his strength, fighting to stop the wind snatching it away, he held the open end to a hole, allowing the fuel to trickle in. It was almost impossible. He kept on getting splashed himself. He could barely see. The blood was pounding behind his eyes and he was terrified that he was a sitting – or hanging – target for the machine guns in the train. They were now less than half a mile behind. He could feel the children gripping his legs. If they let go, he would fall.

The Thermos flask was almost full. Alex didn't know how much fuel he would need. He didn't even know if this was going to work. Maybe Jack was right. Instinct told him that the more he had, the better his chances. But at the same time he knew that for every drop he collected, whole litres of fuel were being sprayed into the darkness and if the coach came to a halt, they were finished. He was struggling to keep the neck of the Thermos still. His hands and arms were soaked. Diesel contains sulphur and nitrogen and it stank. It was on his skin and in his hair. He could taste it in his mouth, and some had even gone up his nose. The ground was rushing past, a blur beneath his head. How much longer could he endure this? Finally, he decided he'd had enough. He kicked with one of his feet. At once the hands around his legs started pulling and he found himself being dragged back inside.

He crumpled into one of the seats, surrounded by puzzled children. He knew he looked awful – but he examined the flask and saw that it was virtually full. He screwed on the lid, then called out to Jack.

"I'm going up now, Jack..."

"Take care!" She couldn't look back. She was staring at the railway stretching out ahead.

"Everyone get back down!" Alex warned. "There may be more shooting but I promise you it'll be over soon."

He climbed out of the same window, this time putting a foot on the ledge and then easing the rest of his body through. Again, the Thermos made the task twice as difficult as it should have been because he couldn't use both his hands. The coach jolted as one of the wheels came into contact with the railway line and he almost dropped it. There was no handrail on the roof. It was a flat surface with nothing to hold on to but at least it wasn't too far away. He pushed himself out of the coach, then jackknifed back with the Thermos gripped above his head.

A second later, he came crashing down and rolled over immediately onto his stomach. He lay there, pressed against the roof, with the wind slicing over his shoulders. He felt sick and dizzy. The taste of the diesel was still in his mouth, working its way down his throat. His eyes were on fire.

Everything depended on Jack.

She had already started slowing down – not so much that the train driver would think anything was wrong but enough to allow *The Midnight Flyer* to catch up with them. Alex lay where he was, recovering his strength, preparing himself for what was to come. He would have one chance. If he missed, then everything he had done so far would be for nothing.

He had a bomb in his hands.

Alex knew that diesel wouldn't normally explode. If he tried to light it with a match, nothing would happen. But he had filled a pressurized container – a heavy steel Thermos – with the liquid and sealed it. If he threw the Thermos into something hot, he thought that might make a difference.

The Midnight Flyer was producing steam with a temperature of around ninety-three degrees Celsius. The whole engine was powered by a blazing furnace on wheels. Every part of it would be white-hot. And it had a wide chimney which led down into its bowels.

That was the plan.

Alex couldn't stand up yet. He had to leave that until the last moment. He wondered if the Grimaldi twins were in the cab. He knew how much pleasure it would give them to tear him to pieces with their machine guns. Still lying flat, he watched the iron monster draw closer. A few seconds ago it had been a quarter of a mile away. Now it was near enough for him to read the number – 1007 – printed on the front. He saw the rushing steam, the glare from the headlights, the iron buffers, the pipes and the couplers. There were two men leaning out of the cab, one on each side. He recognized the Grimaldis. They looked like cowboys in their brightly-coloured checked shirts.

Cowboys with machine guns. They opened fire as one and Alex flinched, his face pressed against the roof as the back window shattered and the metal panels of the coach ripped to pieces just beneath him. But Jack was holding her nerve. She had allowed *The Midnight Flyer* to come so close that it was almost touching. A second later the buffers actually made contact, smashing into the back of the coach and shunting it forward, almost throwing Alex off in the process.

This was the moment he had been waiting for. Somehow he got up – first on one knee, then on his feet. There was no need to throw the Thermos. The locomotive was right in front of him, the smokestack almost within reach. Terrified that he would lose his balance or that the driver would shunt the coach a second time, Alex staggered to the very edge of the roof and leaned over the space between the coach and the train with the track rushing past below. He stretched out. Now he had one foot on the coach and one foot on the front of the train. If the gap between the two of them widened, he would fall to a horrible death. Steam was belching out all around him. He felt the ferocious heat of it scalding his neck, his chin, the skin on his forehead. He had to close his eyes. If he kept them open, they would be burned out. But he had seen his target. He reached as far as he could until the Thermos was over the chimney. Then he dropped it and threw himself backwards, landing heavily on the roof, at the same time pounding it with his fist.

Jack heard the sound and slammed her foot on the accelerator. The coach leapt forward and suddenly the gap between it and the locomotive widened as the driver was taken by surprise. She saw something and gasped. A black mouth had opened up in the hillside ahead of her. She had reached the tunnel! At the same time, a horrible thought flashed through her mind. Had Alex seen it too?

Alex hadn't. He was crawling back towards the window when the round entrance of the tunnel suddenly loomed up on him. It was like the end of the world, a black hole that would swallow him and all life with him. With a yell, Alex dived over the side of the coach. His scrabbling hands found the edge of the window frame and he half climbed, half tumbled down, until he was stand-ing on the lower ledge. He took one last glance over his shoulder. The great blackness of the hill was rushing towards him. He bent down and threw himself forwards into the coach. He actually felt one of his feet brush against the side of the tunnel as, arms flailing, he fell onto the seat below. The blackness of the tunnel smothered him. He didn't know if he had been hurt or not.

The Midnight Flyer had fallen back. It was thirty metres behind. The Thermos flask filled with diesel had been dropped through the smoke stack and had come to rest next to the blastpipe, blocking the superheater header. It was trapped in an iron container that was insanely hot. The diesel boiled. The fumes expanded. The pressure increased.

The whole thing exploded.

The Grimaldis didn't hear the explosion. They didn't even know it had happened. They simply felt a jolt as if some gigantic gust of wind, coming out of nowhere, had hit *The Midnight Flyer* on its side. Ahead of them, they saw the coach disappear into the tunnel. But here was the strange thing. They were no longer following it. Instead, they were hurtling into the rock face on the side of the hill.

Only the driver, Frankie Stallone, understood that one of the pistons had shattered and that

The Midnight Flyer had derailed. There was nothing he could do to prevent the end. His face, already badly burned, distorted one last time in sheer terror as the steam locomotive smashed into a solid wall of rock. Skunk screamed as the boiler was torn open and the boiling water and steam erupted in a white cloud like a nuclear catastrophe. Giovanni and Eduardo had been born five seconds apart and, as it happened, that was the same interval between their deaths. Giovanni was killed instantly. Eduardo had five seconds to realize that everything had gone wrong before he followed his brother into oblivion. The furnace had disintegrated, scattering burning coals all around the mouth of the tunnel. The very ground seemed to be on fire. There was a pause and then what was left of the locomotive tilted and collapsed, dragging the tender with it. Water and fire swilled around it, the one attacking the other. Hissing and spitting, *The Midnight Flyer* lay dying. A great cloud hung over it, blotting out the stars.

Half a mile away, on the other side of the tunnel, the Mercedes-Benz Tourismo finally burst out into the open air, then continued forward, utterly silent, as the fuel finally ran out.

At last, it rolled to a halt and stood still.

NIGHTSHADE

It ended with the two of them in a room on the sixteenth floor.

Alex Rider had been more hurt than he had thought as he dropped the improvised bomb that had destroyed *The Midnight Flyer*. The steam had burned him and his face was streaked with red marks. He had cut himself on the broken window as he had jackknifed back into the coach. He had cracked a rib, falling onto the arm of one of the chairs. It would be at least a week before he could go back to school.

He wondered how he was possibly going to explain where he had been for the past couple of months and why he had once again turned up with injuries that made him look as if he had been involved in a multiple pile-up. But that was for the future. Right now he had to deal with the woman who sat in front of him and who had played such a huge part in his life.

"Alex, I don't quite know what to say to you," Mrs Jones began. "I should have listened to you ...

and to Ben Daniels, for that matter. You both thought we were making a mistake, chasing after the gold. But it all seemed so straightforward. Forty million pounds is a lot of money."

"Two hundred and sixty million is a lot more."

"Yes. The Vospers were working together, of course. She gave him the information he needed and he sold it to the Grimaldis. You might like to know that both the twins are dead, by the way. Derek Vosper has been arrested."

"You've kept it out of the papers."

"Yes. We thought it was better that way. There are a lot of very wealthy and powerful people connected with Linton Hall, and they don't like publicity. More to the point, we don't want to give anyone the same idea. We can't have gangsters targeting our schools! As for what happened on the motorway, there were a great many witnesses but we've managed to persuade them that it was American producers, working on a new film. It doesn't sound very likely, I know. But then the truth is hardly very likely either."

"So nobody knows about me," Alex said. He was pleased about that.

"The general public knows nothing about you. But actually there is something you need to know. The Linton Hall parents have joined together. They know that you were the one who rescued their children and they want to give you five million pounds – as a reward."

"Really?" Alex couldn't help smiling. It seemed like an awful lot of money to have in his bank account. He wanted to buy something nice for Sabina and her parents and now he could afford it.

"If you ask me, it's hardly very generous," Mrs Jones sniffed. "It's less than one-fiftieth of the ransom they would have had to pay if it hadn't been for you – and you got all their children back safely. Well, one or two of them have minor injuries and quite a few of them may have night-mares about that final coach journey. I'm sure their parents will arrange expensive counselling for them. But as to the reward, we've had to say you can't take it. MI6 operatives aren't allowed to receive cash payments."

"I'm not an MI6 operative," Alex said.

"I'm not sure that's true." Mrs Jones smiled for the first time since he had come into the room. "Anyway, you'll be glad to know that we've found a way around the regulations. Jack Starbright was driving the coach and she's the one who's going to take the credit for the release of the children. So the money can be paid to her."

"Jack will like having five million pounds."

"I'm very glad you found her, Alex. When you and I met in Saint-Tropez, I really didn't think she was still alive. Is she going to continue looking after you?"

"I'm meeting her later."

"That's good." Mrs Jones paused. Alex could see

that she had thought hard about what she was going to say next. "In Saint-Tropez I told you to go back to America," she said. "In fact I ordered you. I hope you understand that I meant what I said. I didn't want to put you in any more danger. I wanted you out of harm's way."

"You knew I wouldn't go," Alex said. "You'd already bugged my phone."

"I wanted you to have a choice. You're fifteen years old now, Alex. Things have changed. We can't keep on treating you like a child."

"You mean ... manipulating me."

"That's exactly what I mean. I warned you that danger can become a drug and it seems to me that in your case, it's too late. You're already hooked. You say you don't work for us but a year from now, we could employ you quite legally."

"I may not get any GCSEs."

"In your line of work, you don't need GCSEs. Well, that's not entirely true. In fact, I'd be much happier if you settled down and did some school-work. Passed your exams. Had an ordinary life."

"So what are you saying, Mrs Jones?"

"Just this. If we ever need you again, I'd prefer to ask you properly. Which is to say, you can say yes or you can say no. I don't want you to think of us as the enemy. You've been incredibly help-ful to us on so many occasions, Alex, and we're grateful. Do you understand me? If there ever is a next time, it will be your decision."

Alex nodded. He got to his feet. "You know where to find me," he said.

Jack was waiting for him outside. It was great to see her back in her own clothes, sitting on a bench, reading a paperback. It was as if she had never been away. Seeing him, she closed the book and the two of them jumped in a cab.

"Where are we going?" Alex asked.

"Covent Garden." She gave the driver instructions. "How did it go?" she asked.

"They're paying you five million pounds."

"I know. Ben Daniels told me. I wasn't going to mention it to you. I wasn't sure what you'd say."

"I'm really pleased."

"We'll share it."

"Are you going to stay?"

Jack looked out of the window. They had turned up towards the Barbican, the great blocks of flats on the edge of east London. "A long time ago, before we even went to Egypt, I was thinking of leaving," she confessed. "I didn't want to tell you – but you know my dad's not been well. It seemed to me that you didn't need me so much any more. And you must admit, it's pretty weird the two of us living together the way we do."

"Everything about my life is weird," Alex said.

"This may sound crazy, Alex, but when I was taken prisoner by Razim and then when the Grimaldi brothers came along, part of me thought that I was being punished for wanting to leave you on your own." She stopped him before he could interrupt. "It doesn't matter. I'd already decided. London's my home now and you're part of my life. If I don't have to look after you so much, maybe I can start studying law again. That's the reason I came here in the first place – and I can certainly afford the tuition fees. So if you don't want to get rid of me, maybe I will hang around."

Alex wanted to hug her again. But it wasn't so easy in the back of a cab, and anyway, he'd had enough of all that. It was time to move on. "Where are we going?" he asked.

"I thought we'd start at the Apple store. You lost your laptop in the South of France so I'll buy you another. You need a whole lot of new clothes too. I know that's boring, so we're also going to have lunch and then we're going to a movie, and then after that you should catch up with your friends."

"You've spoken to Brookland?"

"They know you're coming back. They can't wait to see you. The bad news is they've sent a pile of homework." Jack stopped herself and for a moment, the smile faded from her face. "Mrs Jones. What did she say about you and MI6?"

"She said from now on, it was my choice."

"Good. I won't be sorry if we never see her again."

The taxi turned a corner and continued on its journey west.

* * *

She had lied to him.

If we ever need you again, I'd prefer to ask you properly.

If there ever is a next time, it will be your decision.

But she hadn't told him that there already was a next time and that, although it was hard to believe, she already needed Alex Rider.

She took a file out of the top drawer of her desk and laid it in front of her. There was a single word on the cover.

NIGHTSHADE

She opened it and looked at a black and white photograph of a boy of about Alex's age. He was thin, with a long neck and troubled eyes, his hair cut very short as if he were a soldier – which, in a way, he was. There were thirty pages of typewritten text attached to the photograph, each one stamped TOP SECRET. Once again, her eye fell on the page that she had been reading just before Alex came into the room. It was written in the dry, matter-of-fact language of every official report, even though the events it was describing were extraordinary.

It was only a matter of pure luck that the subject was arrested following the successful (and extraordinary) murder of our agent in Rio de Janeiro. The killer had clearly been trained to the very highest standard, being proficient in Ninjutsu, Krav Maga, Muay Thai and at least three other lethal martial arts. He carried about his person several deadly weapons (see Paragraph 37) and was responsible for the deaths of four more agents after he was taken into custody.

The killer carried no ID. His clothes and personal items contained no labels, nor anything that could suggest their country of origin. His fingerprints had been removed with acid. During interrogation, even when threatened with extreme measures, he remained silent. It was only through his DNA that a positive identification became possible.

The killer's name is Frederick Grey. He is the son of Sir William and Caroline Grey. He is fifteen years old. He was presumed dead in a boating accident ten years ago and has never been seen since. His parents were of course shocked that he had been found and were introduced to him (meeting recorded) in a secure cell. They were both certain that he was, indeed, their son. He, however, showed no recognition and did not speak to them.

The subject is now being held at our special facility in Gibraltar. He has so far refused any form of communication and remains extremely dangerous. He has been observed by a psychiatric team and they are currently preparing an in-depth report. Their first impressions are that he is "unique", "a killing machine".

Given his age, his attitude, his weapons and the fact that he has been missing, presumed dead, for most of his life, it is our belief that Frederick Grey has been recruited and trained by the mercenary group known as Nightshade.

Nightshade is currently the most dangerous organization in the world. It has no political affiliations or personal ambitions. It is interested only in money. It has provided highly trained personnel for acts of terror in Munich, Washington, Singapore, Paris, Brussels and Madrid.

"Nightshade" was the last word spoken by our agent in Rio before he died.

We recommend that action should be taken immediately if we are to take advantage of this situation. Threat levels are now at critical levels as intel suggests that Nightshade are lending their support to a global operation (see Reports 7710514AH, 780595J and 215006CNB). Grey is the key that can unlock Nightshade. We must move at once.

Mrs Jones closed the file and rested her hand on the cover. A fifteen-year-old boy who had performed a brutally efficient killing. A boy who was prepared to die to protect the people who had employed him, who said nothing, who had been missing for ten years. She needed to send someone to Gibraltar to get close to him. Somehow he had to lead them to Nightshade before it was too late.

Who better than Alex Rider?

She would let him go home. She would give him time to recover from his injuries ... but not too much time. And, as she had promised, she would let him decide if he was prepared to do this for her or not.

But she also knew she wouldn't let him say no.

READ OTHER GREAT BOOKS BY
ANTHONY HOROWITZ...

THE ALEX RIDER SERIES

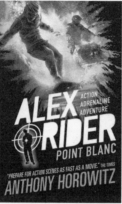

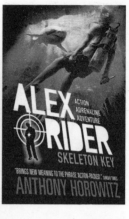

Alex Rider – you're never too young to die…

High in the Alps, death waits for Alex Rider…

Sharks. Assassins. Nuclear bombs. Alex Rider's in deep water.

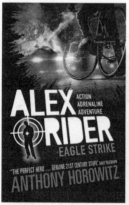

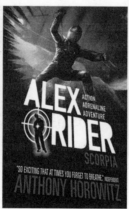

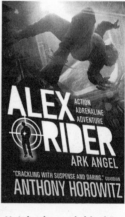

Alex Rider has 90 minutes to save the world.

Once stung, twice as deadly. Alex Rider wants revenge.

He's back – and this time there are no limits.

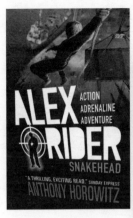
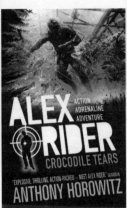
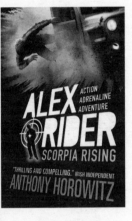
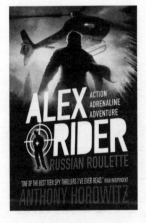